The Executive's Valentine
by Merline Lovelace

A series of small shocks rippled down her spine. Those eyes.

That deep golden tint. The russet outer ring around the dark iris. Wolf's eyes, the former librarian in her catalogued automatically, due to the high incidence of that colour in wolves.

Like… Like…

Like the eyes that had haunted her dreams for years. Mocking her. Taunting her to shed her prissy inhibitions. Tempting her to sin.

It couldn't be him! This high-powered executive *couldn't* be the hot stud she'd given her virginity to. The bastard who'd roared out of her life the next morning, leaving a trail of devastation in his wake.

She couldn't breathe, couldn't think as he approached. Those wolf's eyes never left her face.

"Hello, Caroline. It's been a long time."

Valente Must Marry
by Maxine Sullivan

In the lamplight she lay there for a few seconds, as if she'd been mummified, then gave a nervous laugh. Make that *petrified*.

Of Nick?

No, she was being absurd. Nick would never physically hurt her. Realising she was letting her nerves get the better of her, she sat up against the pillows, only just managing to cover herself with the sheet a moment before Nick opened the door.

His gaze flashed over her. "I see you're already in bed."

She blinked, suddenly confused. Should she have sat on the brocade chair instead? Or stood by the window? What was the protocol on the wedding night of a marriage of convenience?

"I thought this was where you'd want me."

"Oh, it is." An intense look filled his eyes. "I'd want you anywhere, Sasha."

Available in February 2010 from Mills & Boon® Desire™

The Executive's Valentine Seduction
by Merline Lovelace

&

Valente Must Marry
by Maxine Sullivan

Blackmailed Into a Fake Engagement
by Leanne Banks

&

Tempted Into the Tycoon's Trap
by Emily McKay

Featuring a bonus story by Maureen Child

The Duke's Boardroom Affair
by Michelle Celmer

&

Convenient Marriage, Inconvenient Husband
by Yvonne Lindsay

THE EXECUTIVE'S VALENTINE SEDUCTION

BY
MERLINE LOVELACE

VALENTE MUST MARRY

BY
MAXINE SULLIVAN

MILLS & BOON®

First published in Great Britain 2010
Harlequin Mills & Boon Limited,
Eton House, 18-24 Paradise Road, Richmond, Surrey TW9 1SR

The publisher acknowledges the copyright holders of the
individual works as follows:

The Executive's Valentine Seduction © Merline Lovelace 2009
Valente Must Marry © Maxine Sullivan 2009
(Original title: *The C.O.O Must Marry*)

ISBN: 978 0 263 88157 8

51-0210

Harlequin Mills & Boon policy is to use papers that are natural, renewable
and recyclable products and made from wood grown in sustainable forests.
The logging and manufacturing processes conform to the legal environmental
regulations of the country of origin.

Printed and bound in Spain
by Litografia Rosés S.A., Barcelona

THE EXECUTIVE'S
VALENTINE
SEDUCTION

BY
MERLINE LOVELACE

Merline Lovelace, a retired air force officer, served at bases all over the world, including tours in Taiwan, Vietnam and at the Pentagon. When she hung up her uniform for the last time, she decided to combine her love of adventure and flair for storytelling, basing many of her tales on her experiences in the service.

Since then, she's produced more than seventy-five action-packed novels, many of which have made the *USA TODAY* and Waldenbooks bestseller lists. Over ten million copies of her works are in print in thirty-one countries. Named Oklahoma's Writer of the Year and the Oklahoma Female Veteran of the Year, Merline is also a recipient of the Romance Writers of America's prestigious RITA® Award.

Check Merline's website at www.merlinelovelace.com for news, contests and information about forthcoming releases.

Dear Reader,

My husband and I have stumbled across some magical spots during our many years of rambling. Tossa de Mar, on Spain's Costa Brava, ranks right up near the top of our list. We found it by chance during a jaunt that took us from Madrid to Seville to Barcelona to the Strait of Gibraltar.

When we stopped in Tossa, I fell instantly in love with its sparkling bay, crescent-shaped beach and ancient ruins. What made it even more special is that Al and I celebrated an anniversary there. So when I needed a spot to set the stage for *The Executive's Valentine Seduction*, I knew it had to be beautiful Tossa by the Sea.

All my best,

Merline

For my darling,
who explored Tossa de Mar with me all those years ago.
I can't wait for all the adventures yet to come!

One

Caroline Walters had no premonition her world was about to implode that balmy February afternoon.

She stood in the lobby of a new, upscale resort in Tossa de Mar, a seaside vacation spot on Spain's Costa Brava, just an hour north of Barcelona. While Caro breathed in the fragrance of the bloodred gladiolas on the table beside her, she waited for the silver BMW gliding along the palm-lined drive to pull up at the resort's entrance.

The big moment was finally here. Her first meeting with the client who'd had her and her two partners jumping through hoops for the past month!

She used the final few seconds before he arrived

to check the mirror framing the gladiolas. Her honey-brown hair was smooth, with not a single tendril escaping from the heavy twist. Her green eyes gazed back at her with just the right degree of confidence. Her slim, black wool crepe skirt and matching jacket didn't show a single wrinkle.

Satisfied she looked the part of a coolly competent travel consultant and event coordinator, she flipped through the embossed leather folder she'd prepared for Rory Burke, founder and chief executive of the LA-based firm Global Security, Inc. She wanted to make sure she'd included everything Burke had requested.

Final conference agenda, check.

Resort layout, check.

Diagrams showing room setup for general sessions, check.

Additional diagrams for breakout rooms, check.

Arrival times and room numbers of all attendees, check.

Burke's hotel preregistration and room key, check.

Reassured everything was in place, Caroline closed the folder. She was primed and ready.

She should be! She and her partners had worked their buns off since this short-notice job dropped in their laps a few days before Christmas. They'd had just a little over a month to scout locations and pull together a conference plan for the hundred-plus security agents flying in from all parts of the world.

January had passed in a blur of frantic prep work. The flurry of e-mails and phone calls with Burke's people had multiplied exponentially the first week in February. Two days ago Caro had flown to Spain to nail down the final details. In several marathon sessions with the resort's conference coordinator, she'd reconfirmed menus, special dietary considerations, room setups and audiovisual aids.

She'd also tackled the rather daunting challenge of arranging a demo facility for an assortment of lethal weapons. In a last-minute change to the conference agenda, Global Security's head honcho had added a hands-on session to test new offensive and defensive weaponry for the protection of their clients.

As its name implied, GSI specialized in providing threat analysis and personal protection for clients ranging from kings and rock stars to newspaper editors who landed on religious fanatics' hate lists. The company profile indicated its agents were drawn from the ranks of military and law enforcement in twelve different countries.

The company's CEO was equally fascinating. His bio read like a James Bond novel. U.S. Army Ranger. Special Ops duty in war-torn Bosnia. A short stint with an unspecified government agency. Advisor to the Columbian Presidential Protection Unit. Founder and chief operating officer of GSI. Now fielding highly specialized agents in Iraq, Darfur, Indonesia,

Latin America—just about every hot spot on the globe.

Somewhere along the way he'd also managed to complete a bachelor's degree in law enforcement and a master's degree in international affairs. Curiously, neither his bio nor his company Web site had included a photo of Burke or any of his operatives. Caro suspected that might have something to do with GSI's pledge to provide "complete, confidential and anonymous protection."

As a former librarian, Caroline had read more than her share of action/adventure novels. She could admire real-life James Bond types like Rory Burke. Unfortunately, her one brief walk on the wild side had produced such disastrous consequences that she had *zero* desire to emulate their exploits.

So she couldn't help feeling both curious about and just a touch wary of her new client. She didn't allow either emotion to show, however, as the rental car she'd reserved for him at the Barcelona Airport pulled under the resort's vine-covered portico. A polite smile firmly in place, she waited while he exited the BMW and strode through the double glass doors.

Her first thought was that Burke certainly fit the mental image she'd constructed in her head. Despite the pinstripes and Italian silk tie, he wasn't someone she wanted to encounter in a dark alley.

The hand-tailored suit only emphasized his lean, rangy build. He wore his tawny hair cut ruthlessly short. His nose was flattened at the bridge, as if it had taken a direct hit from a club or a gun butt. And when he peeled off his mirrored sunglasses, his amber eyes lasered into Caro.

A series of small shocks rippled down her spine. Those eyes. That deep golden tint. The russet outer ring around the iris. Wolf's eyes, the former librarian in her cataloged automatically, due to the high incidence of that color in wolves.

Like… Like…

Like the eyes that had haunted her dreams for years. Mocking her. Taunting her to shed her prissy inhibitions. Tempting her to sin.

Her heart stuttered. Her breath sliced like a razor blade inside her throat.

It couldn't be him! This high-powered executive *couldn't* be the young tough whose motorcycle she'd climbed aboard one steamy summer night. The hot stud she gave her virginity to. The bastard who'd roared out of her life the next morning, leaving a trail of devastation in his wake.

She couldn't breathe, couldn't move, couldn't think as he approached. Those wolf's eyes never left her face.

"Hello, Caroline. It's been a long time."

Oh God! Oh God, oh God, oh God!

Her mind reeled with disbelief. Everything in her shouted a denial. She gouged her nails deep into her palms and felt her body go ice-cold then blaze white-hot when Burke shot out a hand to grip her upper arm.

"But don't keel over on me."

The gruff command triggered the survival instincts Caro had been forced to develop in the aftermath of that long-ago night. She couldn't quite stop the trembling, but she clamped down on the waves of dizziness and dragged in a breath that cut like jagged glass.

"How…? When…?"

"When did I find out I got you pregnant?" he finished for her. "Three months ago."

His gaze swept the lobby, came back to her.

"This isn't the place to discuss the result of our one-night stand. Let's take it somewhere private. Am I preregistered?"

"I… Uh…" She swiped her tongue over dry lips. "Yes."

"You have the room key?"

She could only nod this time.

"What's the room number?"

"Five…" She forced herself to breathe, to think. "Five oh eight."

He waited to relay the number to the bellman wheeling in his luggage before steering Caro toward the elevators. His hand remained locked around her upper arm. His body crowded hers in the claustrophobic cage.

She didn't say a word on the way up. She was still numb with shock, still fighting desperately to suppress the emotions that bombarded her.

She'd thought she'd put her past behind her. Was so certain she'd wiped out every remnant of her paralyzing fear when she finally realized she was pregnant, her shame at having to drop out of high school, her despair of being bundled off to a haven for pregnant teens.

She'd never gotten over the heartache of delivering a stillborn, seven-month-old baby, however. That stayed with her always. The experience had molded her into the woman she was today. Quiet. Contained. Careful.

And strong, she reminded herself grimly. Strong enough to survive. Strong enough to endure. Certainly strong enough to deal with Rory Burke.

Rory Burke. The name fit the man he'd become, but in no way could she connect it to the cocky, T-shirted eighteen-year-old who'd worked in her uncle's garage for a few weeks that long-ago summer.

"I never knew your real name," she got out through frozen lips as they exited the elevator. "My uncle and cousin always called you Johnny. Or Hoss."

Short for Stud Hoss, her shamefaced cousin had admitted later. By then it was too late.

"John—Johnny—is my middle name. I stopped

using it when I went into the army. The military isn't big on calling recruits by their middle names. Or *any* name except some that can't be repeated in polite company." He stopped at a set of double doors. "Five oh eight. This is it."

She fumbled in the leather folder for the key card. All her careful work—the agenda, the layout, the support setups—went unnoticed as Burke slipped the card into the lock and stood aside for her to precede him.

She'd checked out the lavish four-room suite just a half hour ago. The welcome basket still sat on the slab of polished granite that served as a coffee table. The handwritten note from the resort manager was still propped beside it. The minibar was stocked with single malt scotch, Burke's reported drink of choice. Yet Caro was too numb to absorb any of the details she'd checked so meticulously.

She dropped the leather folder on the coffee table beside the basket. With her arms wrapped around her waist, she turned to the man she'd never expected to see again.

"You said…"

She stopped, cringing at the ragged edge in her voice. She wasn't a frightened seventeen-year-old, dammit! She'd survived the angry recriminations her parents had thrown at her. All those lonely weeks at the home. The wrenching loss of her baby.

In the process, she'd discovered a strength she

didn't know she had. That inner core had pushed her to finish high school by correspondence, work her way through college and attend grad school on a full scholarship. During her junior year in college, she met the two women who would become her closest friends and, ultimately, her business partners. She'd built a life for herself. She owed no explanations to anyone, least of all this man.

But he sure as hell owed her one!

"You said you just found out three months ago I got pregnant."

"That's right."

"How?"

He tossed the key card on the coffee table and yanked at the knot of his tie. "I had dinner with a prospective client. Turns out his wife's from Millburn."

Millburn, Kansas. Population nine thousand or so. The town where Caro had spent the first seventeen years of her life. The town she'd returned to only once in the years since she'd left—for her father's funeral.

"The wife's name is Evelyn Walker," Burke said as he slid the tie from around his neck with a slither of silk on starched cotton. "Maiden name was Brown. Maybe you remember her?"

"Oh, yes. I remember Evelyn Brown."

They'd never been friends. They'd rarely talked to each other in the halls at school. But Evelyn had led the chorus of smirks and snide comments when word leaked that prim, prissy Caroline Walters had gotten herself knocked up.

"I asked the woman if she knew you."

His eyes held hers. Those compelling, dangerous eyes that had made Caro shiver every time he'd looked her over all those years ago.

"She told me you dropped out of high school at the start of your senior year. She also told me why."

"Schools weren't as tolerant of teenage pregnancies back then as they are today."

She could say it without bitterness. She'd never blamed the guidance counselor who'd called her in and told her she had to leave. Never blamed her parents for shipping her off to live with strangers. *She* was the one who'd tossed aside every principle, every precaution drummed into her by parents, teachers and church pastors to climb aboard a motorcycle that sweltering summer night.

"When I heard what happened, I…"

A brusque knock cut into Burke's terse explanation. With a muttered oath, he went to let in the porter with his luggage.

Caro grabbed at the interruption with relief. She turned to stare through the doors that gave onto a wide balcony. The spectacular views had mesmerized her when she was scouting locations for the GSI conference last month. Now she barely registered the medieval castle brooding high on a rocky promontory at the far end of a perfect, crescent beach.

Tourists strolled the wide seawall circling the beach, admiring the remnants of a walkway first laid by the Romans when Hispania was one of its far-flung provinces. Several fishermen sat beside boats drawn up onto the sandy shore, mending their nets in close proximity to the few hearty sun worshippers stretched out on towels or blankets.

It was a picture-postcard scene, one Caro was in no mood to appreciate. But staring at the endless stretch of sky and sea gave her time to squelch her churning emotions before she faced Burke again.

"So Evelyn told you I was pregnant. Do you want to know what happened to the baby?"

"I know what happened. I ran a check of birth certificates."

Birth and death. One and the same for the stillborn baby she'd buried; only the sympathetic manager of the home was beside her.

She fought to keep the bleak memory at bay, but Burke must have seen it in her eyes. He crossed the room and stretched out a hand.

Caro's tight hold on her emotions left no room for touching. She jerked back, and he dropped his arm.

"I'm sorry you had to go through that all alone," he said quietly. "If I'd known, I would have come back to Millburn."

That surprised her. Even more surprising was the fact that he didn't ask if he was the father.

Then again, he knew she was a virgin that night. He had to, given her inexperienced fumbling and surprised yelp when he penetrated her. Then, of course, there was the blood he'd wiped from her thighs with his wadded T-shirt.

"My uncle tried to contact you," Caroline said stiffly, "but he'd always paid you in cash, under the table. He didn't know your Social Security number. Or your real name for that matter. We had no way of tracking you down."

"I'm sorry," he said again.

She knew in her heart it wouldn't have made any difference if he *had* come back. Chances were she still would have lost the baby. And she still would have had to live with her parents' bitter disappointment in her.

"I'm sorry, too. I won't lie to you. The experience changed my life in ways I could never have imagined back then. I was so young, so stupidly naive. But in the end, it made me stronger."

She lifted her chin. This time it was her gaze that held his, direct and unflinching.

"I've put the past behind me. I suggest you do the same."

"That might be difficult, seeing as it just caught up with me a few months ago."

"Try," she snapped. "Try very hard. We're going

to be working together for the next five days. I don't want to…"

She broke off, her eyes widening.

"Oh God! I didn't connect the dots until this moment." Disgusted, she shook her head. "The conference… This job… It dropped in our laps just a little over a month ago. *After* you found out about me."

"I checked you out," he admitted without a trace of apology. "Saw you'd quit your job at the library to launch this business with your two partners. I also saw you sank your entire savings into start-up costs and nationwide advertising. That wasn't real smart," he added in an aside, "considering the three of you could have qualified for a small, woman-owned business loan and kept your personal assets intact."

She brushed over his editorial comment in her outrage over this invasion of her privacy. "How did you get that kind of information?"

"I'm in the security business, remember? I have access to all sorts of databases."

"You had no right to delve into my personal life or my finances!"

"Wrong." His mouth took a wry twist. "I've broken pretty well every rule in the book over the years, but there are a couple I live by. One, I keep my back to the wall. Two, I pay my debts."

Caro didn't think she figured into rule number one. That left number two.

A healthy dose of anger swept through her, scattering the other emotions this man had roused. She wasn't a shy, uncertain teenager anymore! She hadn't been for a long, long time. Becoming the butt of so many malicious jokes and whispers had stripped away her natural shyness and fired an inner core of tempered steel.

"Let's get one thing straight, Burke. You don't owe me a thing. You didn't drag me down to the river that night and have your way with me. I went with you willingly."

Willingly, hell! She'd been so eager, so hungry for the muscled-up kid with the wicked grin and daredevil glint in his eyes that she could hardly think that summer, much less weigh the consequences.

"Whatever price had to be paid for that bit of idiocy I paid long ago. The slate's clean."

"Not hardly."

He reached for her again, giving her no chance to flinch away this time. His fingers tipped her chin. His eyes narrowed as they locked with hers.

"Millburn was just a brief stop on a road that would have landed me in jail sooner or later. I'd probably be behind bars now if I hadn't gotten crosswise of a cop who grabbed me by the scruff of the neck and dragged me to an Army recruiter instead of the police station."

She'd sensed that in him. The recklessness. The hint of danger. They'd only added to his appeal. Prim, proper Caroline Walters had been seduced as much by the age-old desire to taste forbidden fruit as by a pair of tight jeans.

"You said what you went through changed your life," he said grimly. "The Army changed mine. Saved it, I guess you could say. In return, I gave everything I had to my platoon every minute I was in uniform. And when I got out, I went back and found the cop who kicked my ass all those years ago. Harry's now my senior VP of operations."

His thumb brushed the curve of her chin. His compelling amber eyes telegraphed a message she couldn't begin to interpret.

"It's your turn, Caroline. One way or another, I intend to make things right with you."

Two

Rory could see he'd rocked his consultant back on her heels. No surprise there. He'd taken a few hits himself since learning he'd fathered a child in a single, irresponsibly careless act.

The woman who'd had to live with the consequences of that act frowned up at him now. Her heart-shaped face was a study in distrust and disbelief. Her forest-green eyes reflected her fierce struggle to deal with the shock of his unexpected reappearance in her life.

"I… I need some air. I'll let you get settled in. We can talk later."

They'd do more than talk. Rory had already

decided that. But he would give her the space she needed to recover before initiating the next phase of his campaign.

"I'm still on U.S. time," he reminded her. "How about an early dinner? Six o'clock?"

"Okay. Sure. Fine."

"I'll meet you in the bar downstairs."

With a distracted wave, she indicated a leather portfolio on the coffee table. "The conference information is in that folder. I'll see you later."

She certainly would. Rory hadn't spent all those years in the Army without learning to develop contingency plans for just about every situation. He'd put a good deal of time and thought into Operation Caroline Walters.

As the door closed behind her, he tried to reconcile the woman she'd become with the seventeen-year-old she'd been. It took some doing. His memory of that summer was a little hazy around the edges.

With good reason. He'd left home at sixteen after a final, explosive brawl with his drunk of a father. For more than a year he'd drifted across the country on the beat-up Ducati 600 he'd put together from spare parts, picking up odd jobs as he went. Best he could recall, he'd worked for less than a month in the garage owned by Buck Walters. Millburn, Kansas, was too flat, too dusty and way too boring for his taste.

The same couldn't be said about Walters's niece. Rory vaguely remembered a shy smile, an embarrassed blush whenever he caught her eye and *very* shapely legs showing beneath her shorts.

The legs had interested him a whole lot more than her smiles or blushes. He'd been such a horny bastard at that age. Most of the time he'd walked around with a permanent hard-on. So naturally he'd had to strip off his T-shirt whenever the shy brunette came into her uncle's garage. Had to tease a smile out of her. Had to taunt her into a ride on the Ducati.

He'd never really expected her to swing into the saddle behind him the night before he left town. Never dreamed she'd wrap her arms around his waist and lean into his back that hot August evening. And when they'd parked beside the river, he sure as hell had never expected to get lucky.

The next morning, he remembered with a grimace of disgust, he'd left with a casual promise to call the next time he came anywhere close to Kansas. Thirteen years later, he still hadn't been back.

But he was here. Now. With the woman whose life he'd altered so irrevocably that night.

Her stricken look when she confirmed the pregnancy made Rory want to kick himself all over again for not using a condom. Or maybe he had and the damned thing didn't work. All he knew for sure was Buck Walters's niece didn't sleep around. Not back then, anyway. She'd given him ample proof of that.

He'd covered a lot of miles since that night and been with his share of women. As far as he knew, he'd never left one crying or cursing his name. The fact that he'd given Caroline plenty of reason to do both had scratched at Rory's conscience, big-time.

He'd begun developing Operation Caroline Walters the day after he'd learned of her pregnancy. His first objective had been to scope out the target. That hadn't taken long. A few clicks of the keyboard and some poking around in databases he had legal access to—and several he didn't—had verified the basic facts.

His second objective was to arrange the initial contact. He'd debated whether to approach her on a personal basis or through her business. He'd opted for the business angle for two strategic reasons. One, it gave him a hold over her. She couldn't just haul off, slug him in the jaw and stalk away. Second, this angle dovetailed nicely with his corporate plans. With so many explosive events happening all around the world, he'd been planning to pull in his key operatives for a face-to-face.

The third objective involved actually making the contact. Rory could now check that item off his plan. The meeting had gone pretty much as he'd scripted. Except…

He'd expected to experience a welter of emotions when he saw her again. Guilt, yes. Regret, certainly. Relief that he'd taken the first steps to making things right for the girl whose life he'd brought crashing down around her ears, for sure.

But he *hadn't* expected this tug of interest in the woman that girl had become. He'd shocked the hell out of her; yet she hadn't folded, hadn't yielded an inch of ground. This Caroline Walters was tougher than the shy girl he remembered. Tougher than those misty green eyes and soft mouth would lead a man to expect.

Then, of course, there were those smooth, silky legs.

The sudden tightening in his groin had Rory shaking his head in disgust. He wasn't a horny young stud anymore. He'd learned to control his appetites and harness his lust.

Stick to the plan, man! Keep the final objective firmly in view.

With that stern admonishment, he popped the buttons on his shirt and headed for the shower to sluice off the effects of his transatlantic flight.

Caro wanted out of the resort.

She had to escape the confines of her mini-suite. Had to hit the paved walkway circling the beach and let the stiff sea breeze blow away some of her shock and confusion.

She also needed to contact her partners. She had to advise them of this incredible development and get their take on how the heck she should proceed with Rory Burke. Deciding she could talk and walk, Caro dug her cell phone out of her purse and tucked it in her jacket pocket with her room key.

The salt breeze slapped into her the moment she exited the resort's lower level. February wasn't the warmest month on this stretch of Spain's Costa Brava. That didn't deter the determined sun worshippers who flocked from more northern climates to soak up the Mediterranean rays, however. Caro picked up snatches of German, Swedish, French and Russian as she set off along the tiled walk first laid by the Romans.

An elderly Spaniard in a sweater vest and black beret hunched on the seawall, a cigarette dangling from his lips. He stared out to sea with eyes narrowed in his weathered face and displayed no interest in the topless bather stretched out on the beach below. Her generously siliconed breasts had certainly attracted the interest of others, though. Caro had to skirt a small crowd of tourists, all male and all avidly clicking away with their cameras.

Caroline found a sheltered spot at the base of the hill leading up to the castle ruins. Perching on the seawall, she pulled out her cell phone. Luckily, both of her partners were currently in Europe so she didn't have to juggle time zones. Devon McShay had arrived in London just this morning with Cal Logan. The CEO of Logan Aerospace now had her handling all his European connections.

Sabrina Russo was in Rome, busy setting up a satellite office and sorting through an avalanche of potential jobs steered her way by the handsome neurosurgeon she'd fallen for—literally and figuratively!—last month.

Caro speed-dialed Sabrina first and felt her heart lift at just the sound of her friend's cheerful greeting.

"Hey, girl. Wazzup?"

"Hang on a sec. I want to get Dev on the line for a three-way."

She hit the button for a conference call and caught Devon in a limo with Cal Logan, on their way to a meeting with British Aerospace.

"Hi, Caro."

"Hi, Dev. Sabrina's on the line, too."

"Great. I need to update you both on my itinerary. But first... Did you get our new client all meeted and greeted?"

"Yes."

Caro kept her voice even, or thought she did, but the other two women had known her too long. Both picked up on the clipped response.

"Uh-oh. Is there a problem?"

"You could say that."

She couldn't think of any way to break the news except to blurt it out.

"Rory Burke, Global Security's chief exec, is the father of the baby I lost when I was in high school."

Simultaneous exclamations burst through the phone.

"What!"

"No way!"

"Trust me, you're not half as flabbergasted as I was. Still am, for that matter. I'm—I'm not sure how to handle this."

"You don't have to handle it," Sabrina shot back. "You pack up, girlfriend. Right now. Catch the next flight home. I'll zip over from Rome and deliver a hard, swift kick to the bastard's balls before orchestrating the rest of his friggin' conference."

"That'll bring us a lot of future business," Caro said on a shaky laugh.

"We don't need Burke's business," Devon added with equal fervor. "I'm with 'Rina. Tell the jerk to take a long walk off a short pier, and get out of there."

Caro had to put in reluctant protest. "He's not a total jerk. He didn't know I was pregnant. I never told him."

"Because you couldn't find him!"

Their fierce, unquestioned loyalty eased some of the tightness in Caroline's chest. Devon and Sabrina were her best friends as well as business partners. The *only* friends she'd ever opened up to about her past.

She'd met them for the first time at the University of Salzburg, where they'd shared rooms while participating in a Junior Year Abroad Program. Still carrying the emotional scars from high school, Caro had been distant and reserved at first.

The combination of a minuscule apartment, Sabrina's bubbling personality and Devon's passionate love of all things historical had gradually penetrated her shield. Looking back, Caro would always zero in on that year in Salzburg as the point where she came fully alive again.

Now the three of them were in business together. Partners in a fledgling company called European Business Services, Inc.—EBS for short. Since EBS launched last year they'd kept busy providing travel, translation and support services for executives doing business in Europe. Caro had thoroughly enjoyed the clients she'd worked with so far.

This one, though, was in a class by himself.

"Thanks for the moral support," she told her friends with heartfelt sincerity.

"Moral support, hell!" Sabrina grumbled. "I still want to kick some gonads."

"Hold on to that thought," Caro said with a faint smile. Talking through her shock and confusion like this had provided just the shot in the arm she needed. "I appreciate your offer to do the dirty for me but…"

Her gaze shifted to the waves rolling in to the beach. They were endless. Relentless. Like time. Like her past. The only way to deal with it, the only way Caro knew to deal with any problem, was to face it head-on.

"If there's any gonad-kicking to be done," she told her partners, "I'll do it myself."

"You sure you don't want one of us to fly in?" Devon asked, sounding worried and unconvinced.

"I'm sure. I just needed to talk to you guys and let you know there might be a problem with this contract."

She managed to inject more confidence into the calm reply than she was feeling. *Much* more.

"Whatever you decide," Sabrina reminded her unnecessarily, "Dev and I are behind you two thousand percent. Stay in Spain, don't stay. Deck the bastard, don't deck him. Just keep us posted, okay?"

"I will."

Caro flipped the cell phone shut, feeling a hundred pounds lighter and a hundred years younger. She couldn't erase the memories of that awful time. She would live with them forever. But she didn't have to let them cloud her future.

She was in control of her life, she reminded herself sternly. What's more, she was part owner in a firm with a very lucrative contract on the line.

She would use the hours until dinner to shake off the residual effects of coming face-to-face with her past and figure out a way to smooth over this awkward situation. When she met Rory Burke this evening, she vowed she would be cool, calm and completely professional.

Cool and calm went up in smoke two seconds after Caro spotted her client in the resort's trendy bar.

He had a drink in front of him—scotch she presumed, since that's what his administrative assistant had told her to stock his suite with—and was crunching down on an appetizer from the assortment arrayed on the cocktail table.

He must have showered before coming down. Dampness still glistened in his dark blond hair. He was also, Caro saw with a jolt that went through her entire system, wearing a black V-neck sweater and faded jeans. Both items molded a body far more mature and muscled than the one she remembered.

She'd prepped for another meeting with the smooth, polished executive, dammit. She'd rehearsed what she would say, had her conditions for continuing their professional relationship all laid out. Her prepared speech didn't fit the man who rose and strode over to her.

He was too relaxed, too informal and far too dangerous. She didn't trust his easy smile. *Or* her instinctive reaction to it.

"I ordered some *tapas*." He gestured to the colorful display on the table. "Care to indulge?"

"When in Spain…" Caro murmured, trying once again to recover her balance. Rory Burke seemed to be making a habit of throwing her off it.

"What would you like to drink?"

"White wine. Godello, if they have it."

"I'll bring it to the table."

Caroline had spent enough time in Spain to identify most of the appetizers on the small cocktail table. Spaniards had a passion for *tapas,* flavorful bite-size bits that served more as a conduit for socializing in bars and restaurants after work than a source of nourishment.

There were as many variations of *tapas* as there were cooks. The dozen or so small dishes in front of her held aromatic combinations of chickpeas and spinach, clams in sherry paprika sauce, roasted almonds, fried calamari, olives, red peppers with anchovies, garlic shrimp and what looked like chunks of cod wrapped in grape leaves, all staked with wooden toothpicks for easy nibbling.

Paprika seared her palate after one bite of the clams. With her tongue on fire, she reached for the wine Burke brought her with a murmur of fervent thanks. Before she could take a sip, he'd reclaimed his seat and raised his own glass.

"Shall we drink to new beginnings?"

That stopped the wine halfway to Caro's lips. Her eyes met his across the small table. She couldn't interpret the message in their amber depths, but common courtesy demanded she at least acknowledge his toast. Her burning tongue made that courtesy a necessity.

"To new beginnings."

The tangy, light-bodied Godello extinguished the paprika-fueled fire. Able to draw breath again, Caro set down her glass and launched into her prepared spiel.

"Okay, here's the deal. I've spent the time since your arrival trying to decide how best to handle this situation."

"I expect you have."

"First, I don't appreciate the backhanded way you arranged this…this reunion."

He hooked a brow. "You don't appreciate that I dropped a fat contract in your lap?"

"You should have been up-front with me. Told me who you were."

"I didn't try to hide my identity," he countered mildly. "My name is on the contract."

"You knew darn well I would never associate the chief executive officer of GSI with the kid everyone, including my uncle and cousin, called Johnny."

"Would you have taken the job if I'd spelled it out for you?"

"Probably not. And that brings us to the conditions under which I'll continue to work this conference for you."

She edged several of the small dishes aside. Hands clasped loosely on the table, she kept her gaze steady and her tone even.

"I don't want any further discussion of our previous association. Nothing either of us can say will change what happened, so there's no need to rehash it. Agreed?"

He toyed with a tooth-picked clam, trailing the succulent morsel through the dark sherry sauce. Caro glanced down to follow the movement and found herself wondering when and how he'd acquired those thin, faded scars webbing across the back of his hand.

"Agreed," he said after a moment. "As you said, we can't change what happened."

"And this notion that you have to make things right with me… Forget it. There's nothing to make right. I'm content with my life now. Very content. I don't want you charging into it out of some mistaken sense of obligation."

"All right. I won't charge."

Her eyes narrowed in suspicion. The reply was too amiable, too quick.

"Let me rephrase that. I don't want you in my life, period."

"Too late for that," he said reasonably. "I'm here. You're here. We'll be working together for the next four days."

"Then I want your agreement that's all we'll do," she stated emphatically. "Work."

The clam made another slow swirl. He contemplated its dark trail for a few seconds before lifting those russet-ringed eyes to hers.

"I can't promise you that. Who's to say the heat that flared between us back in Millburn won't ignite again? But I can promise this," he added as she went as stiff as a board, "I won't make the same mistakes I made then. And I won't make any moves you don't want me to. You're safe with me, Caroline. I swear it."

"Yeah, right," she muttered. "Isn't that what the big, bad wolf said to Little Red Riding Hood?"

He grinned then, looking so much like the cocky kid she'd mooned over all those years ago that her heart knocked against her ribs.

"Pretty much," he agreed.

Three

Caroline was up at six-thirty the next morning. Since most of the GSI attendees were coming in from the field, their CEO had specified casual attire. Caro had to walk a fine line as the event coordinator, however. Jeans and jungle boots wouldn't hack it for her.

She settled instead on dove-gray slacks and a wide-sleeved cotton tunic in warm tangerine paired with the colorful espadrilles she'd picked up in Tossa de Mar's open-air market. Winding her hair up into its usual neat twist at the back of her head, she anchored it with a clip. A few swipes of blush and a quick pass with lip gloss and she was done.

She rechecked her zippered conference file for the fifth or sixth time. Satisfied she had everything she needed, she hit the door. With the conference set to kick off at eleven, she'd arranged a breakfast meeting with her GSI focal point to go over last-minute details. Caro and Harry Martin had exchanged dozens of e-mails over the past two months. She'd kept hers brisk and businesslike. His had been so succinct as to be almost indecipherable. A man of few words, Harry Martin.

And, according to Rory's startling revelations yesterday, he was the man who'd hauled a smart-mouthed kid into an Army recruiter's office all those years ago and put his life back on track. After what Rory had told her about his senior VP of operations, Caro expected a big, grizzled retired cop.

Martin was definitely big. Six-three or -four at least. He had to stoop to avoid brushing the grape-vines that dangled from the arbor leading to the terrace restaurant. Grizzled, he wasn't. Sleek Ray-Bans shielded his eyes above chiseled cheeks and a serious, unsmiling mouth. His khakis sported a knife-blade crease, and his sky-blue polo shirt stretched across a frame that looked fit and trim. His salt-and-pepper buzz cut gave the only clue to his age.

"Ms. Walters?" He set a notebook on the table and folded her hand in a tough, callused palm. "Harry Martin."

"Good to finally meet you, Mr. Martin."

"Harry," he corrected as he seated himself at the umbrella-shielded table. "Caroline okay with you?"

"Of course. How was your flight from Casablanca?"

She knew he'd flown into Morocco two days ago and from there to Barcelona late last night.

"Fine."

He helped himself to coffee from a stainless-steel carafe and proceeded to dump five heaping spoonfuls of sugar into his cup. Wondering how the heck he managed to stay so trim, Caro watched with some fascination as he stirred the syrupy goo.

"Sweet tooth," he said when he caught her gaze.

He downed a long swallow, replaced the cup on the saucer and slid his Ray-Bans down on his nose. There weren't more than a half dozen other people eating breakfast on the terrace. The faint clink of their silverware and the occasional murmured comment barely carried over the sound of the waves hitting the shore. Still, either from habit or instinct, Martin lowered his voice.

"I talked to Rory when I got in last night."

Caro felt her spine stiffen and her smile slip a notch or two. Martin noticed both reactions with a flicker of interest but didn't comment on either.

"Rory says you have everything well in hand."

She relaxed infinitesimally. "I hope so."

"I hope so, too. We hate pulling over a hundred of our operatives out of the field at one time, but the world situation is so volatile right now that we had no choice. They need to know what's going on around them. So we need to make every minute of this conference count."

"You've certainly packed the agenda."

"It's about to get more packed."

Nudging aside his cup, he flipped open his notebook and pulled out a heavily marked-up copy of the schedule. Caro's heart sank at all the insertions and bold black arrows indicating changes.

"Rory and I went over this again last night. He called in some favors and we now have an expert on Africa flying in to brief us on the situation in Zimbabwe. We want to put him on here, right before the update on Tiblesi."

"Okay."

"And we've added two additional SITREPS on the latest developments in Tibet and Venezuela. We can squeeze them in before the live fire demo tomorrow. I'm thinking we'll do one early, during breakfast, and the other at lunch. Make both meals working sessions."

Caro gulped as her meticulously coordinated meal plans fell apart. She'd have to get with the resort's caterer—and *fast*—to make the requested changes. Masking any sign of dismay, she nodded.

"No problem."

"And speaking of the live fire demo…"

Martin flipped to the agreement signed by Captain Antonio Medina, the officer in charge of the *policìa nacional* armory in Girona. Acting as a go-between for GSI and Captain Medina, Caro had put hours into translating, compiling and forwarding the necessary forms. GSI's senior VP of operations now handed her two more.

"See if you can get Medina's chop on these additions to the demo."

"Ice shield?" she read. "Paraclete vest? What are they?"

"The first is a negative energy defense system. We're looking at it for possible deployment to protect high-vis clients when they have to get out among a crowd. The second is a new-generation vest designed to stop armor-piercing bullets. I've tracked down a source here in Spain for both and can have them delivered in time for the demo tomorrow."

He downed a swallow of his syrupy coffee and eyed her over the rims of his Ray-Bans.

"Think you can handle the changes?"

Like she had a choice? Tapping two fingers to her temple, she gave him a brisk salute. "Yes, sir!"

A faint smile softened Martin's chiseled features. "I have to admit I had my doubts when Rory told me he wanted European Business Services, Incorporated, to handle this conference. I didn't think your company had the resources or the experience to pull it together on such short notice. So far, you've proved me wrong."

Caro shifted a little in her seat. She couldn't deny this job would rake in a fat profit for EBS. Still, she resented the way Burke had used it as a pretext to stage a reunion she'd neither anticipated nor wanted.

"Judging by the little exposure I've had to your boss," she said, working hard to keep the acid out of her reply, "I'd say he's used to getting his way."

"Well, he *is* the boss." Martin toyed with his coffee cup and studied her face with a scrutiny that made Caro distinctly uncomfortable. She suspected those cop's eyes saw more than most people wanted them to.

"Rory's a good man," he said after a moment. "The kind you can trust to do what's right."

Depending on your definition of "right," she thought cynically.

"I'll take your word for that."

She glanced at her watch and swallowed another gulp. "Do you have any other items you want to discuss with me?"

"Not right now."

"Then I'd better skip breakfast and get to work on these changes."

"Go."

After dropping off a USB drive with the revised agenda in the business office, Caro met with the resort's conference planner in her den. She, in turn, called in the executive chef.

Andreas was not happy about scratching the second day's elaborate breakfast of fire-grilled Andalucian ham and house specialty *torrijas*. Frowning, he substituted a simpler sausage-and-egg scramble served with flaky rolls and the region's signature apricot jam. He was even less thrilled about changing the elegant seafood lunch buffet planned for outside on the terrace to sit-down service in the ballroom.

Caro left him grumbling over the changes and rushed back to the business office. To her relief, the efficient staff had the revised agendas rolling off the high-speed printer and promised to place them on the tables for the kickoff session.

Those two tasks well in hand, Caro tried to reach Captain Medina. As she'd discovered in her previous dealings with the police captain, he tended to set his own schedule. Luckily, she caught him this time and extracted his promise to review the forms she'd faxed over.

"I need your reply as soon as possible," she begged in the Spanish she'd studied in high school and college. She was almost as fluent in it as in the German she'd mastered during her year in Salzburg with Devon and Sabrina. *"Por favor, capitán."*

"Sí, sí, le llamaré."

Forced to be content with his promise to call, she headed for the ballroom to make sure everything was set for the general session. To her relief, the audiovisual technicians had their equipment up and running. She also confirmed there was plenty of coffee, tea, water and soft drinks available for the attendees who were starting to trickle in. Snatches of conversation caught her ear as she made a last check of the seating arrangements.

"Ramieriz, you old bastard!"

A brawny redhead in a safari shirt with at least a dozen pockets punched the arm of a bearded Latino.

"Heard you got snakebit on that job down in Panama."

They were joined by a slender Asian in a dragon-red dress slit on one side. A head shorter than the two men, she got their instant respect and an eager demand for the details on the Yang Su kidnapping.

Caro ducked out of the ballroom and into the ladies' room to check her hair and lip gloss. Then she drew in a deep breath, pasted on a smile and re-entered the ballroom.

It had filled considerably in her brief absence. Those present were predominantly male, although she picked out several of the dozen or so women slated to attend. Rory was easily identifiable as he moved among the crowd. He'd dressed for the kickoff session in loafers, black slacks and a pale yellow oxford shirt open at the collar. Caro watched from the corner of one eye while he shook hands and thumped backs in that age-old male ritual.

At least one of Rory's crew got a kiss instead of a back thump. Or more correctly, she kissed him. On the cheek, although it was obvious to Caro that the tall, striking blonde would have preferred a full-frontal lip-lock.

For reasons she didn't have time to analyze, Caro formed an instant dislike for the woman. That lasted only until Rory caught sight of his conference coordinator and brought the blonde over for an introduction.

"I want you to meet Sondra Jennings. She's head of GSI's European division, based in Copenhagen. Sondra, this is Caroline Walters, with European Business Services."

The blonde returned Caro's handshake with a friendly smile. "So you're the one who pulled this confab together. Harry Martin was talking about you when we had coffee together a little while ago." Her blue eyes twinkled. "Knowing Harry, I'm sure he's kept you hopping."

"Pretty much," Caro admitted.

"I've worked with several clients who might be interested in the type of services EBS provides. I'll contact them when I get back to Denmark and spread the word."

"That's very generous of you."

"We girls gotta stick together." Her gaze snagged on the man just entering the ballroom. "There's Abdul-Hamid! I haven't seen him since we tracked the source of those death threats against the author of *Inside the Mujahideen.* 'Scuse me, you two."

She hurried to the door and enveloped the newcomer in a monster hug. He returned it with such obvious delight that Caro was forced to revise her initial impression.

"She's very gregarious."

"When she wants to be," Rory drawled. "Ready to get this show under way?"

She swept a final glance over the tables and now-milling crowd. "I am if you are."

"Let's do it."

"I'll be at the back of the room. Just signal if you need anything."

"That won't work." Shaking his head, he caught her elbow and steered her toward a round table near the podium. "I want you up front, with me."

"But…"

"It'll be easier for us to communicate this way."

After seating her beside Harry Martin, he pinned the mobile mike to his shirt. His voice boomed through the speakers.

"All right, team. Time to get to work."

He waited for the general shuffle of chairs to die down before asking Caroline to stand.

"For those of you who haven't met her yet, this is Caroline Walters. She and Harry are running this show. Any complaints, tell him. Any and all kudos go to her."

Rory held the stage for the next hour. Caroline listened in mounting amazement as he discussed worldwide trends in violence against VIPs, quoting specific facts and figures without once referring to the prepared script. It was obvious even to an out-

sider like her that he had every facet of his dangerous profession down cold.

His message was grim, and the slides that flashed
up on the screen were appalling. They depicted, in
graphic detail, a blindfolded French ambassador with
a gun barrel to his head. The bullet-riddled body of
a candidate for prime minister in Indonesia. The terrified wife of a police captain in Colombia, explo-
sives strapped to her chest, just seconds before drug
runners blew her apart as a message to everyone who
cooperated with law enforcement officials.

Caroline was ready for a break by the time Rory
finished. *More* than ready. She didn't view the world
through rose-colored glasses by any means, but
Rory's grim assessment had brought home just how
dangerous it could be.

Particularly for the kind of high-powered executives her company catered to. Neither she nor Devon
nor Sabrina had fully considered that aspect of their
business. The realization sobered Caro and made her
anxious to impart some of this information to her
partners.

"We'll take a short break so they can set up for
lunch," Rory told his people. "Harry will go over the
latest State Department alerts while we eat."

With palpable relief, Caro signaled the servers to
bring in the paella extravaganza she'd arranged for the
kickoff luncheon. Most of the ingredients had been
precooked in the resort's kitchen, but four chefs in tall

white hats provided the finishing touch. Positioned before waist-high stands supporting huge black frying pans, they sizzled the rice, chopped vegetables and cooked seafood morsels over open flames.

The tantalizing aromas soon drew the attendees back into the ballroom. Caro didn't relax until everyone had filled their plates with heaping servings. At Rory's insistence, she brought her plate back to his table.

"You need to listen to Harry's update on State Department alerts," GSI's chief executive advised. "They could play into your business."

"I was thinking that same thing during your briefing. That was pretty scary information you put out."

"It's a scary world."

Nodding, she speared a morsel of calamari and tuned in to Harry Martin's succinct recap.

The rest of the afternoon passed in a blur of country briefings and individual case rundowns. Caro had to duck out to take a call from Captain Medina. She returned with the welcome news that he'd approved the additions to the live fire demo.

The conferees broke for the day at six o'clock. Dinner was scheduled for seven. Since many of the GSI operatives would be feeling a delayed jet lag, Harry had requested Caro keep the meal short and simple. She'd ordered a selection of *tapas* served in a roped-off section of the bar that gave a magnificent view of the bay, followed by salad and chargrilled kebabs. Dessert was a melt-in-your mouth flan with its top seared to a sugary crunch and drizzled with caramel sauce.

A number of the GSI folks folded their tents immediately after dinner. The rest congregated in groups, exchanging war stories that ranged from the ridiculous to the downright gruesome. Caro tried to move unobtrusively between groups to make sure they had everything they needed, but Sondra Jennings drew her into one enclave, Rory into another. By ten o'clock that evening, the colorful espadrilles pinched her toes and she couldn't *wait* to get them off her feet.

Finally she said good-night and left the last die-hards crammed knee-to-knee around a cocktail table. Rory's gaze followed her as she wound through the lounge. Caro could feel it, and the awareness annoyed her no end.

She'd made a determined effort to keep their past out of her head all day. It wasn't that difficult, given how much Rory had changed. She'd watched a stranger kick off the conference today. Informed, incisive, every inch the boss. She didn't know him, any more than he knew her.

Which didn't explain the prickly feeling between her shoulder blades as she left the bar.

Frowning, Caro stepped out onto the tiled veranda. She fully intended to go up to her room, zing off a quick e-mail to Devon and Sabrina and fall into bed. The full moon hanging over the Mediterranean sabotaged those intentions.

She paused, mesmerized by the path the moon had painted across an incandescent sea. The thought of wading into that liquid silver was too much for someone who'd spent half of her life in landlocked Kansas.

The resort sat only a few short yards from the wide seawall encircling the bay. A quick walk brought her to the stone stairs that led down to the sandy shore. Kicking off the espadrilles, Caroline scooped them up in one hand and crossed the hard-packed sand to the water's edge.

The sea breeze carried a damp chill that made her wish she'd gone back to her room for the colorful Spanish shawl she'd purchased at the same time as the espadrilles. Shivering a little, she curled her toes into the sand. The waves washed out, luring her a little farther, and returned with an unexpected wallop.

"Yikes!"

The water was frigid, far colder than she'd anticipated. And much more powerful. The first wave swirled around her ankles. The second hit before she could retreat and soaked her to her knees.

She leaped backward but couldn't escape the undertow. Like a giant vacuum, it sucked the sand right out from under her bare feet and pulled her in. Thrown off balance, Caro stumbled. She saw the next wave roll toward her and floundered backward for one futile step before she went down with an ignominious splash.

The surf boiled up, soaking her. Salt burned her eyes. Cursing, she let go of the espadrilles and slapped the waves. She made a clumsy attempt to get her feet under her, but the sucking undercurrent had her firmly in its grip.

Great! Perfect! At this rate, she'd wash up on the coast of Libya. Thoroughly disgusted, she dug a heel into the shifting ocean bed beneath her.

She'd just found a toehold when a hand clamped around her wrist. The next second, she was jerked to her feet and landed with a thump against a solid wall of chest.

"Caroline! You okay?"

She flipped strands of wet hair out of her eyes and looked up into Rory's taut face.

"I'm fine. Now."

"I almost had a heart attack when I saw you go under. What the hell were you thinking, wading out this far?"

His grip tightened, anchoring her against the next wave. Frigid seawater swirled around her thighs and floated up the hem of her cotton tunic.

"In answer to your question," she said when the swirl subsided, "I didn't *intend* to wade this far. The undertow got me."

"Jesus!"

Almost as wet as she was, he helped her to the

shallows. His pale yellow shirt was plastered against his chest and shoulders. His drenched khakis molded his thighs.

"You scared the crap out of me, woman." Softening both his tone and his grip, he raked her with a swift once-over. "You sure you're okay?"

"I'm fine. Really."

And mortified, now that the initial scare had passed. Getting dragged up on the beach like a half-drowned harbor seal didn't do a whole lot for Caroline's image as a cool, with-it professional.

"Thanks," she added on a grudging afterthought.

"You're welcome." He grinned at her reluctant gratitude. "Rescuing beautiful women is just one of the many services GSI provides. The charge for this particular service is pretty steep, though."

"Send me an invoice. I'll deduct it from the final amount we bill GSI."

"I have a better idea."

Still grinning, he brushed back a wet strand and hooked it behind her ear. His voice dropped to a teasing, all-too-familiar taunt.

"How about I just take it out in trade?"

The situation was so absurd, his touch so unexpected, that Caro didn't have time to block the sudden onslaught of memories.

In a flash, she was seventeen again, hopelessly infatuated, helplessly captivated. Her heart slammed against her ribs. Her pulse shot off the charts. All she could do was stare up in breathless fascination as Burke curled a knuckle under her chin and tipped her head back.

"This is just the first installment," he warned before he swooped down to cover her mouth with his.

Four

Rory initiated the kiss with a clearly defined set of goals.

He wasn't a perpetually aroused young tiger on the prowl anymore. He could control his appetites, harness his primitive instincts. His intention was simply to show Caroline she could trust him. Now.

Then her mouth opened under his, and his intentions were shot all to hell. She tasted of salt and just a hint of sweet, sugary caramel. Through the wet shield of her clothes, he could feel her breasts, hips and belly against his. The ocean thundered in his ears, or maybe it was the sound of her breathing.

He found her tongue with his, and his world shifted, almost tilting him off his feet. Belatedly,

Rory realized it was the damned sand. The powerful undercurrent was siphoning it out from under him.

He raised his head and allowed himself a brief stab of pleasure at the sight of her. Her hair had straggled free of the tight twist. Water spiked her lashes and made them glisten in the moonlight. Her eyes were huge—and rapidly filling with a welter of emotions that included dismay and unmistakable disgust.

With a chuckle, Rory tried to head off the storm he saw coming. "Sucks you in, doesn't it?"

The double entendre was completely unintentional but not lost on either of them. Her breath hissed out, and he backtracked immediately.

"The sand, I mean. I can feel it giving way. Unless you want to rescue *me,* we'd better head for shore."

The water was only ankle high, but the pull was so insistent that he had to wrap an arm around her waist to help her get to dry land. The moment they gained the beach, she jerked away from him.

He could see her fighting for control, struggling with the raw emotions he saw in her face. Rory expected her to lay into him. Was sure she'd deny that second or two when her mouth opened and her tongue danced with his. To his surprise, she took aim at herself.

"What was I thinking? Why *wasn't* I thinking?"

She sounded so appalled, so dismayed, that he had to suppress a wince.

"I never let myself go like that," she said with a break in her voice. "Never!"

Rory's brows soared. "Are you telling me you don't... That you've never..."

His incredulity snapped her out of her miasma of dismay and disgust.

"Never been with anyone but you?" she finished, her chin angling. "Don't flatter yourself, Burke."

But he *had* been the first. The memory of that night beside the river hit Rory hard, low in his belly, as Caroline raised her chin another inch.

"I don't blame you for that...that bit of idiocy. I blame myself. Trust me. It won't happen again."

The hell it wouldn't. Now that he'd had a taste of her, Rory intended to make some revisions to his op plan. Objectives five and six needed considerable adjustments.

He was reworking them in his mind when Caroline whirled and marched all of two yards up the beach before coming to a dead stop. He heard her gasp and followed her line of sight to a set of lighted, floor-to-ceiling windows.

Well, hell! They were there. Harry. Sondra. Abdul-Hamid. The rest of the crew who'd hung around the bar after dinner. All crowded close to the windows, all watching the scene with avid interest. They'd had ringside seats to the entire episode.

"Oh, no," Caroline moaned, more to herself than to him. "How am I supposed to face them in the morning?"

He didn't even try to tell her it was no big deal.

Rory could take the flak from his frolic in the surf. It would hit Caroline hard, he guessed, and not just because of the professional image she worked so hard to project. The past had left her all too vulnerable to whispers and sidelong glances. He was damned if she would be subject to them again because of him.

"I'll do damage control with my people. You don't have to worry about facing them tomorrow—or any other day."

His flat assurance quelled some of Caro's rioting emotions. He sounded so confident, so matter-of-fact. As if wading into the Mediterranean and getting chest-to-chest with a dripping female was no big deal.

Which it probably wasn't. To him. She, on the other hand, could still taste him on her lips.

They parted just inside the foyer. Caroline punched the button for the elevator and refused to look over her shoulder as Rory peeled off toward the bar. Only after she'd gained the safety of her room did she let loose with the torrent churning up inside her.

"Stupid! Stupid! *STU-PID!*"

She wanted to burst into tears. Pound the sofa pillows. Scream or kick or haul off and slug someone. *Anything* to erase the agonizing embarrassment of the past ten minutes.

She was forced to settle for stalking into the bathroom and yanking her wet sweater over her head. Slinging it at the wall gave her a small measure of satisfaction. The sopping cotton hit the tiles with a loud whap. Her slacks and underwear followed in short order.

She stared at the soggy pile, everything inside her cringing with self-disgust. Everything, that is, except a tiny, rebellious corner of her mind that sparked with a life of its own. A nasty little corner that wanted to relive every second of that kiss, to taste the sizzle, feel the heat.

She hadn't lied to Burke. There *had* been other men. Two, to be exact. The first she'd dated for almost six months before she'd let down the barriers enough to go to bed with him. Unfortunately, the sex hadn't been worth the wait.

Her friend Devon had introduced her to the second. A biologist Dev had met at some Let's Go Green function. Ernie was serious about his work but what made him so endearing was his hopeless addiction to old Dean Martin records and any stray cat that happened across his path.

Caro had wanted to love him. She really had. He was so right for her. So gentle and considerate in bed.

Too gentle and considerate. Try as she might, she couldn't help comparing Ernie's cautious lovemaking to the wild explosion of delight she'd experienced that night beside the river with Rory.

The same wild delight she'd tasted again tonight.

The thrill of it crouched in that forbidden corner of her mind. The excitement was like a fever, swift and all-consuming, straining to break free of Caro's rigid restraints and fire her blood.

Disgusted all over again, she padded on sandy, seaweedy feet to the walk-in shower and twisted the taps to full blast. Face turned to the pounding spray, she let a frustrated groan rip from deep in her throat.

When in *hell* would she learn!

The next morning, she walked into the room set up for the GSI breakfast with a cool smile and her chin high.

She'd had all night to prepare for the smirks and knowing smiles but soon realized that whatever Rory had said to his people must have sunk in. Other than a sideways glance from the male operative with the red hair and a more speculative one from Sondra, everyone was friendly and polite. Gradually, Caroline relaxed.

She snapped wire-tight again the moment Rory appeared. All she had to do was catch a glimpse of him as he strode in and her stomach went into a fast roll. She turned away before he saw her, swallowing a curse when her china coffee cup rattled on its saucer.

She had herself under control by the time he made his way to her side. Exercising iron will, she refused to let either his smile or the faint, tangy scent of his aftershave get to her.

"Morning."

"Good morning."

"You okay?" he asked quietly.

"Fine."

The clipped response didn't seem to faze him. Or keep his glance from drifting downward toward her lips for a few seconds.

"No aftereffects from your late-night swim?"

"Not a one."

The mocking glint that came into his eyes told her he recognized that for the lie it was. Thankfully, Harry Martin came over before he could challenge her on it.

"I've got that situation brief on Venezuela ready to go, boss."

"Let me grab a cup of coffee, and then we'll get started."

As she had the day before, Caroline tried to hang back so she could oversee the meal service. As *he* had the day before, Rory sabotaged her plans.

"After you, Caroline."

The command was politely worded but definitely a command. She thought about saying no for all of three or four seconds. Then she shrugged and accompanied Rory to their designated table.

After the general session detailing the somewhat scary situation in Venezuela, the attendees broke into smaller groups for regional updates. Sondra took charge of the European sessions. Abdul-Hamid orchestrated a series of briefings dealing with the Middle East and Africa. The Asian expert turned out to be a ruddy-faced Englishman with what Caroline could only describe as a seriously warped sense of humor.

Intrigued by roars of laughter emanating from his session, she slipped into the back of the room in time to hear him describe attempts by pirates to hijack a luxury, oceangoing yacht owned by a GSI client.

"They came in under our radar during the night and got close enough to fire their rocket-propelled grenades. Lucky for us the buggers didn't know how to activate the built-in lock-and-launch radar. Bloody grenades came close enough to tighten my knickers, though."

One of the men in the room gave a loud hoot. "Since when do you wear knickers, Basil?"

"It was merely a figure of speech, old chap. Back to our nocturnal visitors...I sincerely wish I could have seen their faces when we whipped the cover off the M61 mounted in the stern, but it was too bloody dark."

Caroline had no idea what an M61 was, but she gathered from the murmurs of approval that it was a powerful weapon. The speaker confirmed that a moment later with his cheerful claim to have blown the buggers right out of the water.

Amazed all over again by the danger Rory's people apparently faced on a daily basis, she slipped out to check on preparations for lunch and finalize transportation to the *policía nacional* armory in Girona.

She had two buses lined up and waiting when the conferees broke after lunch. A truck loaded with sealed crates idled patiently behind the buses. Two of Rory's men had accompanied the crates from the airport and stayed with them for the short trip to Girona.

Caroline had prepped as best she could for the excursion and knew that the ancient city of Girona had been inhabited in turn by Iberians, Romans, Visigoths, Moors and the armies of Napoleon. It had also served as a major center for Kabbalah studies until the Jews were driven out of Spain in 1492. In recent years, Girona had once again become a center of learning for the Jewish faith.

Following directions faxed by Captain Medina, Caroline directed their small convoy to the police armory on the outskirts of town. Antonio Medina strolled out to meet them on their arrival and greeted Caroline in English heavily flavored by his native Catalan roots.

"Good afternoon, Ms. Walters."

"Good afternoon, Captain. Allow me to introduce Rory Burke, president and CEO of Global Security, Incorporated."

Medina thrust out his hand. "I have heard much of you, Mr. Burke. You took part in the international task force that investigated 3/11, yes?"

"I did."

It took Caroline a few moments to make the connection. Nine-eleven was indelibly ingrained on the consciousness of all Americans. Similar horrific attacks had occurred in Spain on March 11, 2004.

Close to two hundred people had died in coordinated commuter train bombings. Almost two thousand more were injured.

She'd had no idea Rory had been part of the multinational task force investigating the bombings. It certainly hadn't been mentioned in his company profile. Then again, maybe that was the kind of expertise you didn't want the bad guys to know you possessed.

It did explain, however, Captain Medina's patience while Caroline had slogged through the reams of paperwork to permit GSI access to his outdoor firing range.

The range was situated in an open field several kilometers from the armory buildings. Medina invited Rory to ride out with him in his vehicle. The rest of the team followed in the buses. Once on the range, the captain, Rory and Harry Martin conferred with the range supervisor. A sense of unreality gripped Caroline as she listened to them discussing laser-directed small-arms fire, armor-piercing bullets and high-impact detonations while swallows chirped merrily in the trees and the bright Catalonian sun warmed the earth.

The first crack of a high-powered, laser-guided sniper rifle sent the swallows flapping. Caro stood well back from the firing line, her ears shielded by cushioned protectors, and felt her jaw drop when a spotter more than a mile and a half downrange signaled back a direct hit.

Even more astonishing was the so-called ice shield. Caro never did grasp the physics involved. Somehow the device activated an intense negative ion field around the target. The hyperactive ions sucked the velocity from most of the bullets fired at the target from various distances. Enough got through, however, for Rory to admit with a wry grin that the device required further testing before being fielded.

After Harry demonstrated the paraclete vest, the GSI agents took turns at the firing line testing an assortment of handguns and ammo. Caroline had no idea she would be included in the live fire exercise until they took a break and Rory beckoned her forward.

"Ever fired one of these?"

She glanced at the blue-steel subcompact nestled in his palm and shook her head. "Nothing that small. I went quail hunting with my father a few times. His double-barrel shotgun just about knocked me flat."

"Given the high-profile clients your firm caters to, a working knowledge of handguns might come in handy."

"I sincerely hope not!"

"We'll start with the basics," he said, calmly brushing aside her objections. "This is the safety. Always check to make sure it's on before handling your weapon."

Fifteen minutes later, Caroline found herself standing between Sondra and Abdul-Hamid on the firing line, peering through shatterproof goggles at a paper target strung from a wire twenty yards away. A borrowed ball cap blocked the sun's glare. Heavy-duty protectors shielded her ears.

Rory stood directly behind her, his body leaning into hers as he corrected her stance. "Don't square off and face the target like that. You won't get good front-to-back balance. You want to form a pyramid, with your power leg forward."

"Which one is my power leg?"

"You're right-handed. You'll naturally favor your right leg. Now angle your pelvis at forty-five degrees to the target. A little more."

Oh, sure! Like she could think pyramids and angles with his hands on her hips and her rear jammed against the fly of his jeans.

"With an automatic, you want to use what we call a 'crush' grip. The harder you hold the weapon, the less it will kick."

"A tight grip also lessens the chance some sleaze-bag can knock it out of your hand," Sondra volunteered.

Caroline diverted her attention long enough to see that a circle of interested observers had gathered to watch the lesson. Then Rory reached around her to steady her arms, and every nerve in her body snapped back to the task at hand.

"Use your thumb to release the safety. That's it. Now tuck your thumb and focus on the front sight.

You want to pull the trigger straight back. Squeeze it or roll it. Don't jerk it. All set?"

"I think so."

He dropped his arms and stepped back. "Fire when ready."

Her first shot went wide of the target and kicked her arms up. The second wasn't much better. With cordite stinging her nostrils, Caroline scowled, tightened her grip and squinted through the front sight.

The next three shots peppered the edges of the target silhouette. The sixth and seventh hit dead center. Cheers and hoots erupted from the observers as Caro lowered the weapon and engaged the safety.

"You're a natural," Rory said after he'd taken charge of the automatic.

"Beginner's luck."

"Trust me. Not all beginners can find a target."

His smile of approval stayed with Caro all the way back to the resort. She felt it almost as much as the disturbing aftereffects of her close encounter with his zipper.

It took Caroline the rest of the evening and most of the night to comprehend her inexplicable reaction every time Rory got within striking distance. When she padded into the bathroom just before seven the next morning and braced her hands on the marble sink, she had it all figured out.

"It's simple," she told the tangled-haired woman

in the mirror. "The man represents temptation. Danger. Forbidden desire. Everything you've gone out of your way to avoid in the years since high school."

She'd worked so hard to suppress her past. With deliberate intent, she'd chosen a nice, safe profession. Dated nice, safe men. Established a nice, safe routine. Not until she'd gotten together with Sabrina and Devon last year and taken a hard look at her life did Caro realize she'd mortgaged her future to her past.

Quitting her job and joining forces with her friends to launch EBS had been a *major* step in a new direction. Admitting that Rory Burke still turned her on after all these years was another.

"There," she threw at the face in the mirror, "you've acknowledged it. You want his touch."

She wanted more than that. With brutal honesty, she could admit she wanted his mouth and hands and lean, hard body all over hers. The realization shook her right down to her core. It also made her turn to the two friends she'd come to depend on for support and advice.

Whirling, Caro stalked back into the bedroom and flipped up the lid of her laptop. She caught her business partners at their computers, checking morning e-mail. A few clicks later, she had their faces displayed side by side. Devon's hair lit up the laptop's screen in a blaze of dark red. Sabrina raked a hand through her tumble of blond curls and demanded an instant update.

"So what's happening with Burke? Have you hauled off and decked him yet?"

"Not exactly."

"I'm still available to do the job for you. So is Marco, by the way."

"And Cal," Devon put in.

Oh, sure. That's all Caroline needed. Their two bristling males confronting a former Army ranger and all-around tough guy.

"The situation has, uh, changed a little."

"Changed how?"

She tapped a nail on the laptop keyboard. How to explain this insidious heat, this growing hunger, to friends who had watched her put her emotions on total lockdown for so many years?

"The thing is, I'm…er…sort of…attracted to Rory."

Talk about understatements, Caro thought ruefully as the two faces on the laptop screen took on looks of almost identical astonishment. While they were still struggling to recover, she told them about the kiss that followed her dip in the ocean and the itchy feelings that had almost consumed her at the firing range yesterday.

"The conference wraps up tomorrow morning," she said. "Part of me wants to just crawl in a hole until Rory leaves for the airport in the afternoon. But there's this other confused, completely idiotic part that doesn't want him to go."

"Well," Sabrina said after a long silence, "sounds like there's something between you and this guy Burke. Call it unfinished business or chemistry or plain old-fashioned lust, the fact that it revved to life after more than a decade says something."

"I *know!* But what?"

"Beats me. Dev, what do you think?"

Devon pursed her mouth to one side. Like Caro and Sabrina, she'd made her share of mistakes, most notably the brief marriage to her jerk of an ex. She hadn't expected to tumble into love with Cal Logan, EBS's first big client. Dev still pinched herself every day to make sure she wasn't dreaming. Caroline suspected that's why she took her time before slowly replying.

"I think… I think Sabrina may be right. This unexpected reunion has stirred emotions you've tried to repress for years. Maybe you should get them out of your system once and for all. Or more precisely get *Burke* out of your system."

"Are you suggesting what I think you are?"

"Look, you said you're still attracted to him. I suspect in your mind you still see the young stud who fed your adolescent fantasies. The man he is now may not live up to those fantasies, but there's only one way to find out."

"Hot, mindless sex."

"If that's what your instincts are telling you. Go with them, Caro. See where they take you."

"We all know where they took her last time," Sabrina protested.

"She was seventeen and a virgin. She's a lot older this time around."

"Thanks," Caroline drawled.

"You know what I mean."

That was just it. She did.

"One thing is for sure," she vowed. "Whatever happens between Rory and me will *not* include unprotected sex. I'm still on the pill, thank God."

She'd never gone off it after nice, safe Ernie. Even then she'd insisted they use condoms. Nothing like a healthy dose of paranoia to flavor a relationship.

"So," Sabrina mused, "the real question is whether whatever happens between you and Burke will include *any* kind of sex."

Caro blew out a sigh. "At this point, your guess is as good as mine."

Five

Rory initiated the next phase of Operation Caroline Walters early on the third day of the conference.

This particular objective required that he get her alone. Away from all distractions. Out from under the curious eyes of his people. He'd planned a private dinner in his suite to "discuss" conference business, but the phone call he received that morning from a potential client in Barcelona provided a much better target of opportunity.

Snapping his cell phone shut, he went looking for Caroline and Harry Martin. He found them together, conferring over yet another addition to the schedule. The kick to his gut when he noted the silky tendril that had escaped her neat twist and curled at her nape resolved any doubts about his course of action.

Harry looked up at his approach and sensed instantly that something was up. The man knew him too well, Rory thought wryly.

"Hey, boss. Need something?"

"Yeah, I do. Check out a guy named Juan Casteel for me. He owns a shipping company based in Barcelona."

"Juan Casteel." He jotted down the name. "What's his angle?"

"He says he needs more protection."

"Who doesn't?" Harry muttered.

"Casteel found out I'm in Spain and wants to meet with me. I've set up an appointment at his office for three this afternoon."

"I'll get on him."

"Caroline, I need you to go with me. Casteel's English is pretty heavily accented. I'd like a second set of ears to make sure I understand him."

Rory ignored the quick glance Harry shot his way. "Pack an overnight bag," he instructed his surprised conference coordinator. "Casteel said something about dinner at his place, so I could meet his wife and see the layout of his house. If they eat as late as most Spaniards, it'll be too late to drive back tonight."

Dinner or no dinner, Rory had already determined he and Caroline would *not* hit the road again tonight.

"Better make hotel reservations," he told her. "We'll take my rental car. I'll meet you in the lobby at noon."

She waffled, clearly uncertain and wary. He didn't give her time to recover.

"Let me know what you dig up on Casteel, Harry."

His deputy gave him a hard look before nodding. "Will do."

Harry delivered a background dossier on Juan Casteel to Rory's suite forty-five minutes later. The Spanish shipping magnate didn't top the list of his priorities, however.

"Let's have it, boss. What the hell are you up to with Caroline?"

Rory paused in the act of stuffing his shaving kit into his carryall. "What makes you think I'm up to anything?"

"Don't give me that bull. I'm the one who kept your ass out of jail, remember?"

"How could I forget? You remind me at least once a month."

Never one to mince words, the retired cop set his jaw. "Caroline's a good kid, but she's not in your league. You hurt her again, and you'll answer to me."

"Again?" Rory echoed softly.

"You think I'm getting senile or something?"

Disgusted, Harry tossed the background dossier to the bed beside the leather carryall.

"I knew there had to be some reason behind your insistence that her company handle this conference. I did a little digging. Didn't take long to figure out you were the one who knocked her up."

Wincing at the blunt assessment, Rory yanked on the zipper of his carryall. "Does it make any difference that I didn't *know* I'd knocked her up?"

"Not to me. Or to her, I suspect. What's your game?"

"It's no game, Harry. I intend to atone for past sins."

"How?"

He couldn't lie to the man who'd become his conscience. "My first plan was a cash settlement. I know money wouldn't make up for what she went through, but it could ease the future for her. If she wouldn't accept it outright, I planned to disguise it by steering business her way. Now…"

Now all he could think of was how Caroline had looked in the moonlight. How she'd tasted, so warm and salty. How much he wanted to taste her again.

"I'm thinking maybe a more permanent arrangement."

"Like marriage?"

"Maybe."

"Little late for that, isn't it?"

"Better late than never. Besides, we both know I would have made a rotten husband back then. I was too young and too much of a wiseass."

"You won't get any argument from me on that. I'm curious, though. Why do you think you'll make a better husband now? You haven't spent more than a few weeks in that empty barn you call home in the past year. Then there's the little matter of your line of work."

With a jerk of his chin, Harry indicated the scars webbing the back of Rory's hand.

"Think you can bust in car windows and haul clients out of burning vehicles indefinitely?"

"Yeah, well, that's part of my rationale."

Rory glanced down and made a fist. He hadn't been able to perform that simple act for months after the job in Seattle went sour.

"We both know the odds, Harry. The higher the profile of our clients, the greater the chances we'll take a hit along with them. Conversely, the greater the risk, the greater the reward. I've got more money in the bank than I can spend in two lifetimes."

"And no one to leave it to," his longtime friend and mentor guessed shrewdly, "except the half dozen charities that hit you up on a regular basis. So you're going to make Caroline a rich widow."

"Not anytime soon, hopefully. But one way or another, she'll be set for life."

"Just out of curiosity," Harry said, "what makes you so sure Caroline will have you?"

"I'm not sure at all. But there's something between us that just won't die. A spark. A flame. Whatever. It's been smoldering all these years."

"Yeah, I noticed you out there on the beach the

other night, fanning the fire." He palmed his salt-and-pepper buzz cut and eyed Rory thoughtfully. "Have you told her about your plans for her future?"

"Not yet."

"When are you planning to spring them on her?"

"I'm not sure. Tonight, maybe, in Barcelona."

Harry nodded once, slowly. "I repeat, kid. Hurt that girl again and you'll answer to me."

"Understood. Now give me a quick recap of what you dug up on this guy Casteel."

Caroline decided the meeting with Rory's high-powered prospective client required more professional attire than the semicasual outfits she'd worn at the conference. She changed into black pumps, her slim black skirt with its matching jacket worn over an aqua silk tank.

She was glad she'd made the switch when Rory met her in the lobby. He, too, had changed and was once again the consummate executive in a hand-tailored charcoal-gray suit and silk tie. He looked almost like a stranger again until his amber eyes met hers and a frisson of unsettling sensation rippled down her spine.

"Ready?"

At her nod, he took her overnight bag and carried it with his to the silver BMW waiting at the front entrance. The smiling valet opened the door for her. It closed with a well-mannered thud, shutting her and

Rory in a cage of cloud-soft leather and high-performance engineering.

Caroline said little during the drive into the city. As they sped along the A7 *Autopista,* snippets from her early-morning colloquy with Devon and Sabrina kept replaying inside her head.

Time's running out.

Do I go with my instincts or play it smart and safe this time?

Her fingers tightened on the directions Señor Casteel had provided to his downtown office. She slanted a glance at the man beside her and found only traces of the teenager she'd hungered for in his rugged profile.

This Rory Burke was so different and so dangerously compelling. The square chin, the crinkles at the corners of his eyes, the nose with the flattened bridge—each of the parts added up to a whole that made Caroline's adolescent desire pale by comparison to the hunger he roused in her now.

It hit her again, a hot rush of desire that made her belly clench and anticipation whip through her like wildfire. They had tonight, she thought. Alone. In a city made for lovers.

Go with your instincts.

See where they take you.

He turned then and met her gaze. Those wolf's eyes seemed to burn right through her. "Is this it?"

"Wh-What?"

"C-33." He tipped his head toward the green highway sign flashing by. "Isn't this where we cut off?"

"Oh. Right. C-33."

Jerked back to her self-appointed navigator duties, Caroline consulted the handwritten directions. Barcelona's sprawling suburbs soon engulfed them, with accompanying traffic and noise.

"C-33 turns into Avenue Meridiana about a mile ahead. We stay on that until we hit Avenue Diagonal." A brown sign snagged her attention. "The Diagonal takes us right past the Sagrada Familia."

"The what?"

"The Sagrada Familia, Barcelona's famous unfinished cathedral. It's one of Antoni Gaudí's masterpieces, along with La Pedrera and Casa Batlló."

She clicked her tongue at his blank look.

"You said you've visited Barcelona twice before. Didn't you see any of Gaudí's work?"

"Not unless he built the bar where I spent the better part of a three-day pass." His grin was quick and unrepentant. "I was still in the Army then. The next time I hit the city, I was on business. Landed at noon, left at seven that night. No time for sightseeing."

"What a shame. Barcelona holds some of the world's greatest architectural treasures. Maybe we can squeeze in a side trip or two while we're here."

"Maybe," he agreed with a look she couldn't quite interpret. "Looks like we're coming up on Avenue Meridiana."

In Caroline's considered opinion, Barcelona was a world-class mecca for art lovers of all persuasions. On previous trips she'd spent hours in the Picasso Museum. One whole afternoon was occupied by wandering Montjuic, site of the 1929 World's Fair and now filled with the wild and wonderful sculptures by Spain's great Joan Miró. But Gaudí's unfinished cathedral had truly left an indelible imprint on her.

Its towers appeared in the distance soon after they turned onto Avenue Diagonal, spearing into the blue sky with the soaring power of the apostles they were intended to represent. Eight additional towers were still under construction. Huge cranes had been an integral feature of the cathedral landscape since its foundation was laid in 1882.

Vowing to get Rory in for a closer look, Caroline directed him down Avenue Diagonal, then onto the city's fashionable north-south artery, Paseo de Gracia.

"There's the fountain Señor Casteel said to look for." She pointed to the five-tiered sculpture shooting jets of silvery water high into the air. "His office building should be on the next block."

Following the directions, Rory turned into an underground parking lot and pulled into the spot that had been reserved for him next to the elevators. Moments later, he ushered Caroline into an eighth-floor corridor flooded with light and stopped dead.

"What the hell is that? A giant chess set?"

She followed his startled gaze to the window at the end of the corridor. The sparkling glass gave a clear view of the rooftop of the building across the street.

"Those are chimneys and air vents!"

Thrilled, Caroline dragged him to the window for a closer look at the dozens of fanciful figures sprouting from the wavy roof. Below the modernistic sculptures was an art-deco-style apartment complex decorated with undulating wrought-iron balconies.

"That's La Pedrera. A series of residences Gaudí designed for the Mila family in the early 1900s. He described the roof sculptures as sentinels in the sky."

"Weird," Rory muttered, fascinated despite himself.

"Ha! If you think those are weird, wait until you see his Casa Batlló. The balconies all look like skulls."

"And you like this kind of architecture?"

"I love it."

"No accounting for tastes," he said with one of his quicksilver grins.

Caroline knew then she was in trouble. *Major* trouble. All the man had to do was flash that killer grin and she went gooey inside.

Just like last time, a voice in her head shouted. All those years ago. When he'd glance up, catch her watching him. One corner of his mouth would lift in a sardonic, knowing smile, and she would fall apart.

She'd ached for him then with a schoolgirl's passion. There wasn't anything the least girlish about the desire that now tightened Caroline's nipples under the silk tank top and stirred a damp heat between her thighs.

Some of that wild hunger must have shown in her face. Rory's smile lost its cocky tilt. The tanned skin stretched tight across his cheeks. He leaned in, his gaze holding hers, and brushed a knuckle over her cheek.

"Let's go take care of business. All of a sudden I've got an uncontrollable urge to see more of this guy Gaudí's crazy architecture."

Architecture was the *last* thing on Rory's mind as he escorted Caroline up the steps of Juan Casteel's palatial town house later that evening.

He'd spent a good four hours in the shipping magnate's office, pumping him for precise details regarding his business, his lifestyle, his current security arrangements and the threats that had prompted him to consider additional expertise.

Now, with the night breeze stirring the soft tendrils that had escaped Caroline's smooth twist and her scent teasing his nostrils, he was seriously regretting that he'd agreed to mix business with pleasure for another few hours.

He shoved aside the regret to note with approval the two cameras that screened visitors from separate angles. After he and Caroline complied with a polite request to hold their IDs up to cameras, a uniformed maid opened the door. She showed them into a three-story foyer dominated by a massive stained-glass chandelier.

"Ah, you're right on time."

Juan Casteel and his wife came down a sweeping circular staircase to greet them. He was a big man in his late sixties, with a loud voice and gnarled hands left over from his early years on the docks. By contrast, his wife was slim and elegant and wore her age with great dignity.

"This is my bride of forty years," Casteel boomed, beaming with pride. "To this day, I don't know why she married a great oaf like me."

"I wonder that myself sometimes," she teased in flawless English as she held out a hand. "You must be Ms. Walters. I'm so glad you and Mr. Burke could join us."

"Please, call me Caroline."

"With pleasure. And I am Elena."

While Señora Casteel entertained Caroline over cocktails, her husband gave Rory a tour of their magnificent home. Built in the 1890s, it was opulently decorated and well guarded. Dinner afterward was a protracted affair in the best Spanish style, with a half dozen courses and fine wines.

As the evening drew to a close, Rory waged a fierce internal debate over the best way to initiate the next phase of his plan. He had several options lined up when he and Caroline checked into the five-star Hotel Grand Royale. She'd reserved separate rooms—a suite for him, more modest accommodations for her.

Not that she'd need them. When Rory keyed the lock to his suite, he'd narrowed his options to two. Neither involved separate beds.

His careful planning proved completely unnecessary the moment he ushered Caroline inside. To his sardonic amusement, this character Gaudí had set the perfect seduction scene.

There it was, the architect's unfinished cathedral, bathed in golden light and perfectly framed in the sliding glass doors leading to the terrace.

"Ooooooh!"

Enraptured, Caroline headed straight for the doors. Rory dropped their bags on the suite's antique rolled-arm sofa and followed. A cold, damp breeze swirled across the terrace, but Caroline didn't seem to notice as she laid both palms on the wide balustrade and drank in the view. Rory positioned himself behind her and slightly to one side, blocking the worst of the wind.

He had to admit the cathedral made an impressive sight as it soared above the city lights. The magnificent structure couldn't compare with Caroline Walters, however. With the reflected glow illuminating her profile and the wind tugging a few strands from the twist at the back of her head, she ignited a slow burn in Rory's belly.

He savored the heat and the sight of her for a few

moments before reaching out to release the clip holding her hair. The rest of her golden-brown mane spilled loose and brought her head turning toward him in surprise.

"I've been wanting to do that for the past four days," he told her, sliding his hand under the silky tangle.

He gave her plenty of warning. More than enough time to pull away. The fact that she didn't was like a hard, swift punch to his gut.

"I've been wanting to do this, too," he muttered, "ever since our little stroll in the surf."

Slowly, inexorably, he drew her closer. Just as slowly, he angled his head. He'd swooped in the other night and caught her off guard. This time he wanted her fully aware and quivering with anticipation.

In almost the next breath, he questioned his plan. One brush of his mouth over hers and every tendon in his body went wire-tight. One taste and he had to fight the fierce urge to devour her.

Then she drew back, looked up with wide, solemn eyes and proceeded to shock the hell out of him.

"I think we should have sex."

Six

Even before Rory recovered from his stunned surprise, he'd formulated two possible responses to the blunt suggestion. He could ask Caroline what had prompted it. Or he could act now and ask later.

He'd always preferred action to words.

In one swift move, he had her in his arms. A moment later he was striding through the living room. Soft lamplight showed the way to a bedroom that might have been designed for just the kind of activities Rory had in mind.

Elegant antiques and lush fabrics gave the room a rich, seductive feel. The king-size sleigh bed had already been turned down. Gold-wrapped Godiva chocolates rested on the mounded pillows while blue bottles of Perrier and a split of French champagne occupied a tray on one nightstand.

Several erotic uses for the chocolates and champagne leaped instantly into his head. Later, he told himself sternly. Much later. Right now his most pressing task was to get Caroline out of her clothes before she started having second or third thoughts.

He eased his arm from under her knees and let her slide to her feet. The friction that generated got him instantly hard. Tight and aching below his belt, he buried a hand in her hair and covered her mouth with his.

She hesitated just long enough to nearly give Rory heart failure before she locked her arms around his neck. To his profound relief, her mouth was as hungry as his, her tongue every bit as eager.

The taste of her went straight to his bloodstream, as powerful and as potent as a shot of whiskey. Mere seconds later he had her suit jacket unbuttoned and the silky top peeled off to reveal a lacy half bra in a pale shade of blue.

Curling a knuckle, he drew it down the slope of her breast, then slid his hand under the soft contour. His thumb flicked the dusky tip just visible through the lace. The nipple budded almost instantly.

He played with it, brushing his thumb back and forth until her breath rasped. Then he turned his attention to her other breast. Supported by his arm, she leaned back to give him freer access. Rory took full advantage of her vulnerable position to bend and nip at her tender flesh.

Palming his hand along the curve of her waist, he tugged down her skirt zipper. The black fabric pooled around her pumps. He wasn't sure what he'd expected to find underneath. The frivolous garter belt almost drove him over the edge right then and there. He couldn't believe it when he heard himself ask, "You sure you want to do this?"

Cheeks flushed, her green eyes bright with desire, she nodded. "I'm sure."

Caroline thought she knew what to expect. The only other time Rory had peeled off her clothes and used his hands and tongue on her, he'd had her writhing and gasping and groaning within moments. The sharp ache when he'd penetrated had generated more surprise than pain. Awkward and untutored, she'd followed his gruff instructions until nature took over and she was thrusting her hips up to meet his.

She'd gained more expertise in the years since. But none of it prepared her for the animal lust that grabbed her by the throat when Rory stretched her out on the bed, unsnapped her garters and slowly, so slowly, rolled down her nylons.

His eyes were as hot as his hands when he stood to strip off his own clothes. Yanking at his tie, he swept his gaze from her breasts to her ankles.

"God, you're beautiful."

Caroline's first instinct was to drag the duvet over and shield herself. Her brief spurt of embarrassment lasted only until Rory's suit coat, tie and dress shirt came off to reveal a chest corded with lean, hard muscle.

"So are you," she gasped as her belly went tight.

He grinned at the compliment. "Please don't repeat that in front of Harry. Or any of my people. Doesn't go with my tough-guy image."

What *did* go with the image were the scars crisscrossing the back of his left hand. Breathing hard, Caroline zeroed in on the faint white web while he unbuckled his belt and tugged down his zipper.

When he shucked his slacks and shorts, she forgot the scars, forgot her thumping heart, almost forgot how to breathe. His jutting erection reminded her that she'd never seen him naked. Neither of them had shed all their clothing that night at the river. She'd been too shy; he'd been too eager. And God knew neither of the two men she'd allowed into her bed since then had looked anything like this!

Yielding to an urge she didn't even try to control, she scrambled awkwardly to her knees and wrapped her hand around his rigid flesh. Rory jerked, obviously surprised by the move. Caroline was almost as surprised as him at her uncharacteristic boldness but wasn't about to back off now.

Tightening her fist, she slid it down, then up again. The semiloose cowl near the tip disappeared. Veins popped out under the hot, velvety skin. Reveling in an incredible sense of power, she cupped his sac with her other hand. When a bead of clear liquid appeared on the tip of his shaft, she conquered the last of her inhibitions and leaned forward to lick it.

"Uhhh. Salty."

Her involuntary grimace earned a laugh from Rory. The next moment she was flat on her back. His weight pinned her to the fluffy duvet. His knee pried hers apart.

"My turn."

Spreading her legs, he slid his hand down her belly and between her thighs. His fingers combed the curls covering her mound. His thumb found the hypersensitive nub at her center. She was practically gushing all over his hand when he nudged her a little farther up on the bed.

The rasp of his tongue against her clit arched her spine. The subsequent sucking almost levitated her off the mattress. Mere seconds later, she climaxed in a white-hot flash of pure sensation.

She rode the crashing waves for moments. Maybe hours. Finally the ceiling stopped spinning, the exquisite sensations subsided and mortification set in.

"I'm so sorry! I didn't mean for it to end that quickly. You haven't… I didn't…"

"No apologies necessary."

A wicked glint came into his eyes as he rolled off the bed and fished a condom out of his wallet.

"We're not done. In fact, Ms. Walters, the night has just begun."

He ripped the foil package open with strong white teeth. Caroline didn't tell him she was taking birth-control pills. The more protection, she thought as heat began to swirl in her belly again, the better.

Rory proved as good as his word. They weren't done. Not by any measure in the book.

Caroline couldn't quite believe her hedonistic responses to his lovemaking. Then again, he was so incredibly good at it. He entered her slowly, stretching her, filling her, and withdrew just as slowly.

The next thrust was harder and faster.

Then slow again.

He soon had her almost weeping with pleasure, but she was determined to take him with her this time. Panting, she used every bit of her strength to squeeze her vaginal muscles. His grunt gave her a fierce, almost primal, satisfaction. So did the fists he buried in her hair to anchor her for another series of swift, hard thrusts that—finally!—sent them both over the edge.

As the last sensations from that unbelievable session drained away, Rory curled her into his side. Together, they sank into total oblivion.

When Caroline resurfaced, sunlight slanted through the crack in the drawn curtains, and a heavy weight encircled her waist.

The weight was an arm, she discovered after a tentative exploration. She ran a hand over its dusting of gold fuzz while her sleepy haze slowly evaporated.

"'Bout time you woke up," a husky voice whispered into her ear.

Her mouth tasted like moldy cheese, and she had to pee in the worst way...until Rory tightened his arm and drew her into the cradle of his hips. He was primed and already poking at her bare bottom. When his hand moved to her breast and teased her nipple into an aching peak, an involuntary slickness overlaid the sticky residue on her thighs.

He wedged a knee between hers and opened her. When he slid in, she was wet and ready.

Afterward, Caroline still had to pee but couldn't summon enough energy to roll out of bed. She lay limp and totally boneless, with just enough strength left to stroke his arm and the hand still cupping her breast.

His skin was tanned and dark against hers. Idly, she drew a nail over his wrist and traced the faint white scars on the back of his hand.

"How did you get these?"

"Busting in the window of a burning limo. My client was trapped inside."

He said it with such lazy indifference. As if dragging a client from a blazing limousine constituted an everyday occurrence.

Maybe it did. After sitting in on some of the

conference briefings, Caroline had gained an out-sider's appreciation of the risks Rory and his people faced every day.

"Now I have a question for you," he said, inter-rupting her uneasy thoughts.

He rested his chin on the top of her head. His breath tickled her ear as he hitched her a little higher in the cradle of his thighs.

"What made you decide we should have sex? Not that I'm complaining, mind you. In fact, I'd already decided we wouldn't need the second room."

"Is that so?"

"Yeah, babe, it is. But I have to say you shocked the hell out of me with your cool pronouncement."

"That was the intent."

"I figured. What I can't figure, is why you decided not to fight whatever this is between us."

"I'll tell you. But first I have to hit the bathroom."

Rory loosened his hold enough to let her scoot to her side of the bed. She dragged the lightweight duvet with her. Its ends trailed after her as she re-treated to a cavern of cool marble and gold-plated fixtures.

She traded the duvet for one of the thick terry-cloth robes hanging from padded hangers on the back of the bathroom door. She would have loved a shower but had to make do with a washcloth and the hotel's scented soap. The basket of goodies on the mile-long vanity also included complimentary toothbrushes, thank God! After finger-combing her tangled hair, Caroline faced her nemesis once more.

He was relaxed against the padded headboard. A tangled sheet pooled at his waist, baring his flat belly. Golden bristles stubbled his cheeks and chin, and his hair stood up in short, disordered spikes.

"I called room service," he informed her. "Coffee and hot rolls are on the way."

He patted the mattress in an unmistakable invitation for breakfast in bed. Caroline shoved her hands in the pockets of the robe and stayed where she was.

"You asked why I decided to sleep with you. It's simple."

"To you, maybe."

"I thought I'd wiped you out of my head years ago. Seeing you again so unexpectedly brought back all the confusion, all the unfinished business. I decided to stop fighting the emotions you rouse and work through them instead. The idea is to get you out of my system once and for all."

Lifting a brow, he regarded her with lazy amusement. "Did it work?"

"I don't know. Too early to tell."

She was lying through her teeth. She knew it. He knew it. Everything in her ached to slide back between the rumpled sheets. Instead, she glanced pointedly at the clock on the antique nightstand.

"It's almost eight. The conference wrap-up is scheduled for eleven."

After which he'd fly back to California, and his people would disperse to the four corners of the globe. Caro would stay over until tomorrow to take care of last-minute details, then fly to Virginia. They'd have a continent between them. The prospect closed her throat even as Rory leered and patted the sheet.

"We'd better hustle, then. Come here, woman."

"We can't. Not again. We'll barely make it back to Tossa in time as it is."

He gave in eventually and scooped up his clothes. As he padded to the bathroom, Caroline assured herself she'd done exactly the right thing.

She'd followed her gut instincts. Spent a wild night in his arms. Now she needed to step back. Let time and distance bring the closure she hadn't known she needed.

A little less than an hour later, they had both showered, dressed and consumed the breakfast Rory had added to the room service order.

"We should beat the morning rush hour," he commented as they took the elevator to the lobby. "We'll be heading out of the city, against the traffic."

The lobby was an explosion of lush palms, marble pillars and gleaming, gold-plated fixtures. Interspersed among the palms were boutiques bearing names such as Cartier and Antonio Miró.

Caroline refused to feel guilty when Rory handed in both keys and signed the tab. It wasn't her fault

GSI would get stuck with the tab for an unused room. Not completely, anyway.

"I called down for my car."

"Yes, Mr. Burke. The valet has it waiting for you at the front entrance."

"Thanks."

The casual hand Rory placed at the small of Caroline's back burned right through her suit jacket and silk top. She felt its heat as they recrossed the lobby and made for the silver BMW parked outside the old-fashioned revolving doors.

They were almost at the entrance when a colorful display in the window of the hotel's exclusive flower shop snagged his attention. Pausing, he eyed the ruby-red crystals suspended by silver ribbons to form a large, sparkling heart. A massive bouquet of red roses blossomed in the center of the heart.

"What's the date today?" he asked Caroline.

"The fourteenth."

"Valentine's Day." He grinned. "Appropriate, wouldn't you say?"

Appropriate for what? A night of erotic sex, after which they would each go their separate ways? Somehow that scenario didn't say hearts and flowers to Caro. As she tried to point out when Rory suggested she wait for him in the car.

"The occasion doesn't call for romantic gestures. You don't need to buy me roses. Besides, we don't have time for that now."

"I won't be long," he assured her.

Okay, so maybe she would take a single long-stemmed rose home with her and press it between the pages of a book. When she took it out years from now, she could finger its dry, brittle petals and remember her second walk on the wild side.

And this time a rose was *all* she'd take home with her.

Relieved and a just a little depressed by the thought, Caroline shrugged and pushed through the revolving doors.

She was chewing on her lower lip and taking a third look at her watch when Rory finally joined her, sans roses.

"Couldn't find what you wanted?"

"Actually, I found *exactly* what I wanted." He keyed the ignition and teased her with a smile. "I thought I'd wait and give it to you later, over dinner."

"Dinner? But I thought you were flying home this afternoon, right after the conference."

"I was. I changed my reservation."

"When?"

"Yesterday, when I found out you were staying over until tomorrow."

She slumped back against the seat, too surprised to comment while he maneuvered into the city traffic. He waited until they were headed north on the wide Avenue Diagonal to shoot her a quizzical glance.

"Did you think I was going to just pack up and leave you here in Spain?"

"Why would I think anything else?"

He grimaced and cut the wheel to move into the left lane. "I suppose I deserved that. But I'm not hopping on a motorcycle—or an MD-80 jumbo jet—and roaring out of town. Not this time, Caroline."

She frowned, trying to get a handle on his motives. Even more difficult to grasp was her own inexplicable reaction to the fact they'd have another night together.

"What makes this time any different from the last?"

"We'll talk about that tonight," he promised. "At dinner."

Thrown for a complete loop, she had no choice but to sit back and count the mileposts on the *Autopista* until they approached the exit for Tossa de Mar.

Seven

They made it back to the resort with barely enough time to change before the wrap-up session.

Caroline raced up to her own room and scrambled into a black ankle-length crinkle skirt and her wide-sleeved tangerine tunic. She had started to clip her hair up in its usual neat twist when she spotted a red mark on her neck.

Well! Looks like she'd acquired a souvenir from her second walk on the wild side after all. A perfect match with the unfamiliar ache in her thighs. That's what she got for overworking muscles that hadn't been exercised in years. Grimacing, she left the dark, heavy mass down and swirling around her shoulders.

The first person she saw when she went downstairs again was Sondra Jennings. The blonde had already checked out of her room and was wheeling her suitcase down the hall toward the conference center.

"Hey, Caroline. We missed you at dinner last night."

"I drove into Barcelona with Rory."

"Yeah, I heard." The wheels rattled over the undulating terra-cotta tiles as she gave Caro a considering glance. "Listen, you can tell me to butt out if you want. There's something you should know, though. If you don't already."

Caroline guessed what was coming and cringed inside. Talk about history repeating itself! One night with Rory and already she was the recipient of knowing glances. Would the smirks and snickers come next?

"What?" she asked with a touch of ice.

"Rory's one of the good guys. The kind you want watching your back. And if you let him," she added with a waggle of her delicately penciled brows, "he'll do a pretty good job of watching the front, too."

Her roguish expression melted Caroline's reserve. Relaxing, she returned the blonde's smile.

"I'll keep that in mind. But you've got it wrong, Sondra. Rory and I had some unfinished business to take care of. That's all."

"Yeah. Uh-huh. Sure. You keep telling yourself that."

The suitcase bumped along for a few more tiles.

"I know him, Caroline. He doesn't go into any

situation blind. He knows exactly what his objective is and how best to achieve it."

No kidding! Rory had made it clear his objective in this particular situation had been to right an old wrong. *Her* objective last night had been to exorcise the sexual pull he exerted on her once and for all. So much for either of them accomplishing what they'd set out to.

"And there's the one whereof we speak," Sondra murmured, tipping her chin toward the man striding toward them from the opposite end of the hall.

He, too, had changed out of the clothes he'd worn for his meeting with Juan Casteel. The suit and tie were gone, replaced by dark slacks and a red polo shirt embroidered with the GSI logo. His smile gave only the barest hint of the hours they'd spent exchanging bodily fluids last night and this morning.

"Harry needs to talk to you," he told Caroline. "He has a question about the exit permits for weapons we brought in."

"Where is he?"

"He was heading for the business office when I left him a few moments ago."

"I'll go track him down. Sondra, I know you have to leave before the wrap-up ends. I've scheduled a car for eleven-thirty. It'll be waiting for you."

"Thanks."

"Have a good trip."

The blonde flicked Rory an amused glance and

leaned forward to murmur in Caroline's ear. "You, too, kiddo."

"What was that all about?" Rory wanted to know as Caro hurried away.

"Girl talk. I hear you're staying in Spain another night. What's up?"

"Just some loose ends I need to take care."

With a sardonic smile, Sondra nodded to a woman disappearing around a bend in the corridor. "Is that one of those loose ends?"

"Could be."

His European section chief cocked her head and studied him with assessing eyes. "She's not like us, Rory. Hard and tough and cynical."

"You think?"

"I'm just saying you might have to alter your approach."

"Thanks for the advice. I've got it covered."

Or at least he hoped he did. He hadn't needed Sondra to tell him Caroline required a different approach, much less Harry's blunt warning that he'd better not hurt her again. Rory made it a point to learn from past mistakes.

And God knew he'd screwed up the first time around with Caroline. Literally. He'd taken what she'd offered, climbed on his beat-up Ducati and hit the road without a backward glance.

This time, he intended to give her the hearts and flowers she didn't think she deserved.

As he took Sondra's bag and accompanied her to the wrap-up session, he reviewed his carefully devised plans for the coming evening. Satisfied he'd covered every base, Rory switched mental gears from a romantic candlelit dinner for two to the grim realities of high-profile kidnappings and murdered hostages.

Caroline spent the better part of the afternoon confirming flights and ensuring the conferees had transportation to Barcelona to make their scheduled departures.

Harry Martin was one of the last to leave. He and Caro had been forced to make several increasingly exasperated phone calls to Captain Medina, but they'd finally gotten the exit permits squared away. The small arsenal of high-tech weapons Harry had shipped in was now on its way to the airport.

Shoving his Ray-Bans up to rest atop his wiry buzz cut, the retired cop took her hand in a thorny palm. "We got a lot done this week thanks to you, Caroline."

"I'd say it was a joint effort."

"I'll put the word out about EBS when I get home. Should bring you some business from other security companies."

"Thanks, I appreciate that."

"What's your next gig?"

"My partner got a call from a publisher who wants to set up a European book tour for one of their big authors. Ten days, twelve cities and who knows how many TV and radio interviews. I may take that job."

Actually, there wasn't much "may" about it. Sabrina was just about to open their Rome office and Logan Aerospace work would keep Devon busy indefinitely. European Business Services, Inc., would have to think about hiring additional help soon.

The prospect sent a little thrill through Caro's veins. She and her two friends had launched EBS less than a year ago. Yet they'd already recouped their initial investment and were showing a small but steady profit. A few more contracts like Logan Aerospace and GSI and they could start thinking investment strategies and 40l(k)s. No small consideration for three women who had walked away from steady jobs with solid retirement plans.

"I heard Rory changed his return reservations," Harry commented.

"You're the second person who's mentioned that to me," she responded dryly. "Does everyone in the personal security business keep track of everyone else's moves?"

"Only those who want to stay alive."

With that careless comment, he slid his sunglasses down to the bridge of his nose.

"Just remember what I told you at the start of the conference. He's a good man."

"You're the second person who's made *that* point today, too."

"Well, there you go. See you around, Caroline."

* * *

Instead of reassuring her, the personal testimonials from Sondra and Harry made Caro nervous. She didn't know what Rory planned to spring on her at dinner tonight, but she suspected it was more than a Valentine's Day card.

What made her even more nervous was that she had no idea what her response would be to whatever he wanted to discuss. She hadn't had time to sort through the wildly conflicting emotions a night in his arms had spawned.

As she took the elevator to her floor, she was forced to admit last night's experiment had failed. Instead of working through her unresolved feelings for Rory, she now had a whole new set to deal with. Not the least of which was the insidious, irrepressible hope that they would end this night naked and sweaty.

Once in her room, she wavered between dressing up and dressing down for the dinner. The voice message Rory had left on her room phone suggesting she wear something warm enough for a walk on the seawall settled the matter.

February days on the Costa Brava could bring enticing sunshine. Nights got a good bit cooler. Especially when the moonlight lured you down to the beach, the undertow sucked you in and you ended up with seaweed in your hair. Lips pursed, Caroline vowed she wouldn't take another dunking tonight.

She kept on the black crinkle skirt but traded the

tangerine cotton tunic for a long-sleeved, cream-colored silk blouse and a wide black belt. The fringed shawl she'd purchased in Tossa de Mar's open-air market provided both a touch of exotic color and the required warmth. Draping one end over her shoulder, Caroline grabbed her purse and took the elevator to the lobby.

Rory was waiting for her. He still wore his dark slacks, now paired with a black turtleneck and a rust-colored sport coat almost the same shade as the ring around his irises.

She thought he might suggest a drink in the hotel bar, but he obviously had other plans.

"You sure you'll be warm enough in that?" he asked, eyeing her shawl.

"I should be. Unless," she added on an after-thought, "you've made reservations at one of Tossa's outdoor restaurants."

"As a matter of fact, we will be eating outside. I requested patio heaters, though."

"Then I'll be fine."

He took her arm and steered her toward the walkway leading down to the seawall. The air was cool but not damp and biting, with just enough breeze to flutter the ends of the shawl.

They joined the others out for an evening stroll on the flat, wide seawall. Their footsteps echoed on the glazed tiles left over from the days of Roman occupation.

The tide was in, Caroline saw. Waves foamed over the shore and lapped at the boats drawn up on the beach and anchored to rings at the base of the seawall. Protected from the sea by the stone walkway, Tossa's trendy hotels and restaurants spilled light, laughter and music into the night.

"Where are we going?" she asked after they'd passed the last establishments.

"Near the base of the castle."

She peered ahead and saw only a faint flicker of light. "There's a restaurant at the base of the cliff? I don't remember seeing one. Only the ruins of a Roman villa."

"That's where we're headed."

"The villa? You're kidding!"

"Nope. The manager at the resort told me they often cater private parties there. He swears it's the most romantic spot in Tossa."

She felt obliged to issue another protest. "I told you this morning I don't need romantic gestures. They're superfluous, given our situation."

"What situation is that, Caroline?"

"You want me to spell it out? All right, I will. Last night was…last night. I didn't expect you to stay in Tossa another night, and I certainly don't expect you to wine me and dine me. Tomorrow we'll fly back to separate homes in separate states. Let's not complicate matters."

"There's nothing that says this has to be the end

of it," he countered. "You told me this morning you wanted to get me out of your system. What if I don't want to get you out of mine?"

"Are you referring to your ridiculous notion that you need to make up for what happened when we were kids?"

"In part," he admitted. "There's more, though. Why don't we talk about it over dinner."

Caroline squashed her doubts and yielded. When they took the stairs leading down from the seawall and stepped through the remains of an arched entryway, she stopped dead.

A linen-draped table sat in solitary splendor in what she guessed was once a mosaic-tiled courtyard. Hundreds of votive candles drenched the scene in soft light. Beyond the circle of their glow, the one wall of the ancient villa still standing provided a stark, dramatic backdrop against the night sky.

"I don't believe this!"

"Believe it," Rory returned with a smile. "The resort manager says they have to get special permission from the Department of Antiquities to set up here. It's worth the effort, don't you think?"

"And then some!"

She'd never eaten in such a historic setting before. This one, she knew from her guidebook, was the real thing—the seaside vacation home of a wealthy Roman merchant who'd found the climate in Tossa very much to his liking.

A waiter materialized out of the darkness beyond the glow of the votives. "Good evening, Senõr Burke. Your table is waiting."

He led them to the solitary table set with fine china and crystal. When he seated Caroline, she noted the rose beside her plate. A red bow was tied around the stem, with the ends of the ribbon trailing across the snowy tablecloth.

As Rory settled into the seat next to hers, Caro fingered the velvety-soft petals with a funny little pang just under her ribs. Okay, so maybe she wasn't as immune to mushy romantic gestures as she thought.

Another waiter appeared then and switched on the umbrella-shaped heater Rory had requested. It shed both light and a soft warmth that enveloped them in a sphere of their own. The second waiter proceeded to fill their water glasses while the first plucked a bottle of champagne out of a silver ice bucket, wiped it with a napkin and held it out for Rory's inspection and approval.

"Champagne," Caroline murmured when the waiter had filled her crystal flute. "A table overlooking the sea. Our own private waitstaff. All we need now is a string quartet."

"It's not a quartet, but…"

At Rory's signal, another figure stepped out of the shadows. Caro's jaw dropped as he tucked a guitar under his arm and strummed the strings with a flourish.

When the opening chords of "Grenada" soared into the night, she turned to her dinner companion in sheer disbelief.

"Hey," he said with a grin, "if you're gonna do something, you might as well do it right."

She waited until the song had spun to a glorious finish, and they'd applauded the performance to follow up on his comment.

"What, exactly, are you trying to do?"

"Set the stage."

"For?"

"For this."

While the guitarist strummed another song, Rory slid a small package wrapped in turquoise paper and tied with a silver ribbon across the table.

"What is it?" Caro asked suspiciously.

"Your Valentine's Day present. I picked it up at the hotel this morning."

Her stomach did a quick flip-flop when she saw the embossed foil sticker on the package. She thought he'd hit the hotel's flower shop. Instead, he'd made a detour into Cartier.

A dozen objections leaped into her mind. Their relationship was too confused, too uncertain, for expensive gifts. More to the point, one night of hedonistic sex did not require a trip to Cartier. Unless he was trying to salve his conscience, she rationalized uneasily. Or pay for services rendered.

As quickly as the thought formed, she dismissed it. Rory wouldn't be that crass.

Or would he?

There was the problem in a nutshell. She didn't really know this man, and she certainly didn't understand why he'd gone to so much trouble to arrange this moonlit dinner. Despite the testimonials from Harry and Sondra, despite the hours they'd spent in each other's arms, he was still an enigma to her.

"I can't accept this, whatever it is."

"Why don't you open it before you decide?"

Taking her lower lip between her teeth, Caroline untied the bow and slid a nail under the foil sticker. Her uneasiness increased when the wrapping paper fell away to reveal a small, square jewelry box.

Okay. All right. No need to make such a big deal. The box could contain earrings. Gold studs, maybe. Or a pin. A pretty bauble to commemorate their trip to Barcelona.

As if she needed a reminder. One glance at Rory's strong, square jaw brought an instant tingle to the various body parts his stubbly bristle had scraped. With a conscious effort of will, Caroline resisted the urge to finger the whisker burn on the side of her neck.

"Shall I serve the *tapas,* sir?"

Rory dismissed the waiter who appeared at the table with a smile. "Give us a few minutes."

The waiter faded into the night. The guitarist continued to strum a Spanish folk song, and Caroline continued to stare at the jewelry box with a mix of wariness and indecision. Finally, her dinner companion assumed the initiative.

"Here. Let me."

When Rory flipped up the lid, Caroline's breath caught in her throat. Nestled in a bed of black velvet was a perfect, heart-shaped emerald edged on one side by diamonds that sparkled even in the dim light. She watched, speechless, as he removed the ring from its case.

"As soon as I saw this, I knew I had to get it for you."

Smiling, he reached for her left hand. Before she could recover enough to whip it away, he slid the ring onto her finger.

"It's a little loose. We'll have to get it sized."

"I can't accept this!"

"Sure you can."

"It's too expensive."

"Not for my fiancée."

Her startled glance shot from the glowing emerald to his face. "Your what?"

"That's my clumsy way of asking you to marry me, Caroline."

Eight

"You've got to be kidding!"

That wasn't exactly the most sophisticated response to a proposal, but it was the best Caroline could manage at the moment.

Smiling at her slack-jawed surprise, Rory brushed his thumb over the back of her hand. "Trust me, I'm a hundred percent serious."

"You can't be! We…We don't see each other for more than ten years, you hear about me secondhand or thirdhand through the wife of a prospective client, we spend a few days together and… Oh!"

She jerked her hand free of his hold. The surprise leached out of her. Understanding and the beginning of a healthy anger seeped in.

"Of course. I forgot. You always pay your debts."

She'd been closer to the truth a few moments ago than she'd realized! He *was* paying for services rendered. Only she'd provided these services more than a decade ago. Her jaw tight, she yanked off the ring and jammed it back into the box. The lid closed with a snap.

"I thought I made myself clear the day you arrived in Tossa. What's done is done. We can't change the past, and I sure as hell don't expect you to—to…" She waved a hand in the air, searching for the right phrase. "To make restitution at this late date."

"What makes you think this is all about the past?"

"Oh, right." Her lip curled. "After one night together, you've fallen hopelessly in love and decided you can't live without me."

His grin slipped out. "You have to admit it was a pretty spectacular night."

"If this is a joke," she snapped, "I don't find it particularly funny."

Sobering, he shook his head. "It's no joke. I told you, I'm dead serious. I want to marry you, Caroline."

"Why?"

"Why not?" he countered. "The heat's still there, even after more than a decade. We haven't found anyone else in all that time. And…"

He paused, his eyes holding hers in the flickering light of the votives. The waiters hovered just out of sight. The guitar player still strummed his instrument, his soft rhythm a counterpoint to the restless waves washing against the seawall.

But it might have been just the two of them, alone in the night, with only the small jewelry box between them.

"I want you, Caroline. After last night, you have to know how much. And I want a family. A wife. Something besides an empty condo to come home to. Kids if we get lucky again."

She flinched, and Rory muttered a curse.

"I'm sorry. That was a poor choice of words. But hearing you'd lost a baby, my baby, made me take a hard look at what I've done with my life—and the changes I need to make in it."

He gathered her hand in his again and raised it to his lips. The utter sincerity in his eyes blunted Caroline's anger even as the brush of his mouth against her skin sent a ripple down her spine.

"I've been pretty much on my own since I was sixteen. Let me come home to you, sweetheart."

The quiet words took her back to that long-ago summer. She could see him in her mind's eye, eighteen again, flexing his muscles under his stained white T-shirt. So cocky, so self-confident and so very much alone.

"You talk about want, Rory. Need. Someone to come home to. What about love? Doesn't that figure anywhere in the equation?"

"The way I see it, they all add up to the same thing."

She had to give him credit for honesty. If pressed, Caroline would have a tough time defining the fragile, illusive emotion poets wrote about herself.

She also had to give him points for the most romantic proposal *ever!* Here they were, seated at the only table set up amid the ruins of a two-thousand-year-old villa, with the moon overhead and guitar music floating through the night.

Caroline couldn't imagine how he'd had time to arrange all this, but she knew that whatever her answer to his astonishing proposal, this Valentine's Day would remain seared in her memory for the rest of her life.

Like that night beside the river.

And the cold, rainy day she'd buried her still-born child.

With a small jolt, she realized this man had figured in two of the three major turning points in her life.

The third was the year she'd spent at the University of Salzburg with Devon and Sabrina. Her friends taught her to laugh again during that year.

Yet not until last night, in Rory's arms, had a part of her she'd thought long dead come alive again. And now… Just the feel of his hand holding hers, the brush of his lips on her skin, sent heat rippling through her veins.

Was he right? Did need and want and love all add up to the same thing? If so, Caroline was knee-deep in the volatile mix for the first time in longer than she could remember.

"Tell you what," Rory said, breaking into her thoughts. "Why don't you defer giving me an answer until after dinner? Or better yet, until tomorrow. I'll use the rest of the night to convince you to say yes."

As if the music and the stars and the churning sea weren't enough! He had to add a husky promise of things to come, which tightened the muscles low in Caroline's belly.

"Tomorrow works for me," she replied, taking the coward's way out. She suspected she would need at least that long, if not longer, to wrap her mind around this extraordinary proposal.

"Good. And until then…" He opened the box and slid the heart-shaped emerald over her knuckle. "So you can get used to the feel of it."

He sat back and signaled the waiter. While they conferred, Caroline tilted her hand until the ring caught the glow of the candles. She was no expert on jewelry by any means. Her biggest splurge to date was a twisted silver bracelet she'd bargained hard for in Mexico. But this…

She didn't need the Cartier box to suspect the ring was light-years away from anything she could afford. The center stone glowed a rich, dark green. The smaller diamonds along the outer edge of the heart sparkled with a brilliance that suggested they cost as much or more than the emerald.

"More champagne, madame?"

With a nod to the waiter, Caroline gave herself up to the evening Rory had gone to such trouble to arrange.

The magic didn't end with dinner.

After coffee and dessert under the stars, they strolled back to the resort along the wide seawall. The wind had picked up, and over Caro's protests, Rory draped his sport coat over her shoulders.

His warmth wrapped around her like a protective shield. His scent teased her senses. As they approached the lights of the resort, his husky promise of things to come had her almost quivering with anticipation.

The anticipation increased exponentially when they took the elevator to his top-floor suite. Rory made maximum use of the short ride by propping a hand against the elevator's paneled wall and leaning in for a kiss.

It started light—a brush of his mouth against hers. It finished with Caroline's hands hooked in his belt, dragging him closer. When the door pinged open, they were both breathing hard and fast.

Thank God his suite was directly opposite the elevator. Caro could barely wait for him to put his key in the door lock. She didn't know whether it was the ridiculously romantic evening he'd orchestrated or the fact that this was their last night together that drove her to such a fever of impatience. Whatever the reason, she couldn't wait for him to flick on the lights.

A warm glow filled the suite. Caroline swept the spacious rooms with a quick glance, taking in once again the rich furnishings, the watercolors decorating the walls, the desk now covered by his open briefcase and a scattering of papers. She also noted the suitcase sitting on the bench at the foot of the bed, waiting to be packed. Spurred by the sight, she went into Rory's arms.

"I have the rest of the night all scripted," he warned between greedy kisses. "Soft music. Cognac. Sipped slowly while enjoying the view of the moon over the bay."

"Does the script end with us getting naked?"

"Of course."

"Forget the music and cognac," she muttered, dragging up the hem of his turtleneck. "I want you without clothes. Now."

As soon as she had his shirt off, her hands went to his belt again. She tugged him toward the bedroom, fumbling with the belt buckle as they went.

He returned the favor by peeling off her shawl and unhooking buttons at the waistband of her long crinkle skirt. By the time she had him backed against the edge of the bed, they'd left their clothing in a haphazard trail from one room to the other.

The embarrassing recollection of how quickly she'd climaxed last night made Caroline determined this session would last considerably longer. She would set the pace, she decided, as she stretched up on tiptoe to lock her mouth with his. She would take him to the edge over and over again and give him at least a partial return on the mindless pleasure he'd given her.

Naked, her body eager and straining against his, she took him down to the bed with her. His weight pinned her, but she wiggled free. Hooking a leg over his, she rolled upright and straddled his hips.

"How about I script the rest of this scene?"

Instant delight glinted in the golden depths of his eyes. "Be my guest."

She could feel him rock hard against her inner thigh. Raising up a few inches, Caroline positioned him between the hot folds of her flesh. Slowly, so slowly, she slid her hips back. Forward. Back again.

The erotic friction closed her throat and kicked her heart into a wild rhythm faster than any flamenco. Her body secreted a warm, wet lubricant in response to the movement. His did the same. Their fluids joined as she increased both the tempo and the pressure.

Rory didn't remain passive for long. His hands slicked over her hips and roamed the curve of her waist before moving to her breasts. He kneaded the soft flesh, then rolled the nipples between his thumbs and forefingers until they'd stiffened to hard peaks.

"I want to taste you, Caroline."

Panting now, she leaned forward and dug her hands into the mattress on either side of his head. The sparkling diamonds edging the emerald distracted her for a second or two. Just until Rory took one aching nipple in his mouth. Alternately sucking and rasping with his teeth and tongue, he generated a series of intense sensations that jolted throughout Caroline's body.

Soon even those incredible sensations weren't enough. She wanted him inside her. Every steely inch. She shifted her hips to one side, but Rory caught her hand as she reached down to position the tip.

"Let me get some protection."

"It's okay," she muttered, too hot to wait. "I'm taking birth control."

"But last night…"

"Double indemnity."

She already had the tip partially in. A slight hitch of her hips and it slid deeper. With a sound that was halfway between a sigh and a groan, she sank lower.

Hazy sunlight crept through the shutters when Caroline drifted awake the next morning.

Gradually she registered the fact that she lay sprawled in hedonistic abandon across Rory's chest. Her left leg was thrown over his. Her arm was hooked over his waist. With a little smacking sound from her dry lips, she snuggled closer.

A large hand stroked her hair, slowly and lazily. Minutes passed in boneless contentment, then Rory's deep voice pulled Caroline from a light doze.

"Well? What's the verdict?"

"The verdict?" She raised her head and gave him a sleepy smile. "Best sex I ever had. Except maybe for the other night in Barcelona."

Laughter rumbled up from his chest. "Happy to be of service, ma'am."

Bending an elbow atop her chest, she propped her chin on her hand. God, he looked good in the morning! Especially with that prickly blond stubble shading his chin and amusement crinkling the skin at the corners of his eyes.

"That wasn't the verdict I was looking for, though."

"Mmm?"

"Did I convince you to say yes?"

Lost in contemplation of his whiskery chin and smiling eyes, it took a moment for the question to register. When it did, she eased into a sitting position and hitched the sheet under her arms.

Rory had gone all out with his over-the-top, romantic proposal. The Roman villa, the guitar, the flickering votives. Caroline had been too surprised, too overwhelmed to think straight last night. In the hazy light of dawn, her more cautious self prevailed.

"I jumped in feetfirst with you once and paid the price," she said, searching for the right words. "I need to… We *both* need to proceed more deliberately this time. Explore our feelings. See if they take us anywhere besides bed."

He waggled his brows in an exaggerated leer. "Let's hope they don't take us anywhere else."

"I'm serious, Rory. I want to slow this train down."

"Okay, I hear you." Frowning, he scraped a palm across his bristles. "Exploration could be a little difficult, though, since you live in Virginia and I operate out of California."

"Difficult but not impossible. Unless you think what we might have together isn't worth the effort."

"Oh, you're worth it. You're most definitely worth it. But I have to warn you that patience isn't my strongest suit. When I decide I want something, I go after it."

"I noticed," she drawled. "So we're agreed? We slow things down?"

"We might have to define 'slow' more precisely," he warned with a quick glance at the digital clock beside the bed. "How about we discuss it during the ride to the airport?"

Nodding, Caroline slid the heart-shaped emerald off her finger and held it out to him. Rory refused to take it.

"It's yours, sweetheart. I want you to keep it as a reminder of your night out in Tossa."

Like she could ever forget it?

After she retreated to her own room to shower and pack, Caroline took a moment to stand at the window before going downstairs. A thin fog had rolled in off the sea, almost obscuring the castle at the far end of the seawall. Below the castle, the one remaining wall of the Roman villa stood like a sentinel in the mist.

Until last night, she would have said her favorite spot in Europe was and always would be Salzburg. This small resort on Spain's Costa Brava now vied with the Austrian city for first place in her heart.

Sighing, she grabbed the handle on her roller suitcase and slung the strap of her briefcase over her shoulder. A few moments later she stepped out of the elevator directly across from the resort's business offices. Her last task was to go over the final charge sheet with the conference planner.

The planner was as efficient as she was observant. While Caroline reviewed the carefully tallied charges, the woman eyed her left hand.

"Your ring is very beautiful," she commented in the musical dialect of the Catalan region.

"Thank you."

"Did you buy it here, in Tossa?"

"No, I, or rather, Mr. Burke, purchased it in Barcelona. It was, uh, a Valentine's Day gift."

"Mr. Burke? The gentleman who arranged the special dinner last night?"

"Yes."

To Caroline's utter mortification, a wave of heat rushed into her cheeks. The blush won a smile from the woman on the other side of the desk.

"Ah. He is very romantic. My husband gave me

only roses and chocolates." Her dark eyes twinkled. "You must come back to Tossa for your honeymoon, yes?"

Mumbling a noncommittal response, Caro signed the charge sheet. She could still feel the embarrassed heat in her cheeks when she took the elevator to the lobby.

Rory was waiting for her at the front desk. He'd dressed casually for the long flight back to LA in jeans, an open-necked shirt and the rust-colored sport coat he'd worn last night.

"I called Delta and had them upgrade your ticket," he informed her as the valet had stowed their suitcases in the trunk of his rented BMW.

"Why did you do that?"

"It's a long flight. You might as well go first-class. I fly all my key people first-class," he added before she could object.

That was true. Caro should know. She'd worked their reservations herself. Still, she felt compelled to point out she didn't qualify as a "key" GSI person.

Unperturbed, Rory tipped the valet. "That's one of those minor details we need to work out. I may have agreed to a long-distance courtship, but I haven't agreed to the terms. Yet."

"Good thing we've got this drive to the airport," Caroline retorted. "Looks like we may have to enter into some heavy negotiations."

* * *

The negotiations ate up a good forty minutes of the trip into Barcelona, primarily because they veered off on multiple tangents.

Topics they hadn't had a chance to discuss came up. Like music and favorite movies and food preferences. Caro admitted to being an opera buff, watching *Phantom of the Opera* every time it popped up on TV and liking her steak rare. Rory preferred bluesy jazz and—of course—Tom Clancy's books and movies.

He'd just confessed a passion for crunchy fried fish when his cell phone rang. Keeping one hand on the wheel, he dug the instrument out of his shirt pocket and flipped up the lid.

"Burke."

Even Caro could hear the high, wailing cry that came through the earpiece.

"You must help us! My husband has been kidnapped!"

Nine

While Caroline sat frozen in the BMW's passenger seat, Rory gripped the steering wheel with one hand and jammed his cell phone against his ear with the other.

"Who is this?"

"Elena!" the woman wailed. "Elena Casteel."

"How do you know your husband's been kidnapped?"

Rory kept his tone deliberate and steady in direct contrast to Señora Casteel's shrill panic.

"Juan called! He told me they took him and his driver! Then someone snatched the phone away. He said I'll find Juan's head on the front steps if I don't pay them twenty million euros!"

"When did you get the call?"

"A half hour ago. Perhaps less. I don't know." Her voice spiraled into a terrified sob. "They said I must not notify the police or alert the media! They'll kill Juan if I do!"

Rory had enough experience with executive kidnappings to know whoever had snatched Casteel wouldn't hesitate to follow through on that threat. He'd also bet they were monitoring the phones and listening to his wife's every word.

"I found your business card on my husband's desk," she cried. "He told me you're good, Señor Burke. He said you know a great deal about this awful business. Please, please! You must help me!"

Rory didn't remind the distraught woman her husband had purchased kidnapping and ransom insurance. Or that the highly specialized insurance company would most likely send in a team of experts to handle the negotiations. No need to alert anyone who might be listening in that Casteel had prepared for this situation. The knowledge would only prolong the negotiations.

Besides, Rory knew from past experience the first few hours in any kidnapping were the most crucial. Confused and frightened, relatives often made decisions that led to disastrous consequences. Until the insurance team arrived, Elena Casteel would need someone on the scene who understood the life-and-death game that kidnappers played.

"Of course I'll help you."

He raked a quick glance at the road ahead. They'd already passed the expressway leading into the city center, but he spotted an exit just ahead and cut the steering wheel. Tires screeched, and a wide-eyed Caroline snatched at the armrest to keep from slamming against the passenger door.

"You caught me on my way into Barcelona," he told Elena. "I'm about twenty minutes away. Your husband's right," he added in an attempt to steady her for the ordeal he knew would follow. "I have a great deal of experience in this terrible business. I'll help you get through it."

"And you'll bring Juan home safe?"

He refused to make promises he couldn't keep and dodged the question.

"You'd better leave the phone line open. If the kidnappers call again before I get there, write down the instructions they give you. Every word. Understand?"

"Yes."

"Is there anyone else at the house who could help you?"

"Only the servants and I'm afraid to tell them about Juan. They might call someone, say something."

"What about a friend? A relative?"

"No, no!" Her despair poured through the phone. "There is no one!"

"Okay, Elena. It's okay. I promise you won't go through this alone."

He saw Caroline pointing urgently at an overhead sign and whipped the wheel again.

"Hang on. I'm just turning onto Avenue Meridiana. I'll be there shortly."

She sobbed her thanks and cut the connection. Rory snapped his cell phone shut, his mind already in high gear.

From the time he'd spent with Juan Casteel, he knew the shipping magnate was extremely security conscious. He kept his picture and that of his wife out of the newspapers. He varied his schedule and route to work every day. He'd sent his chauffeur for special training and had installed high-tech systems to protect both his home and his office. That person or persons unknown had penetrated his security measures suggested that this wasn't a quick snatch by street thugs taking a target of opportunity. It was a well-planned abduction.

The twenty-million-euro ransom also suggested the kidnapping wasn't political. Political kidnappings usually involved a demand for a release of prisoners. *Usually* being the operative word, as a growing number of terrorist groups worldwide were turning to high-dollar kidnappings to finance their operations.

He had to talk to Elena and hear the exact details of the ransom demand before he could get a fix on the situation. And before he did *that,* he needed to hustle Caroline out of the picture.

One glance at her shocked face told him she'd heard enough of his side of the conversation to know exactly what was going down.

"I'll drop you off at a hotel," he told her tersely. "Take a cab to the airport. When you get there, cancel my flight and notify the rental agency that I'm keeping the car indefinitely."

Her brow creased. Rory guessed what was coming before she made a tentative suggestion.

"I don't want to get in the way, but maybe I can help. It sounds like Elena's alone. If nothing else, I could hold her hand while you deal with the kidnappers."

"You don't want to get in the middle of this, Caroline. The tension, the gut-wrenching fear… They wring even trained professionals inside out. And if it goes bad," he added, his jaw tight, "the nightmares will haunt you."

She nodded, acknowledging the grim possibilities, but didn't shrink from them.

"I've had a taste of tension and fear. Not to this extent, it's true, but enough to know I won't fall apart on you."

The quiet assertion sliced into his racing thoughts. Brought up short, he shot her a hard look.

"Let me help, Rory."

His fist tight on the wheel, he weighed the options. He could use a second set of eyes and ears. He might also need a runner to relay messages in a safe zone, away from the house.

"All right. You're in. On one condition. If the situation looks like it might go south, you do what I say, when I say. No questions, no arguments."

"Agreed."

Fifteen minutes later Rory identified the palatial late-nineteenth-century town house where he and Caroline had dined a few nights ago.

He cruised the block of similar residences, noting how they crowded side by side, with only a narrow gate leading to rear carriage houses that now served as garages. Noting, too, vehicles parked on either side of the tree-lined boulevard.

Word of the kidnapping hadn't leaked. There were no police cruisers, no TV crews in sight. Nor any delivery vans or cars with darkened windows. No suspicious vehicles of any sort.

Still, the skin at the back of Rory's neck tingled as he pulled into a space halfway down the block. The kidnappers were watching. They had to be watching. Or they had an inside man to keep tabs on the wife. The possibility coiled Rory's gut into a tight knot.

"You sure you want to do this?" he asked Caroline when they exited the BMW. "It's not too late to jump in a cab and catch your flight back to the States."

"I'm sure."

He skimmed another glance down the street. A young au pair strolled along the opposite sidewalk, leading a toddler by the hand. Two older women walked arm in arm on this side of the street. Bundled in coats and scarves and hats despite the mild February weather, they had their heads together and chatted nonstop. Farther down the block a gardener trimmed the bushes in front of a majestic home.

So calm. So normal. So potentially treacherous.

"Here's the deal," he told Caroline as they approached the Casteels' residence. "The kidnappers may have someone on the inside. Someone who fed them information on Juan's personal habits and travel plans. We'll have to run background checks on the entire staff. Until they're vetted, be careful what you say."

She paled a little but nodded. "I will."

"We also have to assume that the house may be bugged. Or the kidnappers may have set up electronic listening posts. Don't use the house phone or your cell phone to discuss anything related to the kidnapping until we get someone in to conduct a sweep. Got that?"

"Got it."

Hoping to hell he wasn't putting her in danger, Rory rang the bell.

The security cameras swept them, and Elena Casteel herself answered the door. Their sophisticated hostess of a few nights ago had disintegrated into a shaking, white-faced wreck. She didn't question Caroline's presence as she ushered them into the foyer.

"I sent the servants home," she said, clutching a handkerchief in one trembling fist. "The cook, the maid, the gardener... I told them I was sick. That was... That was right, wasn't it?"

"That's fine, but we'll want to talk to them later. And we'll need their names and addresses to run through our databases."

"You don't think... You can't think..." Ashen-faced, she wadded the handkerchief into a tight ball. "Our cook's been with us for ten years. Paolo, the gardener, for three or four. The maid...Maria... She's Paolo's daughter."

"We just need to cover all bases," Rory said gently. "How about we sit down? I want you to tell me what was said in the phone call you received. Word for word."

"Yes. Of course."

Elena led the way into a sitting room decorated with Tiffany lamps and art-nouveau-style furnishings. Her lace-trimmed handkerchief fluttered as she made a pitiful attempt to play the hostess.

"Would you care for a cup of tea? I was just about to make a pot. To steady my nerves," she added with what she no doubt hoped was a smile.

The valiant, if completely unsuccessful, attempt tugged at Caroline's heart. "Why don't I take care of that?" she suggested.

The older woman's eyes flooded with grateful tears. "Thank you. The kitchen is just beyond the dining room. There's tea in the caddy. And coffee. Espresso, if you prefer it."

The Casteels' kitchen blended belle-epoch grandeur and modern convenience with seamless artistry. As in the other rooms in the house, the vaulted ceiling was at least fourteen feet high and crowned with ornately carved medallion. The wrought-iron light fixtures featured Tiffany-style shades and complemented the wrought-iron table and chairs set in a window nook that overlooked the garden.

Caroline dropped her purse on an island counter containing a carousel of spice bottles and a gleaming, stainless-steel espresso maker. The appliance drew a look of intense longing, but she reminded herself that Elena had expressed a desire for tea.

A quick check of the cupboards produced the tea caddy, a heating coil to boil water and a tray for the china cups and saucers she extracted from a glass-fronted hutch. She was slicing a lemon for the tea when the sudden jangle of a cell phone nearly made her jump out of her skin.

For a startled moment she thought it was the kidnappers trying to contact Elena. Only on the second ring did she realize the sound emanated from her purse.

With a muttered curse, she dropped the knife and dug out her cell phone. Rory's grim warning replayed in her mind as she checked the number on the display screen.

Oh, Lord! Sabrina!

Caroline had completely forgotten her promise to check in with her partners before she boarded her plane to the States.

The phone gave another insistent buzz. Scrambling to figure out what she could and couldn't say, Caro flipped up the lid.

"Hi, Sabrina."

"Hey, girl! Inquiring minds want to know. How did it go last night?"

Last night? Her mind went blank for a moment before she remembered the Roman villa and the guitarist. This morning's events had shoved the entire evening right out of her head.

"Look, this isn't a good time to discuss last night. I'll give you an update when…"

"Oh, no! You're not getting off the hook that easily. Come on, Caro. Spill it. What did you decide to do vis-à-vis the ghost from your past?"

"I really can't talk about that right now."

"Why? Is he there with you?"

"No. Well, yes. Listen, Sabrina, I'm not flying home today."

"Huh?"

"Something's come up. I'll tell you about it when I can. Right now I just need you to do me a favor and cancel my reservations. Rory's, too. *Please.*"

The touch of desperation in her voice got through to her partner.

"I'll take care of it," Sabrina said slowly, "but…"

"I have to go. I'll call you when I can."

Caro snapped down the lid. Planting her palms on the counter, she pulled in several shaky breaths. Less than a half hour into this frightening situation and her nerves were already strung wire-tight. And it wasn't her husband being held hostage!

Wondering how in the world Elena would hold up through this awful ordeal, she went back to slicing lemons.

A half hour later Rory had wrung every detail he could from Elena. Leaving her with Caroline, he slipped out the back way and over a garden wall. Once he was out of range of any listening devices, he made three calls.

His first was to a contact at Interpol. Although the kidnappers had warned Elena not to notify the police, Rory knew they would be alerted by the large cash withdrawals required for the ransom. Albért Boudoin, chief of the Kidnapping and Ransom Unit at Interpol, was just the man to coordinate with the Spanish authorities and keep them out of sight.

His second call was to Lloyd's of London, who'd insured Juan Casteel. His third was to Harry Martin.

When he returned a short time later, he sat with Elena and Caroline in the sun-drenched kitchen. His rock-solid calm helped both women through the tense hours that followed.

Around three that afternoon, Rory's cell phone buzzed. He checked the number on caller ID and went out the back door again. He returned a short time later with two men and one woman.

After conducting an electronic sweep of the house and phone lines, the Lloyd's of London team of specialists disabled a jury-rigged wiretap. They then sat down with Rory and Elena for another exhaustive review of the details known so far.

"We agree with Mr. Burke," the team leader concluded. "This doesn't look like an express kidnapping. Your husband wasn't snatched off the street by chance, Mrs. Casteel. The job was well planned and executed."

The second call from the kidnappers substantiated the collective opinion.

It came just past ten that evening. Once again the caller's voice was electronically disguised to strip it of any identifying characteristics. He—or she—flatly refused to negotiate the twenty-million ransom and issued precise instructions as to the denomination, sequencing and delivery of the euro banknotes.

As proof of life, the caller put Juan on the phone for all of ten or fifteen seconds. Just long enough to reassure his wife and rip out her heart at the same time.

"I love you, *querida*. Whatever happens, always remember that I love you."

Elena collapsed after the call. Luckily, the Lloyd's

of London unit included a trained counselor. He consoled the sobbing wife while Rory and the other team members made arrangements for the ransom and discussed options for its delivery.

Caroline made a conscientious effort to stay out of their way but found plenty to do. As the night progressed, the team required endless pots of coffee. And sandwiches. Heaping platters of sandwiches. Thank God the Casteels' cook had stocked the pantry with a loaf of crusty Spanish bread and the fridge with an assortment of meats and cheese.

By three in the morning, Caroline was intimately familiar with every nook and cranny in the Casteels' kitchen. By four, she was feeling the effects of the long day and two—correction, make that three— exhausting nights. Her shoulders slumping, she perched on one of the stools at the kitchen island and sipped a cup of espresso.

"You look beat."

Rory's comment brought her around on the stool. He'd shed his sport coat hours ago and rolled up the sleeves of his once-pristine shirt. The wrinkles in the pale blue cotton matched the tired lines in his face.

"You don't look much better," Caroline observed.

"Yeah, I know. Elena offered us the use of a guest room. Why don't you go upstairs and get some rest?"

"Are you going up?"

"In a while. Maybe."

"How about Elena?"

"She says she couldn't sleep and doesn't want to try." He hooked his chin toward Caro's coffee cup. "Any more where that came from?"

"There is. Sit for a minute, and I'll brew you up some. You want it with or without milk?"

"Without."

When the espresso machine hissed out a stream of dark, scalding liquid, Caro slid the cup along the counter. Rory reached for it gratefully and cradled it in his hands.

The faint webbing of scars drew her gaze. She understood now why he would bust out a window with his bare hands. The Casteels weren't even his clients, yet he hadn't hesitated to respond to Elena's frantic call for help.

He'd been so good with her. So calm and steady and comforting. As Sondra Jennings had said, he was the kind of man any woman would want to have watching her back.

The kind of man who, if he'd known about the baby all those years ago, would have stood square-shouldered beside Caro when she faced her parents. Her pastor. Her high school counselor. Her sniggering friends.

And there, in the Casteels' dim kitchen, with Rory hunkered on a stool across from her, Caroline felt her last lingering regrets about the past slip quietly away.

* * *

At ten in the morning, Elena, Rory and one member of the K & R team drove to the bank. The bank manager had already been alerted by Lloyd's of London. He had the requested denominations of euros stacked and waiting.

At three that afternoon, Rory prepared to deliver the ransom.

Caroline had expected the negotiations to take much longer. But in the past thirty hours she'd learned her Hollywood-style perceptions of how these matters went down had little basis in reality. The single driving purpose of the Kidnapping and Ransom Unit was to get their client back alive, as quickly as possible.

For that reason, Interpol and the police had remained on the periphery, the negotiations didn't drag on needlessly and no one, least of all the K & R team, proposed any shoot-'em-up attempts to rescue the hostage.

They weren't going to just hand over the cash, of course. Rory's Interpol contact had arranged for the banknotes to be sprayed with a coating that would collect invisible but indelible fingerprints. Additionally, the technician on the K & R team had installed microscopic tracking devices in the duffel bag on wheels, which contained the ransom.

He also inserted a microscopic video camera into one stem of Rory's aviator sunglasses. The device relayed startlingly clear pictures via satellite. So clear that Caroline saw her face displayed in digital high-def on three separate computer screens when Rory drew her aside to tell her not to worry.

"Yeah, like that's going to happen! I still don't see why you have to deliver the ransom," she muttered with a glance at the others. "These people are pros."

She didn't need Rory's wry look to know how foolish that sounded. This was his business, his profession. He'd taken charge from the first hour and had been the unspoken leader of the team since it assembled.

"Do you... Do you really think they'll let Juan and his driver go?"

"It's a business, Caroline. These bastards are professionals. They know the insurance companies will stop paying if they don't deliver the hostages as promised. That's why less than two percent of all kidnappings brokered by K & R units end in death."

"So you said."

Several times in fact. Somehow a ninety-eight percent success rate didn't reassure Caro as much now as it had before the first few times Rory had stated that calm fact. Especially after watching him strap on a shoulder harness and an ankle holster.

Her gaze went to Elena, sitting white-faced and numb across the room. Caro knew the worry and fear gnawing at her insides couldn't come anywhere close to the distraught wife's, but they were enough for her to reach up and frame Rory's face with both hands.

The beginnings of a stubbly beard tickled her palms. The emerald he'd slipped on her finger winked in the afternoon light. Caroline registered neither as she pleaded with him, her voice low and urgent.

"Promise me you'll be careful."

"That goes without saying."

"And when you finish with the kidnappers, we'll resume our own negotiations."

A smile crinkled the skin at the corners of his eyes. Wolf's eyes, she thought, her throat tight. About to search out and stalk down their prey.

"That's right. We still have to work out the details of our long-distance courtship."

"Maybe not so long-distance," she murmured, going up on her toes.

"How's that?"

"We'll talk about it when this is over."

Caroline kissed him, hard, and issued a fierce command.

"Come back to me, Rory. This time, you have to come back."

Ten

Caroline didn't draw a full breath for the next three hours. Fear lodged like a jagged rock in her throat as she watched the startlingly clear images sent back by the camera in Rory's sunglasses.

Following the kidnappers' instructions, he criss-crossed Barcelona. They gave him only minutes to hail a cab and race across town or seconds to jump a subway jammed with rush-hour commuters. Two of the K & R team members had tagged him as far as the subway. They lost him when he joined more than ninety thousand rabid football fans pouring into Barcelona's Camp Nou Stadium.

When he finally made the drop and walked away,

Caroline wanted to weep with relief and whoop with joy. Elena's paper-white face kept her from doing either. Still, she couldn't refrain from wrapping Rory in a ferocious hug when he returned to the Casteels' town house.

After that, there was nothing to do but hover over the computers while the K & R team tracked the ransom's erratic progress across northern Spain. As one agonizing hour followed another, a grim silence gripped the entire team. Caroline made pot after pot of coffee. The little that was left of Elena's nerves shredded, but she refused to take a sedative or lie down.

Then, just before midnight, the phone rang with the call they'd all been waiting for. A truck driver had found Juan Casteel and his chauffeur stumbling along a deserted country road. Their eyes, mouths and hands were duct-taped, and they'd each sustained vicious bruises but were otherwise unhurt.

Rory and three members of the team shot out of the house to work the recovery. Caroline and the fourth team member stayed with the sobbing Elena.

By eight o'clock the following morning, Rory's role in life-and-death drama was over. Except, he informed Caroline wryly, for the paperwork.

The Lloyd's of London team would track and, hopefully, recover the ransom. Interpol would take down the kidnappers when and if the bastards showed their hand. Trained counselors would work with Juan, his driver and Elena to help them through any post-traumatic stress. In response to Rory's call the previous day, Harry Martin flew in two skilled operatives to beef up the Casteels' security and guard against future kidnapping attempts.

"All we have to do now is provide formal statements," Rory told Caroline with tired satisfaction.

"I don't see how I can add anything to the team's collective input."

"You were here. You saw and heard everything. You might have picked up details the rest of us missed."

"Not likely. And the way I feel now, your friend from Interpol isn't going to get much out of me."

"I told Albért we were wiped out. He said he'll contact us tomorrow. Think you can find us a hotel room to crash in?"

"Consider it done."

She called the same hotel they'd stayed in before. To her intense relief, the Hotel Grand Royale had a vacant suite and could accommodate an early-morning check-in.

When a still-weepy but joyous Elena heard they were going to a hotel, she urged them to stay at the town house. Rory declined with a smile.

"You and Juan need this time together."

"But we'll see you again before you leave Barcelona?"

"Most definitely."

When Caroline walked out of the Casteels' residence beside Rory, a sudden feeling of disorientation hit her. Blinking, she surveyed the scene.

Sunlight slanted through the chestnut trees lining the wide boulevard. Birds twittered in the branches. Nannies pushed baby carriages and chattered among themselves.

It was all so normal. So sane. As if the terror and human drama of the past forty-eight hours had never occurred.

She sank into the passenger seat of the BMW and let her head drop back against the padded headrest. She'd gone for most of those forty-eight hours fueled by fear, espresso and a few quick catnaps. Now that Juan was safe and the euphoric elation over his return had ratcheted down, exhaustion was setting in with a vengeance.

She rolled her head to the left. Rory looked about as bad as she felt. If he'd slept at all in the past two days, she didn't know when.

"Thank heavens the hotel can check us in this early." She sighed. "I want a bath, a full breakfast delivered by room service and at least twelve solid hours in bed."

"Twelve, huh?"

"Some of those twelve I need to sleep," she warned. "So do you!"

"Let's see how it goes."

She might have challenged that comment if she wasn't already sinking fast.

Rory nudged her awake at the front entrance to the hotel. With a tight grip on her arm, he sleepwalked her through the revolving doors. She blinked owlishly at the flower shop in the lobby and thought she recognized the paneled entrance to Cartier. The brief stop at the front desk was a total blur, however. So was the elevator ride to their floor.

"Come on, sweetheart. We're almost there."

Rory steered her down a vaguely familiar hallway carpeted in green and gold. A porter followed with the luggage and briefcases they'd packed what now seemed like two lifetimes ago for their flights back to the States.

Caroline had realigned her priorities even before she entered the luxurious suite. "Forget what I said about a bath and room service."

Ignoring the view of the cathedral that had so enchanted her their first night in Barcelona, she aimed straight for the bedroom. She stayed on her feet only long enough to fish her cell phone out of her purse and leave a voice mail for her partner Sabrina.

"I'm at the Hotel Grand Royale in Barcelona," she mumbled. "Don't call me. I'll call you. Tomorrow. After I talk to Interpol."

Maybe she shouldn't have tacked on that last bit, she thought as she flipped the cell phone shut. Oh, well. Too late now, and she was too tired to put together a coherent sentence in any case.

She kicked off her shoes, shed her jacket and dropped facedown into the cotton-covered duvet.

When she swam back to semiconsciousness, the drawn drapes let in only a faint, hazy light. Rory lay beside her, sprawled on his back, his breathing deep and steady.

He'd stripped down to his shorts, Caroline noted sleepily. Stripped her down, too. At least she assumed he'd done the deed. She couldn't remember and didn't particularly care. Hooking an arm over his waist, she snuggled against him and dropped into oblivion again.

When she woke the second time, the room was dark and the bed beside her empty. Only a faint light showed under the door to the sitting room. Rolling over, she squinted at the bedside clock. When she saw the time, a smile tugged at her lips. Almost twelve hours exactly.

After stretching until her joints popped, Caroline rolled out of bed. She spotted her clothes draped over a chair. Her suitcase sat on the bench at the end of the bed, with her purse and briefcase beside it.

She should call her partners. She knew her cryptic messages over the past few days must have them worried. The obnoxious rumble her stomach emitted put phone calls in a distant second place to food! Any kind of food!

Fishing out her toiletries, Caroline hit the bathroom. She emerged a short time later wrapped in one of the hotel's plush robes and marched to the door to the sitting room. With a dramatic gesture, she flung it open.

"Feed me."

Rory looked up from the work he'd spread over the desk. "With pleasure. I thought I would starve waiting for you to wake up."

He'd pulled on a pair of khakis and a long-sleeved shirt with the cuffs rolled up and the tails hanging out. His cheeks still sported a bristly stubble, but Caroline saw—with relief—that his eyes were no longer rimmed red by fatigue.

"Do you want to go out or order from room service?"

Caro's glance went to the terrace doors. They framed the view that had so enchanted her the first night. The brilliantly illuminated spires of Gaudí's Sagrada Familia thrusting into the night sky.

She ached to show Rory more of the Barcelona she loved. The city's many restaurants and *tapas* bars would just be coming to life, she knew, especially along the series of teeming, vibrant, pedestrians-only streets known collectively as La Rambla.

But going out would involve getting dressed, slapping on makeup, waiting an indeterminate period at a crowded restaurant. She was too ravenous for any of the above.

"Let's do room service. If we're still here tomorrow night, I'll take you to my favorite restaurant in the Gothic Quarter."

"Sounds good to me."

From under the papers on the desk he extracted a leather-bound binder embossed with the hotel's insignia.

"Why don't you order while I shower and shave. I would have cleaned up earlier, but you were snuffling and mumbling into the pillow and I didn't want to wake you."

"Mumbling? What about?"

"Most of it was unintelligible. I did catch a phrase or two, though. One was my name. I'm pretty sure the other was 'way hot.'"

"You're making that up."

"Maybe." Grinning, he speared a hand into her wet hair. "And maybe not."

He dropped a kiss on her mouth, scraping her chin with his bristles, and left with instructions to order him a steak, medium rare, with all the trimmings.

Caroline took the menu to a chair beside the unlit fireplace. Her legs curled under her, she pored through the extensive list of offerings. It ran to eighteen pages, with the first five devoted to the hotel's incredible selection of appetizers.

She lined up her choices after a lengthy internal

debate. Carrying the menu back to the desk, she shuffled some of Rory's papers aside and reached for the desk phone. A direct line connected her with room service.

She ordered a rib eye with all the trimmings for Rory, grilled lamb kebabs with rice pilaf for her. A bottle of Spanish red wine to go with them. And *tapas*. Lots of *tapas*. Fifteen scrumptious, bite-size delicacies to celebrate the conclusion of a remarkable day.

"Send the wine and *tapas* up right away," she requested. "We'll enjoy them while we wait for dinner."

"Yes, madame."

Her stomach rumbling in joyous anticipation, Caroline replaced the phone in its cradle and closed the menu. When she realigned Rory's papers, one near the bottom of the pile snagged her attention. She blinked, startled by the header printed in bold letters.

Operation Caroline Walters.

"What the heck…?"

Frowning, she slid the typewritten sheet free of the pile. Utter disbelief swept through her as she skimmed the paragraph headings, also bolded.

Phase One—Scope out the target.
Phase Two—Arrange initial contact.
Phase Three—Initiate contact.
Phase Four…

She hadn't heard the shower cut off, but she did hear the bedroom door open. She spun around, the typewritten sheet clutched in her fist, as Rory strolled in. Like her, he was wrapped in one of the hotel's plush robes. *Unlike* her, he was loose and relaxed.

"Did you put the order in?" he asked, then caught her expression. "What's the matter?"

When she didn't answer, couldn't answer, he strode over to her.

"Caroline, what's happened? Did Albért call? Did they take down the kidnappers?"

"No," she got out through frozen lips. "Your friend at Interpol did not call. And yes, I put the order in. In the process, I found this."

Her arm rigid, she held out the sheet of paper. Rory glanced at it and grimaced.

"Oh, hell! That isn't what it looks like."

"Really?"

Drawing on a lifetime of painful, hard-won experience, Caroline clamped an iron band on her roiling emotions. "You'd better enlighten me. What *is* it?"

"What we used to call an operations plan in the military."

She flipped the paper around and skimmed over the contents again. Phrases leaped out at her. Some typed, some scratched out and rewritten in hand. When she lifted her gaze again, her heart felt like a solid block of ice inside her chest.

"So it *was* all scripted. Just like you said. Every

word. Every touch. That…that elaborate Valentine's Day seduction."

He could hardly deny it, given the evidence in stark black and white.

"I only planned the initial phases. Tracking you down. Steering the conference contract to EBS. Flying over to Spain to…"

"To make things right with me," Caro finished in a harsh, dry whisper.

"I told you that was my intention. I never hid it from you."

"No, you didn't."

"What wasn't scripted, what I didn't intend, was the way you threw me completely off stride. I haven't stuck to the plan since that night on the beach, when the undertow almost sucked you in. Instead, it sucked me in."

His eyes held hers, steady and unrelenting.

"I'm in over my head now, Caroline. Way over my head. I…"

The rap of knuckles against the door to the suite cut him off.

"The *tapas*," she forced out through a throat that felt etched with glass. "I asked room service to bring them up first."

Rory muttered a curse and strode toward the entryway. It wasn't room service on the other side of the door, however, but a tall, leggy blonde backed by three companions.

"Are you Burke?" she demanded.

"Yes."

"Where's Caroline?"

"She's…"

"I'm right here!"

Reeling from her second shock of the evening, Caro gaped as her two business partners rushed into the suite.

"Sabrina! Devon! What are you two doing here?"

"What do you *think* we're doing here!" Sabrina retorted, enveloping her in a fierce hug.

The tallest of the three partners, she had a tumble of pale blond curls, mile-long legs and an upbeat personality that recognized few obstacles—not the least of which was a domineering father who'd tried repeatedly and unsuccessfully to mold her into a female version of himself.

"You scared the bejesus out of me with your 'I can't talk now' and 'don't call me.' That bit about having to talk to Interpol didn't help, either. You have some serious explaining to do, girlfriend."

Devon appeared no less worried. Her brown eyes were filled with concern under a fringe of auburn bangs. "'Rina called me in London. Cal had his corporate jet fly us into Barcelona. We all hooked up at the airport and came right to the hotel."

Four inches shorter than Sabrina but no less resilient, Devon had only recently learned to trust her heart again. She owed that to the man who followed her into the suite. Cal Logan was nothing if not persuasive.

"Hi, Caroline." His electric blue eyes skimmed her face. "You okay?"

She had no answer for that. Not with Rory's six- or seven-step seduction plan still wadded in her fist. At her helpless shrug, Cal patted her shoulder.

"Don't worry. Whatever the problem is, we'll help you fix it."

Completely overwhelmed, she stuffed the crumpled paper in her pocket and turned to the fourth new arrival. "You must be Marco."

The drop-dead gorgeous Italian surgeon who'd swept Sabrina off her feet—literally!—less than a month ago smiled an acknowledgment.

"I am indeed. It's good to finally meet you. 'Rina has told me a great deal about you."

"Same here."

Now that Sabrina knew Caroline was alive and still kicking, her belligerence returned with a vengeance. Rounding on Rory, she let fly with both barrels.

"When Caro told us you were the bastard who got her pregnant back in high school, I offered to fly to Spain and deliver a swift kick to your gonads. If you've hurt her again, or involved her in some kind of illegal activity, she's got four friends here who will take immense pleasure in following through on my initial offer."

Rory lifted a brow and glanced from her to the trio

standing shoulder-to-shoulder with Caro. His gaze lingered briefly on Devon, assessed Cal and Marco, swung back to the woman facing him with both fists planted on her hips.

"Thanks for the warning," he said, not sounding unduly concerned. "You're Sabrina Russo, right? Dominic Russo's daughter?"

"How did you… Oh, that's right. You're in the spook business."

"Personal security," he corrected mildly. "And you're Devon McShay."

It was a statement, not a question, but Dev responded with a nod.

"You want to introduce me to your friends, Ms. McShay?"

"This is Cal Logan, CEO of Logan Aerospace."

"Which recently acquired Hauptmann Metal Works in Dresden," Rory commented. "I saw the write-up in the *Wall Street Journal*." His glance shifted to Marco. "And…?"

"Dr. Marco Calvetti," Sabrina supplied. "Aka His Excellency Don Marco Antonio Sonestra di Calvetti, Twelfth Duke of San Giovanti, Fourteenth Marquis of Caprielle and a bucketful of other titles I haven't gotten down yet."

She tossed back her hair and glared at Rory.

"Introductions over, Burke. Now would you and/or Caroline kindly tell us what the hell is going on?"

Eleven

Room service arrived before either Rory or Caroline could comply with Sabrina's demand for an explanation.

While the waiter set up the *tapas* and uncorked the wine, Rory headed for the bedroom to exchange the hotel's plush terry-cloth robe for some clothes. He returned a few moments later wearing jeans and a black polo shirt.

Caro debated changing, as well, but the robe covered her from neck to midcalf. And the aromas rising from the array of appetizers were generating some embarrassing noises from the vicinity of her stomach.

"We haven't eaten since…" She had to think. "Yesterday."

"Sit," Sabrina ordered, pointing a stern finger. "You can talk while you eat."

"There's more than enough for all of us. Everyone, help yourselves."

"First things first," Rory stated. "I need something stronger than wine."

Sabrina gave a huff of impatience, but when he brought a bottle of scotch and glasses over to the coffee table both Marco and Cal signaled their approval.

The men dragged chairs over to form a semicircle around the food and drinks. After everyone had a glass in hand and Caroline had filled a plate with a selection of appetizers, Sabrina infused her voice with exaggerated politeness.

"Now?" she asked.

"Now," Rory agreed. "But before we start, I need your assurance that what we're about to tell you doesn't leave this room."

"Why?"

"It hasn't hit the papers yet. With luck, it won't before Interpol has a solid lead on the kidnappers."

"Kidnappers?" Devon gasped.

She was seated on the sofa next to Caroline. Her brown eyes flooding with dismay, she laid a quick hand on her partner's arm.

"You were kidnapped?"

"Not me. One of Rory's clients. Or rather, a prospective client. We met with him a few days ago here in Barcelona. Elena—his wife—contacted Rory right after she got the call from the kidnappers. We were on the way to the airport and made a swift U-turn."

A stark silence followed. Cal Logan broke it by setting his scotch on the coffee table with a thud.

"Let me get this straight, Burke."

Caroline knew Cal had played football in college. According to Devon, the aerospace CEO could also be as ruthless as the next man when it came to business. But none of the three women had ever seen him square his shoulders and look so intimidating.

"Your prospective client is kidnapped," he said, his tone dangerous, "and you drag Caro into the middle of it?"

Marco wasn't any happier. His dark brows snapped together, and his voice cut like a scalpel. "You should have put her on a plane immediately, Burke."

"I don't know about your women, gentlemen," Rory drawled, "but mine has a mind of her own. The only way I could have put Caroline on an airplane was to hog-tie her and stuff her into a suitcase."

The possessive pronouns generated instant and very diverse reactions from the women they'd been applied to. Sabrina snorted at the blatant sexism. Devon shook her head. Marco and Cal turned toward Caroline.

She chose to ignore their speculative glances. *And* the unspoken question of her relationship with Rory.

She needed time to sort through that crazy business about his so-called operations plan before she could answer that. Instead, she speared a spiced onion from her plate and downed it before sharing more details of the frightening ordeal.

"Rory and a team from Lloyd's of London negotiated with the kidnappers, in coordination with the Spanish authorities and Interpol. Rory delivered the ransom yesterday afternoon. Juan—the man who was taken—and his driver weren't released until late last night. Or I guess it was early this morning. I've kind of lost track of time. I'm not even sure what day this is anymore."

"What an awful thing for you to go through," Devon commiserated.

"It wasn't as bad for me as it was for Juan's wife, but I'll admit those were the scariest forty-eight hours of my life." Her eyes lifted to Rory. "Especially after you strapped on a gun and went to deliver the ransom."

"They were a little tense for me, too," he admitted with magnificent understatement. "You did a helluva lot more than stay on the sidelines, though. Elena couldn't have gotten through the most terrifying forty-eight hours of *her* life without you, sweetheart."

He'd done it again. Staked another claim too obvious to ignore. Caro flushed but refused to acknowledge the casual endearment.

"Yes, well, I'm just glad it's over."

"No kidding!" Sabrina muttered.

Setting her plate on the coffee table, Caro slewed sideways to face her partners.

"I received some up-close-and personal training on executive security this week. Given the kind of clients EBS caters to, we need to take a hard look at how we would respond if one of them is kidnapped."

The comment shot Cal upright in his chair. "Respond, hell!"

"I didn't mean we would shoot it out with kidnappers. But Dev and Sabrina and I need to look at how we would protect ourselves if we're with a high-risk client and something happens."

"From what 'Rina has told me of your business," Marco said, frowning, "all of your clients are high risk."

That was true. The three men in the room were prime examples.

"Something we'll definitely have to think about," Sabrina agreed, her mind clearly on other matters. "Marco, why don't you and Cal go down to the lobby and see about getting us rooms? Take Burke with you."

"No need for me to go," Rory commented with a dry look at the blonde. "I already have a room."

Immune to sarcasm, she flapped a hand. "Then have a drink in the bar with the guys."

"Please," Dev said a little more politely. "Sabrina and I would like to talk to Caro."

She could guess what they wanted to talk about. The subject of their conversation was sitting directly across from her, waiting for her to call the shots on this one. Slowly, she nodded.

"The triumvirate has spoken," Cal said as he rose with an easy grace that belied his size. "Come on, Burke. I want to hear more about your business."

"And your assessment of the risks to our women," Marco added as the men headed for the door.

When it closed behind them, "their women" rolled their eyes. Sabrina's and Devon's expressions held a touch of resigned amusement, but Caro's morphed quickly into wariness as her friends made themselves comfortable. Obviously, they weren't going anywhere until they got some answers. Caroline wished she had some to give.

"I can tell this is going to be a long session," she conceded. "Dev, pour us another glass of wine while I load up our plates. We'll eat, drink and gab."

"Just like we used to."

For a moment the years seemed to melt away. They could have been college juniors again, snuggled up in their tiny apartment in Salzburg to discuss men, plans for the weekend, the latest museum Devon had dragged them to, the city's upcoming international music festival and classwork—usually in that order.

Time and maturity hadn't altered the priority, Caroline acknowledged with a rueful smile as she bit into a garlic-flavored olive. Men still topped the list.

"It's just us girls now," Devon announced unnecessarily as she followed Sabrina's example by kicking off her shoes and curling her legs under her on the sofa. "What's the deal with you and Burke?"

"Okay, here goes." Caro pulled in a deep breath, blew it out. "I followed your advice, Dev, to trust my instincts and see where they took me. In short order, they took me to…"

She held up a hand and ticked off the tumultuous events of the past week, one by one.

"The hottest sex I've ever had. A romantic Valentine's Day dinner under the stars. A guitarist playing flamenco music. An emerald and diamond ring. A marriage proposal. Another night of hot sex. A kidnapping. A…"

"Whoa, whoa, whoa!" Sabrina jerked upright. "Back up there, missy."

"To?"

"To the ring."

"And the marriage proposal!" Dev exclaimed.

"I was as shocked as you are," Caro admitted. "I totally didn't see it coming, although Rory and I agreed the sex was great. Okay, spectacular. Then he said almost exactly what you said, 'Rina."

"Oh, Lord! What did I say?"

"It has to mean something that the spark is still there after all these years. Since I was most definitely feeling the heat, that struck home."

Frowning, Caro speared a shrimp swimming in

curry sauce. Reducing everything that had happened between her and Rory into a few sentences took concentrated effort.

"He also reminded me he's been on his own since he was sixteen. He's decided it's time for a wife. Kids. Someone to come home to," she finished quietly.

"So tell him to get a dog," Sabrina declared without a shred of sympathy.

Devon responded more slowly. "What about love, Caro? I know it's hard to believe it can grow so quickly, but Cal and I are living proof. Sabrina and Marco, too. Maybe Rory fell hard after seeing you again. Maybe his proposal came from the heart."

"I wouldn't have such a hard time believing that if I hadn't found a copy of his operations plan."

"His what?"

"Here it is." She pulled the crumpled paper from the pocket of her robe. "Operation Caroline Walters. Read it and weep. I almost did."

Sabrina sprang out of her chair. Her sun-streaked blond curls brushed Dev's dark red bob as she leaned over her partner's shoulder.

"Scope out the *target!*" she exclaimed. "Is that you?"

"Evidently."

"Arrange contact," she read incredulously. "Initiate contact." Her brows soared. "Ensure appropriate restitution?"

Caroline let out a long breath. "Rory told me right

up front that he always pays his debts. He also said he intended to make things right with me."

"By marrying you?"

"I guess. Maybe. Oh, hell, I don't know. I found that piece of paper, like, two minutes before you guys knocked on the door. I haven't had time to absorb all the implications yet."

She shoved a hand through her hair, struggling with a whirlwind of emotions.

"My first instinct was to throw his damn plan in his face. Then I remembered all the trouble he went through to arrange that ridiculously romantic dinner. And how good he was with Elena. And how I go up in flames whenever he takes me in his arms."

Talking through her confusion helped, Caroline realized. A lot!

"And now all I can think about is how I felt when he left to deliver the ransom. The terror almost ripped me apart. I swear to God, I couldn't breathe the whole time he was gone."

"Well," Devon said after a long silence. "That pretty much answers how you feel about the man. The question now is whether he feels the same about you."

"I know he wants me. I *think* he loves me. In Rory's mind, they're the same thing."

She looked at each of her friends in turn. The three of them had shared so much. So many highs, such devastating lows. Now Sabrina and Devon had found the loves of their lives. They *had* to know the answer to the question still gnawing at Caro's heart.

"Is he right? Do want and need and love add up to the same thing?"

Five stories down, Rory was nursing his second scotch of the night.

So were Cal Logan and the doc, but they hadn't gone almost twenty-four hours without eating. Nor were they coming off the adrenaline rush of recovering a client from kidnappers. And they hadn't just had the damn rug yanked out from under their feet because of a minor misunderstanding.

The scotch was biting into Rory's empty stomach. So were frustration and a growing sense of indignation.

"I mean, what's the problem with making a plan?" he threw at the other two men.

Logan was sprawled comfortably in one of the hotel's lounge chairs. He was wearing a business suit, but he'd stuffed his tie in his pocket and popped the top two buttons of his white shirt.

The doc—he'd told Rory he preferred that to the string of titles Sabrina had rolled off—was more casually dressed in slacks, a thin sweater and a suede bomber jacket. Evidently the tawny-haired witch he'd fallen for had barely given him time to change out of his scrubs before hustling him to the airport in Rome.

Both men had regarded Rory with undisguised hostility at first. In the past half hour, however, their hostility had given way to a rueful sympathy that only fueled his indignation.

"What's wrong with devising a plan?" he asked again, feeling aggrieved. "I knew what I wanted and went after it. You'd think Caroline would appreciate all the effort I put into finding her and setting up our reunion."

"You'd think," Logan agreed.

"I didn't intend to pull my people in for a conference until later this year. I moved up the schedule and set the meeting here in Spain to give her company the business. It wasn't just a ploy to get to her," he insisted. "EBS made a bundle off that conference."

The doc swirled his scotch. "I doubt the company's bottom line concerns Caroline at the moment. Or 'Rina or Devon."

"Yeah, well, it should. I checked their financials. EBS didn't start showing a profit until they landed Logan here as a client."

"They secured another big client this morning," Calvetti announced calmly. "With all the worry over Caroline, Sabrina hasn't finalized the details yet. But it appears EBS has been chosen to work the International Neurosurgical Institute's annual convention in Milan."

"And that's another thing!"

Scowling, Rory thumped his glass on the table and glared at the other two.

"Caroline says Logan here has Devon tied up working exclusively for his corporation. You talked Sabrina into opening an office in Italy. I suspect you'll *keep* her in Italy by feeding her more conventions like the one in Milan."

"That's certainly my intention."

"So where does that leave the third partner in their enterprise? Jetting all over Europe to handle the remainder of EBS's business? I'm here to tell you, gentlemen, it ain't gonna happen."

"How do you figure to make it 'un-happen'?" Cal Logan asked curiously. "Or has that objective bit the dust, along with the rest of your op plan?"

"I haven't given up on the plan. Not completely. Although looking back, I see now I might have made a tactical error in proposing to Caroline so soon."

"Might have?" Logan echoed dryly.

"I really thought I'd set the scene." Frowning, Rory tried to decide how his carefully scripted evening had gone wrong. "Dinner under the stars. Music. Candles all the hell over the place. Most women would have…"

Even before he finished the sentence, it hit him. Caroline wasn't like most women. The women he knew, anyway. She'd taken what life had thrown at her without complaint and emerged with a quiet, unshakable strength.

She didn't need Rory to protect her or shield her, much less atone for past sins by making her financially secure for the rest of her life. What she needed…what *he* needed was to put the past where it belonged. In the past.

"Hell! I've got this all ass-backward."

His chair almost toppled over as he shoved out of it.

"I'm going upstairs. Without an escort," he added when the other two started to rise. "I'll send Devon and Sabrina down here."

"Good luck with that," Logan drawled, settling back in his chair.

When Rory stepped out of the elevator, he came face-to-face with the two women he'd been prepared to eject from his suite.

"Caroline sent us to find you," Devon said. "She wants to talk to you."

"Good. I want to talk to her, too."

He tried to read their expressions for an indication of what he would have to deal with when he hit the suite. The redhead's face was carefully neutral. The blonde, on the other hand, didn't try to disguise her feelings. Her earlier belligerence was gone, but she issued a challenge so fierce that it seared the air.

"You've got this one chance to get it right, Burke. A slim chance. Don't screw it up."

Her expression softened for a moment. Just long

enough to give Rory a glimpse of the woman who could inspire such passionate loyalty in her friends and bring a cool customer like Calvetti to his knees.

"Good luck."

He nodded his thanks and strode down the hall. By the time he'd unlocked the door to the suite, he'd marshaled his arguments and put them in priority order.

Every damn one of them flew out of his head when he spotted Caroline. She was standing at the window, her hands shoved in the pockets of her robe, her gaze fixed on the illuminated spires of that character Gaudí's masterpiece.

The sound of the door closing brought her around. "I've been thinking."

"So have I."

"Maybe…"

"Wait, Caroline. Let me go first. Please."

At her nod, he crossed the room. "Your friends warned me I had only one chance. They also warned me not to screw it up. The fact is, there's no way I could screw things up any more than I already have."

"You think so?"

"I know so." He shook his head, wondering how the hell he could have been so dense. "I thought I could cover all the options. Work out the details in advance. The problem is, I was working from an outdated database. You didn't… You *don't* fit any of my prescripted parameters. You're not the girl you were then, Caroline, any more than I'm the hot young stud I thought I was."

She gave him a ghost of a smile. "Young? No. Hot? Well…"

"What I'm trying to say is that I see now I've made a mess of this. My only excuse is that I've never been in love before."

Surprise flickered across her face. Moving swiftly to take advantage of it, Rory raised a hand and cupped her cheek.

"I know, I know. I fed you a load of crap about not knowing the difference between lust and love. I discovered the difference real fast when you found that damn op plan. I thought I would lose you. Thought I *had* lost you. Then your friends burst onto the scene, and I had to stand there with my guts hanging out."

She bit her lip. "That's…that's one way to describe love."

"Here's another." Bending, he brushed her lips with his. "I want to be part of your life, any way you'll have me, for as long as you'll have me."

When he raised his head, the tears shimmering in her green eyes slammed into him like a fist to his chest.

"Christ! You have to believe me, Caroline. I never meant to hurt you."

"I know."

The tears came faster, spilling freely. Rory's heart hit the carpet with them. Cursing his clumsiness, he swiped his thumb across her cheek.

"It's okay. Don't cry, sweetheart. I understand. I blew it."

"You idiot!"

He flinched, then melted with relief when she broke out in a radiant smile.

"These are tears of joy."

She threw her arms around his neck, grinning and sniffling at the same time.

"I love you, too. I knew it before we left the Casteels' house, but that idiotic plan threw me off balance. I just needed a little time to talk through the shock. Sabrina and Dev helped with that."

"I owe them," Rory said fervently. "Big-time. And I always…"

"Pay your debts," Caroline finished, laughing. "We've already had this conversation. Several times. Let it drop, and kiss me instead."

Rory was more than willing to comply. When they came up for air, however, he insisted on resolving one final matter.

"I know I said I'd give long-distance courtship a try, but we've already let too many years build up between us. Marry me, Caroline. Tonight. Tomorrow. The day after, if you need time to shop for a dress."

He was back, Caro realized with a hiccup of mingled laughter and chagrin. The take-charge Rory who'd steamrolled into her life after so many years.

"What about blood tests?" she protested. "A

license? And wouldn't we need to ask someone from the U.S. Consulate to witness the ceremony?"

He had the grace to look embarrassed for a moment.

But only a moment.

"I, uh, already planned for those contingencies. Just say yes, and I'll take care of the details."

Oh God! She loved this man. She had, she realized with a pang of sharp, piercing joy, since that long-ago summer when their lives first collided.

"Yes," she said, surging up on tiptoe to cover his face with kisses. "Yes, yes, yes, *yes!*"

Twelve

At the vehement insistence of Devon and Sabrina, the wedding took place three days later.

They demanded the extra day to add the small touches Rory hadn't factored into his plan. Like six solid hours spent roaming Barcelona's exclusive boutiques. And a full afternoon in an exclusive spa to pamper the bride.

At *Caroline's* vehement insistence, the wedding was conducted on the beach at Tossa de Mar.

Harry Martin took care of flying Caro's mother to Spain. She sat in the front row with Sondra Jennings, looking slightly dazed by the fact that she wasn't in Kansas anymore.

A dozen or so GSI operatives filled the folding chairs behind them. Across from them sat Captain Antonio Medina and a sprinkling of the resort employees Caroline had worked with during the week of the conference.

Elena and Juan Casteel were there, too. They'd arrived several hours early so Elena could come up to the bride's room and "lend" her an exquisite lace mantilla.

"Something borrowed, something blue," she said with a smile. "That's the custom in your country, isn't it?"

Since Caro had decided on a simple, off-the-shoulder white satin dress and a wreath of white baby's breath in her hair, Elena draped the mantilla around her hips.

"You and Rory are right for each other." Her eyes misting, she tied the ends in a loose knot. "Like Juan and me. I hope you have as many happy years together as we've had."

Caro enveloped her in a fierce hug. "I hope so, too."

The mantilla fell around her hips in graceful folds as she took Harry Martin's arm to walk from the hotel to the beach. The retired cop had risen to the occasion. In Caro's admittedly biased opinion, he looked like an older and *very* sexy version of James Bond in his white tie, tux and Ray-Bans.

"I told you Rory was a good man," he said with a grin.

"So you did."

At the first, sultry notes of a flamenco, Harry escorted Caro down the steps to the beach. Sabrina and Dev preceded them. They'd indulged their individual tastes as bridesmaids. 'Rina's backless, strapless dress in eye-popping red turned every head in the rows of folding chairs. Devon was more subdued but every bit as stunning in pale lavender. The color had a special significance for her. Something to do with ski suits and headbands. Sabrina and Caro didn't quite get the connection but promised faithfully to adopt the color for Dev's wedding to Cal in May. Sabrina's would take place just a few short weeks later.

For a giddy moment, the three friends had contemplated a triple ceremony. All for one and one for all. In Salzburg, of course, where they'd first met.

Rory had gulped and made an obvious effort to rein in his impatience to get Caroline to the altar. Aid came from an unexpected quarter when Marco suggested that his mother the duchess would be very unhappy if he and Sabrina didn't have their wedding at the family's palazzo in Naples.

So here Caroline was, floating on Harry's arm, with the sun sparkling on the Mediterranean and Tossa's medieval castle brooding in the distance.

And there stood Rory, aligned alongside Marco and Cal. All three looked impossibly handsome in their tuxes, but Caroline had eyes for only one man. In the space of a few weeks he'd shocked and confused and confounded her. Yet all she had to do was see the wind ruffling his hair and the smile in his amber eyes to know Elena had it right. She and Rory had been meant for each other from the moment they'd met.

Her heart singing, Caroline gave thanks for her past as she went eagerly to her future.

* * * * *

VALENTE MUST MARRY

BY
MAXINE SULLIVAN

Maxine Sullivan credits her mother for her lifelong love of romance novels, so it was a natural extension for Maxine to want to write her own romances. She thinks there's nothing better than being a writer, and is thrilled to be one of the few Australians to write for the Desire™ line.

Maxine lives in Melbourne, Australia, but over the years has travelled to New Zealand, the UK and the USA. In her own backyard, her husband's job ensured they saw the diversity of the countryside, from the tropics to the outback, country towns to the cities. She is married to Geoff, who has proven his hero status many times over the years. They have two handsome sons and an assortment of much-loved, previously abandoned animals.

Maxine would love to hear from you and can be contacted through her website at www.maxinesullivan.com.

Dear Reader,

I imagine it would be difficult being the middle child in a family. On the one hand you may not be given the greatest responsibility like the oldest, but then you aren't given as much leeway as the youngest either. You have to find your own place in the world.

And that's exactly what Nick Valente has done. Being the middle son in the dynamic Valente family has its own special challenges. As middle brother, Nick needed to find something for himself. He doesn't realise it at first, but his father's ultimatum to marry or lose the beloved family estate ends up being the best thing for Nick. It leads this middle son to finding true love with the one woman he can't forget – Sasha Blake.

I hope you enjoy this story, no matter your place in your own family.

Happy reading!

Maxine

To Mum and Dad
"Love Forever"

One

"What are you saying, Dad?" Nick Valente asked his father, Cesare, as they sat on one of the terraced courtyards on the Valente estate.

"I'm saying I've been retired over six months now and while I've loved it here, this place is getting too big for us. Isabel and I have decided to move into an apartment in town."

The statement sucked the wind out of Nick. This place was *home*. He'd grown up on this estate in the Hawkesbury district of Sydney. His own mother had given birth to him here before taking off for greener pastures, leaving his father to meet Isabel six months later.

"The estate is yours," Cesare continued. "If you want it."

Something leaped inside him. Did his father even have to ask? Of course he wanted it. He wanted it so badly he had to turn his head away and look down over the cultivated lawns, lest his father see how *much* he wanted it.

And there was the crux of the matter.

He didn't trust his father.

Cesare was a crafty old devil who'd had a long reign as founder of The House of Valente, an Australian perfume dynasty now branching out in the rest of the world under the control of the eldest son, Alex, with their new perfume, "Valente's Woman." Cesare was used to getting his own way.

"And if I don't want it?" he said, playing it cool, just like he did every day in his job as Chief Operating Officer for the family business.

"Then I'll give it to Matt."

Damn.

He was close to Matt, but his younger brother liked living in the center of the city, and this place would end up neglected. Matt would die out here on the far outskirts of Sydney, no matter that he could commute.

He, on the other hand, would appreciate the break away from his city apartment and from the constant round of hard work and equally hard play.

He casually turned his head to look at his father. "Matt's never liked this place much," he pointed out coolly.

Cesare inclined his gray head. "I know that."

"So why give it to him?"

"I haven't…yet. It all depends on you."

His misgivings were increasing by the moment. "What's the catch, Dad?"

Cesare's lips twisted wryly. "You know me well." A calculating expression took over the older man's face. "You can have the estate on one condition. You have to get married."

Nick straightened in his chair. "What the hell!"

"This place needs a young family again."

"So I'm supposed to get married *and* have a family, too?" he said, sarcastically.

"That's usually the way it goes."

Nick shook his head. He had no plans to get married just yet. No woman was going to tie him down, and he'd be damned if he'd bring a child into the world whose parents didn't love each other.

"What about Alex and Olivia?" It was the most acceptable option to him. At least they would give this place the care it deserved.

"No, they have their own house now and wouldn't want to move. It would unsettle little Scott."

Yes, that was true. Alex and Olivia had adopted

eight-year-old Scott at Christmas. They wouldn't want to move again so soon, if at all.

Suddenly something clicked in Nick's brain as he looked at his father. "Tell me you didn't have anything to do with Alex marrying Olivia."

Cesare didn't even flinch. "I'd be lying if I said I hadn't."

Nick's mouth tightened. "Does Mum know what you've been up to?"

He'd always considered Isabel his mother. She was elegant, charming, loving, and quite formidable when riled. She'd been the only mother he'd known—until his real mother had started turning up during his childhood, causing havoc.

"Isabel and I have agreed to disagree. She knows my feelings on this, and I'm not about to change my mind. It's too important to me."

Nick swore. "Dammit, I'm not marrying some woman just to satisfy your perverted sense of power."

"Then Matt gets the estate."

His stomach tightened. "Matt won't want it once I tell him what game you're playing."

Cesare took a sip of his coffee before putting the cup down on the table. "Then I'll have to sell, won't I?"

Nick swallowed hard. His father thought he had it all figured out, did he?

"Just who the hell am I supposed to marry anyway? Should I just pick a woman from my Rolodex?"

"Sasha Blake."

Nick's brain stumbled. He hadn't thought about that name in years…hadn't thought about *her* in years…hadn't thought about that kiss.

Well, rarely.

"She isn't in my Rolodex," he snapped, not wanting to think about her at all. That kiss had been a minor lapse in judgment.

"She's perfect for you."

"I'm glad you think so."

Displeasure furrowed Cesare's brow, then cleared. "You'll see. Once you marry her you'll—"

"I'm *not* marrying her, Dad." If he was getting married—and he wasn't saying he would—*he'd* choose the woman. "Besides, isn't she in England?"

"No, she's back. She's an interior designer now, and I've asked her to redecorate this house."

The surprises just kept on coming, didn't they?

"This place is fine the way it is."

Cesare considered him. "You've always loved it here."

Nick shrugged. "It's home."

"And that's why I'm offering it to you."

"But only if I marry Sasha Blake, right?"

"It'll be good to join the two families. Porter and Sally Blake have been our friends for years."

"I've never trusted Porter." Sally was a nice enough woman, if a little too submissive.

"Forget Porter Blake. It's his daughter you're marrying."

"I'm not marrying anyone. Period."

There was a small pause. "Sasha will be here tomorrow morning checking things while we're in the city. It might be a good time to talk to her."

"No."

His father went very still. Then, "I think Matt will be more than happy to change the whole look of this place, don't you? And Sasha must have some innovative ideas she's picked up from living in London."

Nick swore. "Why are you doing this, Dad?"

Cesare looked at him, a hint of vulnerability in his eyes. "I've had one heart attack already. I want to see you married before I die."

"It was a mild heart attack," Nick rasped, remembering.

"And the next one may be fatal, *figlio mio*," *son of mine*, he said, lapsing into Italian.

Nick felt an inward shudder at the thought and knew his father had him right where he wanted him. He could fight Cesare on everything but this. That heart attack had really shaken up the whole family, and *he* wasn't about to be responsible for any further attacks.

Marrying to please his father may sound ridiculous in this day and age, but he'd been raised with strong family values. He'd do what was necessary.

But did it have to be Sasha Blake of all people he had to marry?

A shapely female bottom and matching long legs in white trousers greeted Nick when he opened the front door to his parents' house the next morning. They belonged to a gorgeous female figure standing in strappy sandals on a chair near the staircase.

At least they were until the woman turned, saw him and gave a squeal of fright, then started to topple off. He raced forward and caught her as she fell back into his arms.

For a moment she stared up at him. "Nick?" she whispered, almost as if his name was a secret.

He looked down at the beautiful blonde and wanted to lie and say no, he wasn't Nick. And he'd never kissed her either. Nor did he want to again.

She was Trouble.

And he had to ask her to marry him.

"Hello, Sasha."

She continued to stare up at him with eyes good at robbing a man of his thoughts. He'd forgotten the impact of those long sweeping lashes featuring eyes the color of green satin. Even when she was growing up there was something about them that tried to pierce his defenses. It had taken a constant and concentrated effort not to let her succeed.

Their kiss had come close.

"What on earth were you doing up there?" he growled, setting her on her feet, fascinated despite himself at the visible pulse beating at her throat and a faint blush dusting her cheeks. She'd been a pretty teenager before, but now she'd grown into a very beautiful woman.

She pushed against him and stepped back. "I thought I saw a crack in the wall, so I was checking it out."

The impact of her touch lingered. And so did the scent of her perfume—Valente's Woman. Somehow he was glad she wore his family's perfume.

"I hear you're an interior designer now," he said for something to say.

"Yes, I am." She seemed to pull herself together, and an excited light entered her eyes. "And I'm so happy your father chose me to redecorate this place."

Remembering, he shot her a dark look. "I don't want this house redecorated. It's fine how it is."

Disappointment crossed her face before she gave a tiny smile that held a touch of defiance. "Then it's as well this isn't your house, or I wouldn't have a job."

Tension rocked his stomach. "Look, let's go into the salon. I'll get Iris to make us some coffee."

Her expression grew wary. "I'm supposed to be working."

"Then add an extra hour's wages to the bill. My father can afford it."

She tipped her head to one side, her straight blond hair swaying like a sheen of silk over her shoulders. "You're very generous with your father's money."

"He wants me to talk to you."

She tensed. "Oh. I see. He's firing me, is he?"

"No, it's not that at all." But she was going to wish it was.

Relief fluttered across her face. "Then what can you possibly say to me that he can't himself?"

Marry me.

He opened his mouth to say it but realized it would be a bit too much all in the space of a minute. No need to break a record with this.

He gestured toward the salon. "The coffee first." He waited for her to precede him, then used the intercom to ask Iris to bring in some coffee.

When he turned to look at Sasha she was standing by the fireplace. Suddenly he couldn't take his eyes off her. It was crazy but she looked so right standing there in tailored white pants and a soft-knit green top, slim and refined and such a contrast amongst all this heavy, ornate furniture.

"It's not polite to stare."

Her words broke through his thoughts. "You're

different from what I remember." It was more than a physical difference, but he wasn't sure what it was yet.

Her eyelids flickered. "What do you remember, Nick?"

"Our kiss."

She gave a soft gasp. "It's not gentlemanly of you to bring that up."

"I was only being honest."

"Ever heard of being too honest?"

"I don't work like that."

"True. You were nothing less than honest after that kiss, weren't you?" she said, a wry twist coating her lips.

"If you mean that I didn't profess everlasting love, then you're right. I'd prefer not to sugarcoat things." It had been a kiss—a stunner of a kiss—but that's all it was. "Why, did I hurt your ego?"

"What? No way," she said quickly, perhaps too quickly. "It was my first kiss by a man, that's all. Up until then they'd all been boys."

"No doubt you've been plenty kissed since then."

"I'm not naive."

"Yes, I remember Randall. You had a fling with him, didn't you?"

Strangely, the thought of her with other men—with Randall Tremaine—had always unsettled him, but he forced himself to ignore it. She could kiss whomever she liked, make love to whomever she liked. And she had. It had nothing to do with him.

Until now.

She gave a shaky sigh. "I can't believe the first thing we talk about after seven years is kissing."

"I can."

A blush rose up her cheeks but just then Iris appeared in the doorway with the tray of coffee, interrupting the moment. They exchanged a few pleasantries, then Iris put the tray down on the coffee table and left the room.

"Shall I pour?" Sasha said, taking a seat on the sofa.

"Thanks." He sat down opposite, watching as she poured with an elegance that was innate. Once again he had the feeling she looked right in this setting. He grimaced to himself. Or perhaps it was just because his father had implanted the idea in him.

"So how long has it been since you left for London?" he asked as she passed him the cup and saucer.

"Five years."

"You were twenty when you left. That's young to be in a big city by yourself."

"I wasn't by myself," she said, and just for a moment his breath stopped at the thought of her living with another man. "I have an aunt who lives there, so I stayed with her for a few years. Then I got my own place." She picked up her own cup and saucer but didn't drink from it. "Our fathers are friends. I'm sure your father would have told you all this."

"He probably did," he said without thinking, angry at himself for caring even for a moment that she may have lived with some guy.

"But you didn't bother to listen, right?"

He didn't like being put on the spot like that. *He* was usually the one putting people on the spot. "It's been five years. I'd probably forgotten it long ago."

She held his gaze for a moment. "I'm sure." Her tone made him stiffen but before he could analyze her response, she put her coffee cup down on the table. "Now. Please give me the message from your father. I need to get back to work."

Fine. So did he.

He placed his own cup on the table, then leaned back on the sofa, giving himself a full view of her face. He needed to see her reaction. "It's not a message exactly. It's more a request."

Her smooth brow crinkled in a frown. "He wants me to do something?"

"Yes." He paused, trying to find the words that had been going over and over in his head all night. "Did he tell you he and my mother are moving into a smaller place in the city?"

She blinked in surprise. "No, he didn't." Her forehead cleared. "So *that's* why he wants me to re-decorate. He's planning on selling."

"No, he's not selling. He wants to keep it in the family. He wants *me* to have it."

Her eyes lit up, making her look even more beautiful. "Oh, that's wonderful, Nick. This place is gorgeous. I've always loved coming here."

Something wavered inside him. "Then perhaps you'd like to stay."

Her enthusiasm paused. "What do you mean? Rent it from you or something?"

"I mean share it with me."

"Sh…share it with you?" she all but squeaked.

"He wants me to marry you, Sasha."

She sucked in a sharp breath, then slowly let it out. "Good Lord."

His sentiments exactly. His father's ultimatum had been one of the few times in his life he'd had the rug pulled out from under him. He didn't like the feeling. Not one bit.

"Why?" she said in amazement after a moment or two.

"He wants to give me this house to carry on the Valente name but he knows I don't want to settle down so he's blackmailing me. If I don't marry you he'll give the house to Matt."

She shook her head. "No, this place doesn't suit Matt. It suits *you*."

He warmed to her.

"But Nick, I don't understand why he's chosen me for your wife."

He shrugged. "For some reason he thinks you're perfect for me."

Her eyes softened. "He does?" Then she stiffened and began to shift uneasily. "That's sweet of him, but we both know that's ridiculous. I've just come along at the right time, that's all."

"It seems that way," he agreed, happy to see she had a clear head on her shoulders. This was going to be easier than he'd expected. They wouldn't have to get mixed up with all the emotional trappings other married couples had to worry about.

"So what are you going to do, Nick?"

"Marry you."

The blood drained from her face but she soon gathered herself together. "Oh, really?"

He'd made up his mind to do this, and he didn't expect any resistance to the idea. "He's dead serious, Sasha. He wants a Valente to live in this house, and he wants our families to be joined."

She shook her head. "No, Nick."

"I don't like it any more than you do. Frankly, marriage was never in my cards. I like being single."

"So do I."

That surprised him. Career women or not, most of his lady friends had wanted more than a sexual relationship. Most had wanted marriage, despite their declarations that they didn't.

"You may not know this, but my father had a heart attack six months ago. It was only a mild one," he assured her, seeing her slight alarm, "but he's worried he'll have a major one and won't see me married before then. That's why he's come up with this plan."

"Nick, I'm sorry about his heart attack, but I can't do this."

His mouth tightened. "Then this place will go to Matt. I suggest you get ready for some heavy modernization when you redecorate."

She winced. "Talk to your father, Nick. He may let you marry someone else."

All at once he didn't want any other woman. "I know my father. He won't want anyone but you. He can be stubborn."

"So can I."

"Sasha, look—"

She sprang to her feet. "Nick, stop it." Then she straightened her shoulders, her eyes showing a spirit only hinted at while growing up. "Now, if you don't mind, I need to get on with the job, no matter whom the redecoration is for."

She hurried out the door, her high heels clicking on the timber floor as she headed down the hallway toward the kitchen.

Nick sat back on the sofa and contemplated what had just happened. There weren't many women who would actually refuse to marry him. Hell, he didn't think there were any.

But if he was getting married then so was Sasha Blake.

To him.

He just had to find a way to make it happen.

He smiled grimly. Making things happen was one thing a Valente did extremely well.

Two

Sasha finished taking measurements at the Valente mansion, then left as soon as she could. She kept expecting to turn around and find Nick there, ready to pressure her into marriage.

A marriage he didn't want.

And neither did she.

So why was she worried? With his father giving his stamp of approval she was just a convenience, that's all. Nick would go find someone else to marry, and Cesare wouldn't really care as long as it was someone suitable.

Of course if Nick *did* marry then she'd have to

work with Nick and his new wife to redecorate the house. Could she do it, knowing how much she'd been in love with him all those years ago?

Not that she was in any danger of loving him now.

No, it would be a matter of pride.

Unable to concentrate on any real plans for the redecorating until she knew what would happen to the estate, she spent the rest of the afternoon helping her mother around the house. She was preparing dinner around seven when her father walked into the kitchen earlier than usual.

In all the years she'd lived here previously, her father rarely got home before eight. Sasha suspected back then he hadn't always been working late, and that feeling hadn't abated since her return from London. She didn't know how her mother coped with it all.

"I never thought a daughter of mine would be so selfish," Porter Blake snapped with an accusing glare at her.

Sasha's forehead creased as she glanced across at her mother, then back to her father. "What do you mean, Dad?"

"Nick Valente. He asked you to marry him, didn't he?"

Her heart sank. Had Nick gone running to her father? "How did you know that?"

"Cesare told me. And you said *no*. For the love of God, why?"

She tried not to let him make her feel guilty. "I have that right."

"No, you don't. Your mother and I have given you everything, and you can't even do this one thing for us."

Sally Blake started toward him. "Porter, what are—"

"Be quiet, Sally," he all but growled.

Sasha hated the way he talked to her mother in private. In company, butter wouldn't melt in his mouth.

"Dad, don't speak to Mum that way."

Porter made a dismissive gesture. "This isn't about your mother and me. This is about you and Nick. Dammit, girl. It's not like Nick isn't a good-looking young man."

Sasha could only stare at him in dismay. "I don't understand why you want me to marry at all."

Her father's eyes darted away, then back again. "The Valentes are our closest friends. It would be nice to join the two families."

That was a crazy reason to get married. Nobody did that sort of thing anymore, or if they did *she* wasn't about to do it.

"Dad, I'm not going to marry a man I don't love just to bring two families together."

The wind seemed to leave Porter and he sat down

heavily on a chair, looking defeated. "If you don't, then say goodbye to this house and everything we have."

"What are you talking about?"

"If I don't close a deal with the Valentes soon, I'll lose my shipping business. If that happens we lose everything."

Sasha ignored her mother's gasp. "But Cesare's your friend. He'll give you the deal."

"He's a businessman first. If anyone undercuts my offer he'll go with them." He paused. "Unless you're his daughter-in-law and then he'll want to keep it in the family."

"You don't know what you're asking," she whispered.

Her father sighed heavily. "You're right, but it's the only chance we've got."

Sasha shook her head. No, she couldn't do it. It was too much to ask of her.

Then she caught her mother's pleading eyes. "Sasha, darling," Sally began. "Do you think it would be so terrible to marry Nick?"

She drew a painful breath. "Oh, Mum, no. Don't ask this of me."

"Darling, I have to. If not for your father's sake, then mine."

Sasha hated seeing how her mother always put her husband first, and no amount of talking on her part could change her mind. It was part of the reason she'd gone to London. She'd had to get away from her parents.

And from the memory of Nick Valente.

She sighed with defeat. "Do you have Nick's address?"

Her father's face lit up and so did her mother's. "No, but I can get it right now." He jumped to his feet, then hesitated. "Thank you, Sasha," he muttered, then strode out of the kitchen.

Sasha looked at her mother, who was blinking back tears of happiness. "Darling, I'm sorry. I know—"

"Mum, please don't say anything right now."

Her mother flushed. "Okay. If that's what you want."

"It is."

Sasha went to get her purse when her father came back with Nick's address. It was small comfort to know she could help her parents.

At what cost to herself she wasn't sure.

An hour later she stood in front of Nick's apartment and rang the doorbell. Right now the cost seemed much too high a price to pay.

Oh God, if only this had been seven years ago. She'd have given anything for him to ask her to marry him back then.

She remembered that kiss in the gazebo in the summer rain. It had just happened and she'd almost melted in a puddle at his feet. He'd surely felt everything she'd felt, she'd told herself as it ended and she'd moved in closer for another one. He'd realize he loved her and couldn't live without her and any moment he'd tell her so.

Instead he'd held her back from him, obviously appalled he'd kissed her. She'd seen it in his blue eyes that had turned from light blue to dark in a matter of seconds.

And then he'd left her there, gone back up to the main house to the party and casually taken another woman home, just like he'd been exchanging his Ferrari for another model. It had devastated her, but she'd never let him know it.

Right at that moment the door opened and Nick stood there, devastatingly handsome and undeniably male, and nothing on his handsome face giving away any of his thoughts.

He moved back to let her enter the apartment. "My father said you'd be stopping by."

"Word gets around fast."

She stepped through the doorway, trying to shake her feelings of the past. It was the present…now… that should concern her.

He gestured to the leather couch. "Make yourself comfortable. Would you like a drink?"

"No, I'm fine." She couldn't sit, and if she tried to drink anything she'd probably choke. Her throat ached with pure defeat.

His blue eyes rested on her. "So what made you change your mind?"

"My parents." She didn't want him to think it had been for any other reason. "I'm their only child and they really want our families to be joined." She swallowed hard. "I can't deny them that."

Cynicism twisted the corners of his mouth. "I'm sure your father's delighted."

Her heart thudded inside her chest. Could Nick know that her father's shipping business needed this deal?

Then she realized he didn't know. If he did, he'd have certainly blackmailed her into marriage. Nick wouldn't hesitate to use any leverage he could to get her to do what he wanted.

Still, she felt the need to defend her father.

She angled her chin. "Why do you say it like that?"

"Your mother's a nice woman. I'm sure she wouldn't pressure you into a marriage you don't want."

She realized he didn't know her mother that well. If her father wanted something, then her mother was usually the go-between.

He held her gaze. "I don't think I can say the same for your father."

"And that's so different from *your* father?"

Surprise flickered in his eyes. "True."

She briefly appreciated her feeling of triumph. "*Both* my parents are happy about this marriage, Nick."

He scrutinized her. "Why do I believe you?"

"Because it's the truth." She couldn't confess her mother was happy for Porter's sake, or Nick might get suspicious.

"Okay, let's get down to business. First, I want to assure you that if things don't work out we can always get a divorce later on."

She winced inwardly at his insensitivity, or his honesty, as he liked to call it. It was the same this morning when he'd asked if his rejection had hurt her ego in the gazebo that night.

Could a man be so hard-hearted to a young woman in love with him?

Hadn't he been able to tell she'd put her heart and soul into that kiss?

Of course he hadn't.

"Are you reassuring me or yourself?" she asked cynically.

He scowled. "I just don't want either of us to feel totally trapped."

"How nice."

He shot her a hard look, then, "Do you want children?"

Her heart skipped a beat and all her cynicism disappeared. "Do you?"

"One day. Not yet."

"Me, too." She hadn't thought about children. They were a lifetime commitment, and one that connected her to Nick for the rest of her life.

She wasn't sure she could do that.

Wasn't sure she *wanted* that.

He started toward a small table where there were a bunch of papers. "Right. Looks like we have a wedding to plan."

She took a quick breath. "Hold on. I have one condition of my own before we settle this."

He stopped to look at her, his eyebrow winging upward. "And that is?"

"You remain faithful to me," she said without hesitation. "I won't accept the humiliation of you having affairs. If you can't do it, tell me now."

Something shifted in his expression. "It's not that I can't do it. The question is whether I *want* to remain faithful."

She tensed. "I'd suggest you've probably had enough affairs to last a lifetime anyway."

"You know me so well," he drawled.

She raised her chin. "I'll accept nothing less, Nick."

There was a lengthy silence as their eyes held and locked. This was the one thing she wouldn't relent on, it was too important to her.

Then he expelled a breath. "You may be surprised

to know this but I do take marriage vows seriously, and mine especially. I can assure you I will remain faithful."

She let out a quiet sigh, but wasn't sure if it was relief or despair. Her only chance to refuse to marry him had just dissolved into thin air.

On the other hand, at least she could do this one thing for her mother. She had to keep remembering that.

"The wedding will be in three weeks."

She swallowed past her dry throat. "That soon?"

"The sooner we get this over and done with the better."

"Yes," she said, giving in to the inevitable.

She felt the same as Nick, but probably for different reasons. She suspected Cesare wouldn't let his sons sign the deal for her father until after their marriage vows had been taken. Cesare wasn't a fool.

If only he was.

Nick was pleased with himself after Sasha left his apartment. He'd known he wouldn't have to do a thing except tell his father she had refused his offer. Cesare had immediately got on the phone to Porter and offered regrets that they wouldn't be in-laws.

And that's all that was needed. Porter knew what side his bread was buttered, and the last thing he would want was to offend Cesare.

Nick gave a snort of derision. Porter Blake was a

wimp. If the Valente family didn't have money, the other man wouldn't be hanging around being Cesare's friend. No, Porter would be out with his latest lady friend. The man was a rake of the worst kind, his affairs the worst-kept secret.

No wonder Sasha was insisting on fidelity in their marriage. She had to know about her father's numerous affairs.

Or did she?

He hadn't asked her straight out in case she didn't know. Not that he was protecting Porter. It was merely that if Sasha didn't know, then he wasn't about to tell her.

He only hoped he didn't live to regret giving his word. Women were notorious for having an angle for everything, and he suspected Sasha did, too.

Was she marrying him for reasons other than her family?

More prestige?

More money?

Better contacts for her work?

Time would tell, but he'd be ready for her if that happened. No one pulled the wool over his eyes. If they did, it didn't happen a second time.

Three

At eighteen Sasha had dreamed about a white wedding to Nick in a beautiful church in Sydney—the perfect setting for their perfect love for each other.

Now at twenty-five, a stylish ceremony on the sun-drenched lawn of the massive Valente estate was more than lovely, but a marriage of convenience to a man who'd never given her a moment's thought wasn't quite the same.

And that was never more prominent than on her wedding day. She'd been nervous in her responses throughout the ceremony but Nick hadn't missed a beat. Obviously she still didn't affect him in the slightest, least of all by marrying him.

"I now pronounce you man and wife."

Oh God. Sasha's knees threatened to wobble, making her grateful for her white wedding gown hiding them from view.

"You may now kiss the bride."

She swallowed hard as she turned to fully face Nick, looking so handsome in his black tuxedo. She'd melted the last time he'd kissed her all those years ago but until his lips were on hers again she wouldn't know for sure how she'd react.

His blue eyes gave nothing away as he lowered his head. Their lips touched and Sasha nervously held her breath, waiting for something…anything… to kick in. It was pleasant, but she didn't melt.

Thank God!

He broke off the kiss and they stared at each other. She was so relieved that she broke into a small smile. His eyes narrowed, making her wonder what he was thinking.

Everyone started to clap, bringing the world back into focus. She turned toward their beaming guests seated on the largest of the private courtyards surrounding the main house. Everyone loved a wedding, it seemed.

Everyone but the bride and groom.

People surrounded them with congratulations

and before too long a string quartet began playing music and waiters started circulating with glasses of champagne.

"You've made your mother and me very happy, Sasha," her father said, kissing her cheek, pride shining from his eyes. It was silly but despite everything, Sasha felt teary that she'd done something to make her father proud of her.

"We're so glad," Nick responded, his voice holding a touch of sarcasm.

His words spoiled the moment for Sasha and she blinked the moisture out of her eyes in time to see Cesare send Nick a warning glance. She wondered again why Nick didn't like her father.

Cesare leaned forward and kissed her on the cheek. "Isabel and I are very happy, too," he said, speaking for his wife, who was seeing to their guests. Then he slapped Porter on the back. "We're all one big happy family now, *amico mio*."

And Porter beamed. "Yes, our two families have been joined together at last, my friend."

Sasha swallowed back a hysterical comment that perhaps her father should have married Nick, but then she saw her mother's happy face and forced herself to relax.

She had done this for her mother.

After that the late afternoon rolled into evening, drawing the hours closer to when she and Nick would be alone. Thankfully their two hundred guests kept her occupied and stopped her thinking about it too much.

"Everything's gone very smoothly, don't you think?" Isabel asked, rescuing Sasha from an older relative and leading her over to the tables laden with wedding gifts beside the open French doors.

Sasha really liked her new mother-in-law. Isabel had always been one of her favorite people. "You've done wonders, Isabel. Thank you so much. I know it took a lot to get it all done in time, especially when you had to move into your new apartment, as well."

Isabel looked pleased. "Anything for you, Sasha. And Nick, of course." Then as quickly she frowned. "I still don't condone what Cesare has done, but after his heart attack I don't want to upset him too much. I've tried all I can, but he's a law unto himself."

Sasha had appreciated it when Isabel had taken her aside two weeks ago and asked her if she knew what she was doing. The other woman had known her husband was blackmailing Nick into marrying her and for a while she'd been very vocal about it.

Knowing she had to do this, Sasha had hurriedly assured her it was okay, and things had proceeded with alarming speed.

"Being a law unto themselves seems to be a trait of the Valente men," Sasha said.

"Yes. And Nick has assured me he knows what

he's doing." She squeezed Sasha's arm. "I'm so happy to have you in the family."

"Thank you," Sasha said huskily. It was lovely to be welcomed so warmly. If she and Nick were truly in love…

"And you know," Isabel's voice cut through Sasha's thoughts, "when I see how happy Alex and Olivia are now, it appears that Cesare knows what he's doing."

Sasha regarded Nick's older brother across the courtyard. Alex was here today with his wife and their adopted eight-year-old son, Scott. Olivia was the daughter of movie legend, Felicia Cannington, and was just as beautiful as her famous mother, and more than gracious. The love between Alex and Olivia made Sasha catch her breath.

Yet just because last year Cesare had blackmailed Alex into marrying Olivia and somehow the two had fallen in love didn't mean it would work for her and Nick.

It wouldn't.

For love to grow there had to be a basic need for love within that person. Nick had no need for love from any woman, and especially not *her*.

"They certainly look very happy," Sasha agreed, keeping quiet about her thoughts. Isabel loved Nick and only wanted the best for her second stepson she'd raised since he was a baby.

Isabel nodded. "You know, I don't think Nick got

any sympathy from Alex about it all." She gave a wry smile. "Especially when he's marrying *you*."

Sasha forced herself to smile back. She didn't think of herself as a beauty, but she knew her looks were probably the only thing she had going for her with Nick.

"Matt must be getting worried that he's next," Sasha said, trying to take the focus off herself.

A worried gleam entered Isabel's eyes. "He says he's not. He told his father he wouldn't be coerced into anything. Of course, when Cesare wants something…" she trailed off, just as Nick came strolling up to them.

"Somebody wants something, Mum?" Nick said, coming up next to them with a smile that must be more for Isabel, Sasha decided. If he ever smiled at her like that…

"Me. I need a drink," Isabel quipped, shooting her new daughter-in-law a look that said it was time to move on. Sasha wanted to beg her not to leave, but that would look foolish.

"I'll do that for you," Nick offered, about to turn away.

"No, honey, that's fine. I want to see your father anyway. I need to make sure he's taken his medication."

The line of Nick's mouth tightened at the mention

of his father. It was easy to see he hadn't forgiven Cesare for all this.

And rightly so. *Both* their fathers had a lot to answer for, Sasha knew. It was the one bond they had in common.

Nick turned the charm on for some of their guests who had come up to say they were leaving. A charm that wasn't false but neither was it for her benefit.

Still, she gratefully accepted the distraction to say goodbye, fielding more questions about not having a honeymoon. No one had dared ask about the haste of their marriage, but if they thought she was pregnant they'd soon find out she wasn't.

And if they wondered about the lack of affection between her and Nick? Maybe then they would guess the hasty marriage was for convenience. She didn't want anyone thinking it was for love.

Certainly not Nick.

Once all their guests had departed, Sasha left Nick talking to Matt beside his Aston Martin, but not before she saw the scowl on Nick's face and suspected he was probably warning his younger brother to watch out for their father. Though by the confident set of his head, Matt wasn't too concerned for his future.

She almost felt sorry for Matt. Just as no doubt Nick was feeling sorry for *himself* right now for having to marry *her*. She felt an instant's hurt but quickly dismissed it.

She had to keep busy.

Walking into one of the smaller dining rooms, she began tidying up, gathering the few remaining glasses and stacking them at one end of the table for the caterers to collect. It had been a good idea of Isabel's to use the room for some elderly relatives as a quiet place to get away from all the commotion and noise of the wedding.

And didn't she know exactly how they felt? If only she could have hidden in here permanently, away from Nick, away from the night ahead.

"Leave it."

Her head shot up to find Nick standing in the doorway. Panic stirred inside her chest. "But—"

"The catering crew will clean up."

"I know but—"

"You'll get that beautiful dress dirty," he pointed out, his enigmatic gaze pausing over her.

"Oh." She glanced down at the smooth white satin of her simply styled wedding dress. She'd been so anxious she'd totally forgotten she was wearing it. Any other bride would be horrified at the treatment.

Of course, who could call her a typical bride?

"Come on," he said brusquely, interrupting her thoughts. "Let's go upstairs. Iris will see everything is put right here."

Swallowing hard, she placed the glass down on

the table and started to walk toward him. "Has Matt gone?" she said for something to say.

His jaw clenched. "Yes."

Then he cupped her elbow and led her up the sweeping staircase, his touch sending a shiver through her that she tried to ignore. There would be more touching soon, more exploring, molding her softer curves to his hard body.

"Relax. You look like you're going to the guillotine."

"Maybe I've already lost my head," she quipped.

His eyes narrowed as he glanced sideways at her. "What does that mean?"

She blinked. Oh heavens. He surely didn't think she was talking about love?

"Nothing, except that I'd have to be crazy to marry you, that's all."

A moment crept by while they continued up the stairs and she held her breath but he said nothing further.

Soon they came to one of the large bedrooms they would use until she could renovate the master bedroom. The bed had already been turned back for them.

Suddenly she felt overwhelmed and she hung back in the doorway. Part of her wanted to know what making love with Nick would be like. Another part of her wanted to run for the hills.

Nick walked over to the large windows and stood looking out for a few seconds, his back to her. "Come here."

Her breath stopped. This was it.

Not wanting to appear childish or afraid, she started across the plush carpet but when she got close he didn't reach for her as expected.

He stood looking out over the estate's magnificent lawns and gardens deeply shadowed by the setting sun.

"Thank you for helping me keep all this," he murmured, the rough edge of emotion in his voice.

Oh.

Pleasure swept through her. "You belong here, Nick."

He turned and put his hand under her chin, lifting her face up to him. "That's the nicest thing anyone has ever said to me."

And then his lips descended.

She wasn't expecting it right then and she didn't have time to prepare. All at once he was there and the second his mouth touched hers she slid into his kiss. It was soft and slow and she melted for him like a frost in the morning sun.

Just as unexpectedly, he took the kiss deeper, pulling her with him into a world she'd dipped into only once before, many years ago. It was a world that tilted on its axis and began to spin out of control.

His tongue gave her strokes of pleasure, his hands sliding down to her hips and pulling her up against him, his body telling her he was a man who wanted, and that she was the woman to give.

And then he eased back.

And the world righted itself…slightly.

He lifted a strand of hair off her cheek. "Want to take a shower?" he asked huskily, his blue eyes holding a dark glitter.

"Er…together?"

He eased into a smile. "Is that an offer?"

She felt her cheeks wash with pink. "No."

He leaned back further, his eyes softening with understanding. "You're shy?"

She swallowed past her dry throat. "Only the first time," she whispered, hoping he'd take the hint so she wouldn't have to say it in words.

"And after that?" he teased.

"I don't—"

He chuckled and stepped back before she could finish. "Don't worry. I'll shower in my old room so that you can have some privacy." He strode away but stopped at the door and looked over his shoulder, his eyes no longer teasing. "This time."

Sasha stood there until she no longer heard his muffled footfall on the carpet along the landing.

She slowly exhaled. Oh God. How could she

know if she would be shy after she made love with him? She'd never made love with any man.

She was a virgin.

And a virgin who'd never felt anything for any man what she had felt for Nick all those years ago.

Nick whose kiss had blown her away just now. How could their wedding kiss earlier today have felt so different…so mild…yet this one be so mind-blowing?

This was like the kiss in the gazebo.

And unlike the episode after the gazebo, Nick wouldn't be going off with another woman. *She* would be the woman in his bed tonight. And all the nights ahead.

For now.

With a shaky hand she managed to unzip her dress and step out of it, carefully placing it over a chair. Then she headed for the shower, aware she was leaving behind more than her wedding dress. Tonight she was going to be a married woman in every sense of the word.

But would Nick even notice?

Or care?

Thankfully, when Sasha came out of the bathroom Nick was nowhere to be seen. Feeling awkward, she took off her silk robe and slipped beneath the covers in her nightgown, pulling the sheet up to her chin.

In the lamplight she lay there for a few seconds

looking like she'd been mummified, then gave a nervous laugh. Make that *petrified*.

Of Nick?

No, she was being absurd. Nick would never physically hurt her. Realizing she was letting her nerves get the better of her, she sat up against the pillows, only just managing to cover herself with the sheet a moment before Nick opened the door.

His gaze flashed over her. "I see you're already in bed."

She blinked, suddenly confused. Should she have sat on the brocade chair instead? Or stood by the window? What was the protocol on one's wedding night of a marriage of convenience?

"I thought this was where you'd want me."

"Oh, it is." An intense look filled his eyes. "I'd want you anywhere, Sasha."

"That wasn't what I meant."

"It's *exactly* what I meant."

"Nick—" She stopped speaking as he came toward her carrying a bottle of champagne and two glasses. He wore a navy bathrobe, his long legs bare and masculine. She could feel herself grow hot.

"I like the way you're looking at me," he said huskily.

Her gaze darted away, then back as she tried to get some sort of mental balance. "It feels strange being here like this with you," she said, her excuse lame but all she had.

"Why?"

She should tell him now.

She took a deep breath. "Perhaps because I—"

"Hell, you don't think of me like a brother, do you?"

His question took the wind from her sails. She blinked. "No." That was the last way she'd ever think of him. Hadn't those two mind-blowing kisses told him that, if seven years between?

"That's a relief." He was joking but she knew the question had been partly serious.

He held out a glass of champagne toward her. "Here, this should help you relax a little."

Grateful for something to do, she accepted it and took a sip, letting the bubbles slide down her dry throat. Perhaps drunk was the way to go, she mused, then dismissed the thought. If she were drunk she might say too much.

He sat down beside her on the bed, a sudden predatory gleam in his expression. "Why did you look shocked after I kissed you before?"

So he'd noticed she'd been taken aback by the power of that kiss.

"Um…at the wedding?" she said, deliberately misunderstanding him.

"No, not that placid little kiss I gave you at the

wedding ceremony. I mean the one just before by the window over there."

She cleared her throat, then decided on the truth. "I guess I didn't expect to…enjoy it so much."

"I did."

"Nick, I—"

"Have the most delectable looking mouth I've ever seen," he murmured, then put his glass down on the table beside the bed and did the same with hers. He leaned toward her. "I want to taste it again."

She moistened her lips, wanting to tell him about being a virgin but a mere second later his mouth settled on hers and she forgot everything but him. He nibbled on her lips until she sighed with delight, then took advantage by slipping his tongue inside.

In one swoop he was a part of her.

She shuddered. The kiss deepened and stole the breath from her lungs, sending excitement zinging to every pore in her body. She'd never known a kiss to be so all-inclusive.

And then he slowed the kiss and edged back a little to stare into her eyes, probing even. "There's something very unusual about you, Sasha."

She held her breath. Had he guessed?

"You haven't slept with many men, have you?"

"Um…no." She swallowed. "Does it make a difference?"

"Oh, yes," he rasped.

She couldn't read his expression and suddenly she was terrified he *wouldn't* make love to her if he knew she was a virgin. And that would be the biggest waste of her life. She was married to him, yes. And they would make love eventually, yes. But she'd missed out on her dream wedding. She didn't want to miss out on her honeymoon, too.

Not tonight.

"Kiss me, Nick."

A light flared in the back of his darkened eyes. Without hesitation, his mouth found hers again and he kissed her with a hunger that filled her with new awe. This kiss took her to places she'd never been before. She didn't want it to end.

She held her breath, her heart tilting with relief as he feathered kisses along her chin and down her throat. She couldn't bear him to leave her now.

He placed his lips at the center of her cleavage and murmured, "I've always thought your name suited you. Soft, sexy Sasha."

She shivered, never expecting this man would say something like that to her. It was the talk of a lover…a soon-to-be-lover.

He moved back and slid the thin strap of her nightgown off her shoulder, exposing one of her breasts to him. His hot gaze lingered on her for a long moment. She gasped when he began tracing her nipple with his fingertip, then held it between his fingers for his mouth to take over.

He suckled, and she almost came apart. She'd never realized her breasts were so sensitive to touch…to Nick. Oh God, this was *Nick* making love to her. *Nick* drawing on her nipple with his mouth. *Nick* who was sending such delicious sensations rippling through her. Everything he did, every move he made, was overshadowing everything else in the world.

The suckling continued, and she felt an odd sort of curl start at her toes and run its way upward. It tightened as it climbed higher through her thighs…higher and tighter still as it reached the core beneath her panties. She stiffened as something marvelous took hold and held her there, making her exhale in little gasps that seemed in rhythm with her body.

It was over almost before it began, the tightness diminishing, then disappearing as quickly.

Nick was looking at her curiously. "Did you just climax?"

"I…I think so. A little." She could feel herself blush. She wasn't sure. "Can we turn out the light, please? I'm embarrassed."

"No need to be embarrassed. Nothing should embarrass a man and a woman when they make love."

"The light, Nick. Please."

"No, I want to see you. I *need* to see you, sweetheart. All of you." And with that he took the hem of her nightgown and lifted it over her head.

Lamplight shone through the room, showing her naked body to him for the first time. "Beautiful," he murmured, reaching out and resting the palm of his hand on her stomach, leaving it there as if soaking up the touch of her skin. Her pulse shimmied through her veins, building anticipation. She wanted him to touch her more.

So much more.

Instead he leaned down and placed his lips against her *there* and just as she recovered from the shock of it, he gave a deep groan and pushed himself off the bed.

Her gasp was not because he'd left her, but because he was shrugging out of his bathrobe. In the blink of an eye her focus was on him, her sensibilities shocked at seeing a man in his full glory for the first time. Transfixed, she reached out to touch him. She could see her hand shaking but once she slid around him, he was her rock.

The air grew thick.

"Sasha," he said in a guttural voice.

She thrilled to the sound of him, to the sight of him, and now if she could just keep on…

"I need to touch you, Nick."

He made a low sound deep in his throat and that

was all the encouragement she needed. Tentatively she ran the tip of her finger over the head of his erection. She wanted to see what power she had over him.

He jerked. "No more," he growled and took her hand off him, twisting away to take a condom out of the bedside drawer and roll it on himself, entrancing her by his very masculine action. She'd read about all this in magazines, but the reality was overwhelmingly intimate.

"Slide over," he ordered, and he joined her on the bed, where he grasped her waist and rolled her on top of him.

She felt a rush of heat at the full length of his body against her own for the first time, and the feel of his hands cupping her bottom.

Their eyes met.

She wanted to look away but couldn't. Not when she could feel that curl starting in her toes again, making her want to tighten her legs and grind herself against him.

Suddenly he rolled her over and slid on top of her like he was meant to be there. And then he nudged her legs apart and pushed inside her a little.

She winced at the slight pain.

He stilled, his eyes widening in shock. "You're a *virgin?*"

She wanted to deny it. Wanted to say that she was

experienced so he would keep making her feel this way. Only she couldn't lie.

"Yes."

He swore but amazingly didn't pull out. He took a deep breath and then began to move slowly, his eyes never leaving her face. Carefully he filled her, and when he was fully inside her he stopped.

"Okay?" he asked hoarsely.

She nodded, too emotional to be able to speak. Nick had made her a woman.

His woman.

He began to move, and the world faded away. No one else existed, and nothing mattered. It was just the two of them, and when she climaxed Nick followed, and they came together in their own private world.

After Nick returned from the bathroom he sat on the bed and took her hands in his. "Why?"

Sasha swallowed. "Why didn't I tell you? You said it would make a difference and I…well…I wanted you to make love to me."

His mouth softened with tenderness. "You silly goose. The difference would have been in the way I made love to you, not in whether I made love to you at all."

"Oh."

"Your first time needs to be handled gently." A moment later he grimaced.

She saw the hint of regret in his eyes. "Nick, you were very gentle with me. Thank you."

He kissed her briefly. "Thank you for saying that." Then he leaned back with a penetrating look in his eyes that made her uneasy. "I seem to remember you telling me that you'd slept with Randall Tremaine."

She'd been prepared for this.

"Yes, I did say that. But I was eighteen, and I didn't want you thinking our kiss meant anything to me so…" she lifted one shoulder in a shrug, "I made it up."

"You were saving face?"

"Yes."

He considered her. "Why haven't you ever slept with anyone?"

"Perhaps I wanted to save myself for my husband."

A tic beat in his jaw. "And I've taken that away from you."

"No!" She swallowed, feeling bad for him. "Nick, look, we've both lost a lot of things from this marriage but we've gained some things, too. I'm glad you were my first, okay?"

His gaze took on a piercing look that held hers for long moments. Then just as quickly it changed to a sensual warmth that made her heartbeat stutter.

He got off the bed and scooped her from the sheets. "Nick! Where are you taking me?"

"To the shower."

She didn't ask why. It became obvious when he stood her in the cubicle and began to wash her with tenderness and care, and with a gentleness that almost brought tears to her eyes. This rich, arrogant playboy had a capacity for caring she hadn't really expected.

Then his hand and fingers replaced the soap, creating a lather that had nothing to do with bathing and everything to do with making love.

Four

For a moment Nick was confused when he woke up the next morning. He could hear car doors shutting and voices talking, and usually he didn't hear those sorts of noises from his tenth-floor apartment in the city.

Then he remembered.

He was married now. And this wasn't his apartment. He was at the Valente estate and the sounds he heard were the caterers clearing up the last of the wedding reception.

Sasha!

He lifted his head to find himself weighted to the bed by the naked female sleeping against his chest.

He looked down at the top of her blonde hair, and heat surged through his veins.

God, she'd been a virgin.

Amazingly there was something totally satisfying about knowing *he* was the only man to ever touch her like he had. Knowing he was the first man to be inside her like he'd been. He'd never thought he'd be the sort of guy who indulged in that sort of thing. He wasn't usually some sort of he-man who beat his chest in triumph.

Yet this time he wanted to do exactly that.

A virgin, for Pete's sake!

And of course that meant she'd lied to him all those years ago when she'd told him she'd gone out and slept with Randall Tremaine. It had been a few weeks after the gazebo incident and at the time he'd put it down to the fickle ways of a woman not knowing her own mind.

It hadn't stopped him wanting to knock the other man out when he'd seen them talking together briefly at a party. He remembered thinking Randall had been playing it so cool. No wonder. The poor guy had been an innocent pawn in it all.

Totally innocent.

Just like Sasha.

Hell, was he blind or what? Everything had pointed to her being a virgin, only he hadn't been looking. He'd just thought her a little inexperienced.

He could see it all now. The shyness in her, her first climax, wanting the light turned off.

The thought of being inside her again made him groan softly, and he knew he could wake her up and take her again. And it would be good for both of them.

Damn good.

But this wasn't a woman he could make love to, then kiss goodbye. This was his *wife*.

That thought had him easing out of bed and heading for the shower. He'd already given up his freedom for this marriage. He wasn't giving up his work, too.

But tonight…yes, tonight…he was going to enjoy teaching Sasha more about making love with a man.

Sasha opened her eyes to find the sun streaming in through the windows and an empty bed next to her.

She was a woman in every sense of the word now. And her heart was still intact.

She'd been terrified last night. Deep-down terrified that somehow Nick's lovemaking would open up the floodgates on the love she'd had for him years ago. It had been a very real fear.

But she'd had nothing to worry about, thank heavens. Nick's expertise in bed had made it so very special for her, and while lingering memories of her teenage love may have played a part in her enjoyment, pure physical attraction had saved the day.

It was such a relief!

Yes, she could cope with a physical relationship, she mused, throwing back the sheets and taking a couple of steps, then felt herself blush at how pleasurably sore her body was in all the places he'd touched.

And kissed.

Her hot shower should have soothed her but she kept remembering Nick carrying her in here last night. The thought of it brought a lump to her throat. How gentle he'd been.

And caring.

By the time she was dressed she was ready to face the day. The main thing was that she didn't love Nick nor had he guessed she'd been in love with him years ago.

And that was something to celebrate, she decided, as she went down the staircase to the kitchen. Today was business as usual for her husband, and it would be for her, too. She had her own work to do.

She had plans.

Lots of them.

Her fingers itched while she ate breakfast on the terrace, her mind racing with excitement, eager now to get back to the designs she'd started a few weeks ago.

The house was an interior designer's dream. It had a grand salon with picture windows and French doors looking out over spectacular gardens and courtyards. There was also a formal dining room and family living areas with five bedrooms and bathrooms, a study upstairs and one downstairs, and a kitchen with modern conveniences in an old-fashioned style.

Before too long she'd spread herself out in the downstairs study, her ideas and thoughts spilling onto the paper, her enthusiasm for the project continuing to bubble as she worked past lunch.

"Have you been here all day?" Nick said from the doorway.

Startled, she looked up and her heart skipped a beat at the sight of him. He was so handsome, and she'd been intimate with him last night. The thought made her feel warm all over.

She quickly dragged her gaze away to her watch. "Is it six o'clock already?"

He started to scowl as he stepped into the room and came toward her. "You're working on plans for the redecorating?" A muscle ticked in his cheek. "So you're still going ahead with it?" he asked, stopping in front of the desk.

That warm feeling disappeared at his tone. She

leveled him a look. They hadn't discussed it further, but she'd assumed he would still let her redecorate.

"I guess that's up to you. You're the boss."

His eyes narrowed. "This is your home, too, now, you know."

"I guess it is."

Not for a moment did she think she owned this house. How could she? It was Nick's. It would always be Nick's even if she stayed married to him for fifty years.

Her breath stopped at the thought.

He leaned over the paperwork and looked at her plans for the main dining room. A minute later he grudgingly admitted, "They're good."

Despite herself, she felt a thrill at his praise.

She shrugged. "They're just ideas. There's still a lot to be done."

He studied her. "This means a lot to you, doesn't it?"

"Yes."

There was a tiny pause. "Fine. Then you have carte blanche to do what you like."

"Really?" Excitement rushed through her, but she quickly reined it in and said more primly, "Thank you."

"But my old bedroom stays as is."

"Oh?" She didn't say she'd planned to turn his room and the one next to it into a larger suite. "If that's what you want."

"It is."

"Okay." She'd allow him that. After all, she had the rest of the house.

"I'm going to shower and change before dinner," he said, a possessive gleam in his eyes sweeping over her, making her panic.

She swallowed. Was he asking her to join him?

"Um…I want to finish something here first. I'll freshen up in a minute."

A knowing look in his eyes, he turned toward the door. "Don't be too long."

"I won't."

They both knew she wasn't about to follow him upstairs. As much as she suspected being in his arms was addictive, she had to keep her distance or risk becoming his sex slave.

She smiled to herself. Would that be so bad?

Reality returned. Perhaps she ought to remind herself that she hadn't even warranted an "I'm home, honey" kiss. Whether he wanted her in his bed or not, it was clear he wasn't going to treat her like a real wife outside the bedroom. Not when they were alone anyway.

Shades of her parents' marriage?

No, she wouldn't think that.

The thought was too painful to contemplate. Sasha looked down at her designs and started working on them again. Work had always helped her concentrate on the moment, holding unhappy thoughts of the past or the possibility of a lonely future at bay. Work had been her salvation.

Now, if only she could get the color just right for…

"Dinner's almost ready," Nick said, startling her again.

She looked up and saw he'd showered and changed and she wrinkled her nose at herself. "I totally forgot the time again, didn't I?"

"Obviously you're not falling over yourself to be with me?" he drawled, not looking in the least put out about that.

No doubt he'd have plenty of women who *would* fall over themselves to be with him, she mused. Well, she wasn't one of his women.

She held her head high. "No, I'm not."

He considered her. "You're not like other women, are you?"

Was that a compliment? She wasn't sure.

"I guess not."

His face closed up. "You've got ten minutes," he said gruffly before striding away.

For a moment she just stood there. What was all that about? Her virginity? Was he feeling guilty about it? There was no need.

After that she hurried to shower and re-apply a light coating of make-up, leaving her straight blonde hair to fall loose past her shoulders. Taking her cue from Nick's dark trousers and polo shirt, she didn't dress up too much for dinner, instead slipping on a summery dress made from soft material that fell just above her knees.

Fifteen minutes later she joined him in the dining room. The hint of pleasure in his eyes made her heart race as she walked to where he held the chair out for her.

They sat down at the table. Iris served dinner before mentioning that Cesare had called to remind him about the English launch of "Valente's Woman." Then the older woman left them to eat.

Sasha was curious. "When is the U.K. launch?"

"In a couple of weeks."

"It'll do well over there."

He nodded. "It'll do well everywhere."

She had to smile at that.

"What are you smiling at?" he asked.

"Your arrogance."

His mouth quirked at the corners. "It's the Valente way."

"I know."

Some lazy moments passed while they ate in silence. Sasha was still amazed she was now actually married to Nick Valente. Who would have thought it?

Not her.

Aware she needed to move away from such

thoughts, she made herself reflect on how much effort went into launching a new perfume. "You should go with Alex. He may need you with him."

"Alex can handle it. He and Olivia will make sure it goes off with a bang."

All at once she didn't want him staying home for her sake. "Just because we're newly married doesn't mean you have to stay home with me."

His lips twisted. "Are you trying to get rid of me so soon?"

"Of course not. I'm just thinking you have other commitments and being married shouldn't change that."

He held her gaze for a moment, then, "If I thought Alex needed me, I'd go. But he doesn't and frankly, I'd prefer to stay home."

She noted he didn't say "stay with *her*."

Strangely she was rather glad he wasn't going away and leaving her alone. She seemed to have had too much aloneness these past few years.

Had he?

She didn't think so.

They began to talk about the wedding—was it only yesterday?—and before too long Iris was serving dessert, and then not long after, they finished their dinner.

She wondered what was next....

Coffee?

Tea?

Bed?

"Would you like to watch television?"

She ignored the look in his eyes. He'd known what she was thinking. "That would be nice." She got to her feet, and Nick stood, too.

"You go ahead and I'll be with you shortly. I've got a couple of calls to make first."

She felt a smattering of disappointment, but she quickly pushed it aside. Time alone would let her pulse slow back to its normal beat.

An hour later she was still waiting for Nick to join her. Her favorite sitcom hadn't held her attention, and now a rather boring program was about to start. She could go get her designs and continue working, but she needed a break from them. What's more, she didn't want to interrupt Nick in the study. He could be on an important call.

She yawned.

She felt so tired.

Perhaps she'd just close her eyes for a moment or two.

The next thing she knew a pair of strong masculine arms were lifting her up and carrying her. She tried to clear her mind but she felt warm and protected and she just wanted to snuggle closer.

"Nick?"

"Yes."

It was so hard to open her eyes. "Put me down," she murmured. "I can walk."

"No."

She let out a small sigh. It was too much trouble to argue, especially with her cheek pressed against his chest, his heartbeat beneath it.

He was climbing the stairs now and he smelled so good, his clothes fresh but mixed with his own male scent, his breath retaining a hint of coffee. She'd never been carried by a man before. There was something to be said for all those movies that made it look so romantic being swept off her feet like this.

And then she realized something and she started to giggle. She couldn't help herself.

At the top he paused to look down at her. "What's so funny?"

"You're a little out of breath."

A gleam of amusement twinkled in his eyes. "Are you saying I'm too old to carry you up the stairs?"

"Would I dare?"

"Yes."

All at once she noticed his firm mouth curve up at the corners.

His eyes held a certain glitter. "I'm not too old…or out of breath…to make love to you, my sweet," he murmured, then carried her into their bedroom, kicked the door shut and stood her up against it.

His blue eyes smoldered for her in the lamplight

as he bent his head and kissed her. And he kept right on kissing her until it became a game between them that neither would give up. In the end she had to break away to catch her breath.

He gazed at her triumphantly and before too long he'd stripped the clothes from her body and kissed her again in much more intimate places.

And if he was out of breath by the end of it, he didn't show it. The only thing he showed was a passionate hunger for her that took her by surprise.

Sasha was in the pool when Nick returned early from work the following evening. She'd meant to be showered and changed by now but summer was almost over and she'd wanted to take advantage of the warm weather.

He sat down on the deck chair and loosened his tie, looking handsome but with dark shadows beneath his eyes. She felt guilty for keeping him awake last night, even if it *had* been mutually beneficial.

She trod water in the middle of the pool. "You look tired."

He seemed surprised she'd noticed. "Yeah, I guess I am."

She frowned. "All that driving into the city and back is taking a lot out of you." Commuting to the city took an hour and a half each way, not to mention putting in a full day's work.

He shrugged. "I'll get used to it."

"You shouldn't have to, Nick." She tilted her head at him. "Why don't you get yourself a driver? Your father's had one for many years."

His brow creased in consideration. "Hey, that's not a bad idea. I could hire a permanent driver and that way I can work while I'm in the car and not waste time." He gave her a smile. "Good thinking."

She gave a quick shiver as a late afternoon breeze skipped over her. "Thanks, but I'm sure you would have thought of it yourself."

His gaze dropped to the water lapping at the top of her breasts. "Probably," he said, his distracted tone giving the comment less arrogance.

Her nipples tightened beneath the pink bikini top at the sudden sensual look in his eyes.

He stood up and started undoing his shirt.

"Er…what are you doing?"

"Joining you." He discarded shoes and socks, then his hand went to his belt buckle. Soon he had stripped down to black boxer briefs that fitted him like a second skin, leaving nothing to her imagination.

Her heart thumped erratically. "It's getting a little cold in here."

He gave her a wicked grin. "Then I'll warm you up."

He dove into the pool and she watched him come toward her in the water like a torpedo. The urge to turn and swim for the other side was strong. The temptation to stay and have her defenses annihilated was more exciting.

In one whoosh he came up close to her body and rose to the surface, so close she felt him like a caress. He shook the water from his face and smiled, his wet hair plastered to his head, his sooty lashes spiked with moisture.

"Fancy meeting you here," he drawled, looking what he was: a drop-dead gorgeous male who'd caught the biggest fish in the pool.

Her.

Of course, she was the *only* fish in the pool.

"Yes, fancy that."

The late afternoon sun showed a mischievous gleam in his eye and all at once she knew he was up to something. "Nick," she warned, trying to escape, the water hindering rather than helping.

He laughed playfully and caught her by the waist, before lifting her in the air and tossing her backward. She took a breath just as she went under the water, her mind already on sweet revenge.

She'd get him back, she promised herself as she burst through to the surface. "Nick, you'd—" She gasped. "My bikini top's come off!"

"Really?"

She ignored the relish in his voice and started looking around. Then she saw a pink blob of material near the edge of the pool.

"There it is." She started to swim toward it, aware that Nick was swimming with her. She thought he was merely trying to help her, until they reached it at the same time and he snatched it up and threw it onto the concrete outside of the pool.

"Nick!" She glared at him as she covered her breasts with her hands.

"What?" His eyes danced with the devil.

"How am I going to get out of the pool now?"

"No one's around. Iris is in the kitchen and Leo's gone into Richmond for supplies."

"I'm not a prude but—"

"Yes, you are." He chuckled. "Look at you. I know your body intimately now and yet you're still covering yourself from me."

"You're still a stranger, Nick," she said without thinking.

His smile disappeared. "Am I?" His blue eyes deepened in color. "Then we'd better do something about that."

Without hesitation, he caught her by the waist and pressed her up against the side of the pool.

And then he kissed her.

At first his lips were cold from the water but they soon turned warm enough to have her melting against him. For long, languid moments she reveled in having his mouth take advantage of hers, but eventually he eased back from the kiss.

"Still think of me as a stranger?" he said, a very masculine expression of satisfaction on his face.

A minute ago she'd felt very feminine, but now his words brought her back to reality and she didn't feel in the least like being coquettish. "There's more than knowing a person physically, Nick."

His face closed up. "It'll do for now," he said and turned away. "Stay here. I'll get us some robes."

Sasha watched him heave himself out of the water and stride over to the cabana, all male muscle and sinew. She swallowed hard. What on earth had made her say something so deep like that? Maybe she really *was* a prude and saying that had been her only defense?

He came out wearing a thick white robe and carrying one for her. "I'll cover you as you get out."

Thankful he was still being conscious of her sensitivity, she began climbing up the ladder. It was probably silly to be overreacting but she'd never been one to flaunt her body outrageously and merely because she was no longer a virgin didn't change her way of thinking.

Just as she reached the top of the ladder she looked up in time to see Nick's eyes flicking over her naked breasts. Unable to stop herself, she flushed.

"Put your arms in here," he said huskily, and she did as she was told, feeling more secure once she had the robe cinched in at the waist.

Nick cleared his throat and stepped away from her. "It's still balmy. Would you like to have dinner out here?"

She'd half-expected him to make some excuse to retire to the study. After all, he'd frozen up when she'd started talking about feelings. Fool that she was! The last thing she needed to bring out in the open was any sort of feelings.

To hide her surprise, she pushed back her wet hair. "That would be lovely."

"Good. I'll tell Iris."

"And I'll go dress."

"Let's not bother."

"Er…okay."

He started toward the house, detoured slightly and stopped to pick up something, then came back and handed her the pink bikini top.

Their eyes met and she blushed. "Thanks."

"You're welcome." He turned and walked back toward the house.

She watched him for a moment with her heart thudding, unable to stop herself from admiring those firm legs beneath the bathrobe. She liked the dark hair that was just-so-manly and just-so-touchable and if she dared, when he came back she would love to run her palms up his legs, caressing them, caressing *him*.

All at once she realized she was squeezing her

bikini top. Giving it one last squeeze she dropped it in the pocket of her robe, then went to sit down at the table, her own legs kind of shaky.

And he'd called her a *prude?*

Not any longer.

A few minutes later Nick came back. "Iris will bring out dinner shortly. In the meantime…" He held out two glasses of wine and passed one to her, then went to sit in the chair opposite.

Made selfconscious by her thoughts, she looked away, pretending to concentrate on the guest cottage and glasshouse that could easily been seen from here. Mercifully, the gazebo where they'd shared their kiss was on the other side of the house.

The sound of clinking glass from behind told Sasha that Iris had come out on the patio area. She turned around and smiled as the other woman came toward them pushing a trolley. Before too long she'd left and Sasha and Nick were tucking into their steak and salad.

"How are the designs going?"

She glanced up and saw he'd noticed the paperwork on one of the small tables. She'd been working on them before deciding to take a swim.

"Really well." She hesitated. "Would you like to look over them after dinner?"

"Sure."

After that she turned the conversation to some of the problems she was having with one of the contractors, then they began to talk of the family and other general things.

Nick stood up as soon as they'd both finished eating, and walked over to her designs. Sasha followed him, her heart thumping, wondering if he'd like them. She'd gone to great lengths making sure everything suited the house just right.

"I'm very impressed with these. You've kept the charm of the place without taking too much away from it all."

A swell of relief filled her. "My intention was never to make major changes. I love this place as it is, too, Nick."

His eyes riveted on her face. "Yes, I can see that."

She flushed with pleasure, feeling her cheeks turn almost the same pink as the bikini she wore.

Or *didn't* wear, she mused, pulling the robe tighter over her breasts, seeing his gaze drop to where she pretended she wasn't naked underneath.

"You surprise me," he murmured, lazy seduction seeping into those blue eyes. "I'd have thought you'd put your bikini top back on."

All at once she felt a touch defiant. "Maybe I'm not quite the prude you think I am."

Taking her by surprise, he placed the tip of his finger at her chin. "Hmm, maybe not," he murmured, sending her heartbeat thudding into a mad gallop. Then his finger slithered down her throat to rest on her wildly beating pulse. "You look so damn sexy in that robe."

She moistened her lips. "Nick—"

"I could strip it off you here and now and you wouldn't stop me...would you?"

She was very much afraid he was right.

"And I could slide those tiny bikini bottoms off you and you wouldn't say a word...true?"

Heavens, yes! He could take her this very moment and she'd let him. He made her want to do things she normally didn't do.

How she wished she could lie. "Nick, you know you're right but—"

He dropped his hand away from her throat. "But?"

"Afterwards I would feel totally embarrassed if I thought Iris or Leo had seen us."

His eyes filled with satisfaction. "So you *are* a prude?"

She started to frown. "Are you pleased because I've admitted it? Or because you're right?"

"Both. I like to win."

And he would never give in until he did, she was sure.

Suddenly he said, "I can't help who I am, Sasha."

She looked at him and saw no apology, just a simple statement that made her succumb to her need for him. No, he couldn't help being who he was.

"Nick, please. Take me to bed."

Five

Every evening after that was like a mini-honeymoon for the rest of the week. The weather remained quite warm and Nick would come home and they'd swim in the pool, eat a lazy dinner until dark, then retire to the bedroom.

There Sasha learned she wasn't really a prude at all. She'd just needed to let go of her inhibitions, and with Nick's instructions she did.

And her heart was still intact.

Then one morning she ended up walking past Nick's old bedroom and for some reason she stopped and went in. The room had a large bed and furnishings befitting a teenager of wealth, done out in shades of light and dark brown. On the dresser there were school trophies for cricket, soccer and swimming.

She wasn't sure what she expected to find, but there was something more here, something that made her believe Nick was much deeper than she had previously believed.

She just didn't know what that was.

And perhaps it was best she didn't find out.

Let him be who he was, and leave it at that. She didn't want any more complications in her life.

And speaking of complications, Sasha got a sinking feeling in her stomach when her mother arrived a few hours later right at lunchtime, supposedly to see how things were going. There was nothing for it but to invite her mother to lunch. Not that she minded. It was just that today she seemed to have an agenda.

And Sasha had the feeling it was to do with her father.

"So, you've recovered from the wedding?" Sally asked as they sat down to a light lunch.

"Yes, I have." Until this moment Sasha hadn't let herself be upset that her mother hadn't called since the wedding. *Nick's* mother had managed to call several times.

"I'm sorry I didn't phone you, darling," Sally

said, as if reading her daughter's mind. "I just thought it best I leave you to…adapt."

Sasha gave a remote smile. "Thanks."

"Darling, it's always good to leave a newly married couple to their own devices."

"Is that what the wedding manuals say?" she muttered, then felt bad when she saw the crushed looked on her mother's face. "Mum, I'm sorry. All · this has been a bit of a strain. I never expected to get married. Not for a long time anyway."

Sally nodded. "It's okay. I understand. But please remember that you've made your father and me so happy. I love that he's smiling again."

Ignoring the thought that her father probably had a new girlfriend, Sasha squeezed her mother's hand. "Then I'm glad."

Sally's grateful smile turned to a frown. "Darling, there *is* one thing…" she began, making Sasha tense. "There seems to be some sort of delay in closing the deal with Cesare. Your father can't wait much longer, I'm afraid."

"They're pretty busy with the launch in the U.K. and all, I'd imagine."

Come to think of it, she wasn't sure of the reason for the delay herself.

"I was sort of hoping you could ask Nick. Not straight out, mind you. Just see if there's a problem and what it is. I wouldn't ask if it wasn't so important."

Sasha swallowed. "Mum, this is an awkward position you and Dad are putting me in."

Again.

Her mother didn't seem to notice. "Nick's your husband. He'll tell you everything."

There were just so many things a mother could ask a daughter to do. "Nick and I are not in love, Mum. He keeps things to himself. I can't guarantee anything."

"If you could just try, darling."

Sasha sighed. "Okay, I'll see what I can do."

Her mother left straight after the meal, probably in case she said anything to change her daughter's mind. Sasha saw her off with a heavy heart. She loved her mother dearly but she'd never understand her love for a man, which totally submerged her own personality.

That would *never* happen to her.

Never.

And to prove it to herself, she would broach the dreaded subject with Nick at dinner this evening.

"My mother stopped by for lunch today."

Nick looked up from his meal and felt pleased for Sasha's sake. "Good. I don't think you've heard from her since the wedding, have you?"

"She's been busy."

"I'm sure." No doubt looking after Porter's every whim.

And at the expense of her daughter, Nick thought with a frown, surprised at the lack of attention Sally had actually given Sasha since their marriage. Wasn't a mother supposed to fuss over a newlywed daughter? Or was he just being a bit too old-fashioned?

Sasha moistened her mouth. "My mother does have a concern, though. She thought I might be able to help."

"And that is?"

"My father's waiting on a shipping deal to go through with the House of Valente, and apparently it's been delayed. He's not sure why."

Nick leaned back in his chair, and his lips twisted. "And he's sent *his* wife to ask *my* wife why?"

Sasha swallowed, looking uneasy. "He just needs to know, okay? Otherwise he might have to look at other avenues."

"Other avenues?" He almost snorted out loud. Porter was too lazy to go elsewhere when he had Cesare Valente on his side.

"This is business, Nick."

"Exactly."

Her chin angled. "What's that supposed to mean?"

"Stay out of the family business, Sasha."

She gasped. "I thought I *was* part of the family now."

His mouth tightened. "Not the business. That's got nothing to do with you."

"I see." Her green eyes turning cool, she placed her napkin on the table and stood up. "Then perhaps you should have made me sign a prenuptial. Then I won't be able to touch any of your precious family business if we ever divorce." On that note she walked out of the room.

Nick frowned as he watched her leave. They'd only just gotten married, so why the hell was she already mentioning divorce?

Or perhaps she really *had* married him for the money? No, he didn't think that any longer. Why, he couldn't say.

Besides, there was nothing to worry about. No way would she ever get any part of the House of Valente. The legal side of the business was wrapped up tighter than a ball of string.

Dammit, she should stay out of all this anyway. She had her job, and he had his. And what the hell was Porter playing at? The man had no scruples in hiding behind his wife and daughter's skirts. He never had.

It was just a pity the man was so good at detecting trouble. He was obviously suspicious about the delay in signing the contract. And with good reason.

Nick and his brothers couldn't quite put their finger on it, but there was something not quite right about the deal. None of them liked Porter, though this was more than not liking the man. It was a gut feeling that the wool was being pulled over their eyes. But with no real evidence, and unable to share their concerns with Cesare because of his health, they weren't going to be able to postpone the deal much longer.

Damn Porter Blake.

Suddenly Nick realized that Alex should be told the latest development. Yet he didn't want to say any of this on the telephone in case Sasha overheard him and reported back to her father. He grabbed his car keys and left the house.

After that he spent a couple of hours at Alex's place where they talked over the shipping deal once again, trying to find the reason it just didn't feel right. Nothing came to mind, and they reluctantly moved on to the upcoming launch in the U.K.

"Another cup of coffee, Nick?" Olivia asked, sticking her head around the study door.

He smiled at his sister-in-law. "Perhaps one more, Olivia, thanks."

Olivia's gaze slid to Alex. "What about you, honey?"

"No, nothing for me."

Olivia's gaze darted back to Nick, then Alex again, then she smiled oddly and left. Nick knew they were wondering why he wasn't eager to go home to his new wife.

"Problems with Sasha?" Alex said when they were alone again, a speculative look in his eyes.

Nick rubbed the back of his neck. "Just teething problems."

"I understand."

Nick thought about that. "Yes, you do, don't you?"

There was a moment's pause, then Alex said, "Sasha's turned out pretty good, considering what her father's like."

Nick shot him a twisted smile. "Whose side are you on?"

"I'm sure you'll work it out."

Nick suddenly had the urge to go home. So Sasha had only been trying to please her father. He shouldn't have snapped at her like that.

He stood up. "I think I'll give that coffee a miss."

Alex grinned. "I'll tell Olivia."

By the time Nick got home, Sasha was asleep. He showered and slid into bed beside her, careful not to wake her though he was tempted to pull her close. In the end he fell asleep. It had been a long day.

Sasha kept busy the next day going to various stores, but her mind was on Nick and his reaction last night. Stupid hurt had ripped through her at his response. She had hated to ask about the shipping contract but that's all she'd done. It wasn't a major crime. So why was he being so defensive about it?

Of course that threat of hers about a prenuptial had been a childish thing to say, but it served Nick right for drawing such a line in the sand. She already knew he didn't care for her. She hadn't needed to hear that she should stay in the background like a good little wife. It smacked too much of her father.

"You're late."

She almost missed her step as she came through the front door and looked up. Nick was waiting inside and demanding to know where *she'd* been? After he'd left her wondering last night if he'd gone to see an old girlfriend or two.

She placed her handbag on the hall table. "So we're keeping tabs on each other now?"

An odd sincerity flickered across his face. "I was getting worried, that's all."

Her anger cooled. "Okay, if you must know I've been out seeing some contractors. It took longer than I thought it would."

His eyes clouded and all at once he turned toward the living room, his movements somewhat jerky. "Well, I'm glad you're home."

Sasha frowned at his back. Was he embarrassed because he had worried? At the thought, a hint of tenderness trickled through her.

"You could have called me on my cell phone," she suggested quietly, following him into the room.

"I don't know the number."

Her little bubble burst.

"You only had to ask."

"I know."

It said a lot for their relationship.

"Anyway," he continued, "I phoned Iris earlier and told her not to cook dinner. I thought I'd take you out to a local restaurant."

Was this his way of apologizing?

"That would be lovely."

He looked pleased, then, "I'm sorry I snapped at you last night, Sasha. I wanted to apologize when I came home from Alex's, but you were asleep."

So, he'd been at Alex's place. Could she believe that now? Strangely, yes. She just wished she'd known that last night when she'd been upset and pretending to sleep.

"I'm sorry, too," she found herself saying. "I shouldn't have asked. I was worried for my parents' sake, that's all."

"I understand. I should have understood that, too. I—" His cell phone rang. "Damn. I have to take this call."

"Then you do that. I'll go get ready."

He was answering the call even before she'd finished speaking, but Sasha didn't mind. She climbed the stairs, excited now about going out to dinner with her husband.

Thank goodness the wedge between them seemed to have disappeared. She'd hated that her parents had come between them. Hated that Nick had stormed out and left her wondering. And hated it even more when he'd come home and hadn't taken her in his arms.

She was in the shower ten minutes later when the glass door opened and Nick, naked and somewhat aroused, stood there. "Move over, Mrs. Valente."

She didn't need to be told a second time. She willingly moved aside but only a little. Just enough to let him get up close and personal.

Later at the restaurant she and Nick were given a warm welcome by the owner, an Italian man called Angelo.

"I read in the papers that you marry, so tonight I'll cook you both something very special." He beamed at them, then hurried away.

"He seems like a nice man," Sasha said, making small talk as she looked around the restaurant. "You must come here often."

"I used to date his daughter."

"And he's still talking to you?" she joked.

His wry smile conceded the point. "It was very platonic. Angelo knew that."

"He must think highly of you," she said, then pondered the comment while the waiter poured their wine. Italian fathers weren't known for being liberal when it came to their daughters, especially when it came to playboys.

Yet this man had trusted Nick with his daughter? It didn't add up.

When they were alone again, Nick was the first to speak, "So, tell me about living in London. I know you said you lived with your aunt for a while, but you must have liked the place to stay so long."

She was surprised by his sudden interest.

"I loved it. It's such a vibrant city."

His brow arched. "You don't find Sydney vibrant?"

"Yes, but in a different way." She lifted one shoulder. "I guess I was ready to spread my wings and try new adventures."

"You evidently didn't try *too* many new things," he drawled, hinting at her virginity.

She shot him a smile. "I tried enough to keep me happy," she said, then laughed to herself when she saw him frown.

Let him wonder.

Then he said, "Your mother must have missed you."

She felt her smile dim. "I imagine my father did, too."

His eyes shuttered at the mention of her father. "I've been to London quite a few times. I should have stopped in to see you. We could have seen a show together."

"That would have been nice."

She pushed aside the hurt that he hadn't bothered, despite her knowing it was best this way. Having him drop by to see her would have been a painful reminder of the past.

Just then there was a commotion near the front door as people greeted each other with a lot of enthusiasm, giving Sasha the chance to concentrate on something other than the past. Italians really knew how to welcome each other. They were so warm and friendly and—

"Sasha?"

She turned back to Nick. "Yes?"

"I said I have a surprise for you."

"A surprise?"

"You'll be happy to know that we'll be signing the contract for your father tomorrow. Now you can tell your mother not to worry."

Intense relief washed over her, then as quickly restrained itself. "Thanks, but I'll wait until it's signed."

His glance sharpened. "You don't trust me?"

"Of course I do."

"Then you don't trust your father."

She hardly dared to breathe. "What makes you say that?"

His eyes narrowed. "I've just realized something. This deal of his was why you changed your mind about marrying me, wasn't it? It wasn't only about merging our two families. Your father wanted to make sure the deal went through, so he forced you to marry me."

Her brain stumbled. Her father would kill her for admitting this, but she couldn't lie.

"He was worried, yes. He thought he might be undercut by a competitor."

"So he made sure he wasn't," Nick said cynically.

Sasha couldn't argue with that. Still, she had to stand up for her father. "I think it's understandable he'd be worried about losing the tender."

Nick's eyes riveted on her, and all at once a mask came down over his face. Perhaps he knew the conversation was leading them places neither of them wanted to go.

He inclined his head. "You're right."

Thankfully Angelo appeared with their meal, and Sasha smiled and praised the food but somehow the evening had been spoiled. Talking about their families always caused friction.

They ate in silence for a while.

"By the way," Nick said eventually. "I've invited a couple of people to dinner Friday night. If you could coordinate it all with Iris that would be great."

All at once she felt a chill. "That's only a couple of days away."

"I know, but they're visiting from Europe and only have Friday night free."

"So it's a business dinner?"

"Yes."

"And you want me to arrange it all and host it as well?"

"Of course."

Her heart sank at his assumption that she would drop everything for him. Not only did she have a late afternoon appointment with one of the contractors, but it reminded her of her parents, her father snapping his fingers and her mother jumping to it.

She'd sworn never to be like her mother.

"You're quiet," Nick said after a few minutes more of silence.

"Am I?"

He looked at her sharply. "What's the matter?"

Her disappointment in him was immense. She should have known not to let herself get close to him again. She would only get hurt a second time.

"You brought me out to dinner to sweeten me up, didn't you?"

His brows drew together. "What are you talking about?"

"Actually I'm surprised you even did that," she scoffed. "Did you think I would say no, Nick? Well, you're right. I *am* saying no."

His face hardened. "No to what?"

"To arranging your business dinner and playing your hostess."

"You're my wife."

She bristled. "Yes, not your slave to be told what to do and when to do it."

He sat back, his eyes assessing hers. "Where's all this coming from?"

"I'm sick of being expected to drop everything for everyone else. First my parents expect me to give up my freedom for them, and now you think I should just fall in with whatever plans you make."

And truth to tell, she was sick of being a nobody to Nick. Because that's what it all came down to. He hadn't been interested in her years ago. He still wasn't interested in her.

Not as a person.

A pulse began to beat in his cheekbone. "I didn't mean to treat you like your father does."

She gave a silent gasp. Clearly he thought of her as her father's lackey as well. "Thanks very much."

"You know what I mean."

Hurt gnawed at her. "Unfortunately, yes, I do."

His gaze rested on her face with a hint of regret. "Sasha, I'm sorry. I'll take them to a restaurant in the city. You don't need to come."

She sighed, suddenly feeling bad yet knowing she shouldn't. "Nick, if you were to *ask* me, then I don't mind hosting the dinner. I just don't like the expectation that I have to do it."

He considered her across the table. "Then would

you mind being my hostess on Friday, Sasha? I'd really appreciate it."

Her heart thudded at the sincerity in his tone. "Yes. I'm happy to help." She would reschedule her appointment with the contractor.

His shoulders relaxed a little, and there was an odd amusement in his eyes. "You're quite fiery when you're upset. I never noticed that when you were growing up. You were always quite shy."

Shy and in love.

Her stomach did a flip at the thought. "Perhaps I didn't want you to notice back then," she lied.

"And now?"

She took a moment to answer as past hurts rose in her throat. "I'm older. I want respect."

"You always had my respect, Sasha."

"No, Nick. I didn't."

He went still, his eyes probing hers. "Then I'm sorry if I made you feel that way. It wasn't intentional."

"I know." And therein lay the crux of the matter. It was another example of her meaning less than nothing to him.

Angelo reappeared to check that their meal was enjoyable and Sasha welcomed the interruption. She'd said more than enough. If Nick didn't think she mattered, then she wasn't going to force him to change his mind.

She had her pride after all.

Six

Nick phoned Sasha late the following morning to tell her the deal had been signed and that Alex was calling her father now to tell him the news.

Enormously relieved, Sasha thanked him for letting her know, then waited for her mother to call and share in the good news and perhaps say thanks.

Her mother didn't call.

"No doubt your parents were relieved," Nick said when he came home.

"No doubt they were."

He froze. "You mean they haven't called you?"

A lump lodged in her throat. "No, but they were probably busy."

"They weren't too busy to ask you to spy for them," he rasped.

She sucked in a sharp breath. "It wasn't like that."

A pulse beat in his cheekbone. "Not on your part, but they got what they wanted from you. They used you, Sasha."

He was right, and on one level she was warmed by his concern for her, but loyalty to her mother kept her quiet. "Let's forget that for now."

"Can you?"

"No." If she thought about it the pain would overwhelm her. She'd always known she came second with her mother, but until recently she hadn't realized just how low down on the scale she was compared with her father.

She pretended to dismiss it all. "Come on. I want you to pick a color scheme for the study. I can't decide by myself."

He made a dismissive gesture. "Any color will do."

"No, Nick. You'll be using it a lot, so it's important I get your input."

"You'll be using it, too."

"Exactly. It's something we need to choose together."

He suddenly broke into a sexy half smile. "You're very good at getting your own way. Subtle but very effective."

She found herself smiling back. "That's always been my policy."

The rest of the week went quickly and before she knew it, it was Friday. She was nervous about hosting their first dinner, and of course she helped Iris arrange it all, but there was a difference in doing it because she wanted to and not because it was expected of her.

"You look beautiful," Nick said when she'd finished dressing in a blue dress that hugged her body in all the right places, her blonde hair up in a chignon, delicate diamond earrings at her ears.

Silly delight rippled through her. "Thanks." Her eyes slid over his dark suit and white shirt that did him full-on justice. "You're looking quite spiffy yourself."

He smiled. "Spiffy, eh?"

She smiled back then saw him fiddling with his tie. "Here, let me do that for you."

"You don't mind?"

"No, I like doing up men's ties," she quipped as she stepped close to him and began working on the tie.

His smile vanished. "Just how many men's ties have you done up?"

"The odd one or two."

He stared down at her, then must have seen her lips twitching because he broke into a grin. "I think you're making that up."

"Am I?"

"You'd better be," he pretended to growl, sending a thought flashing through her mind. He *liked* being the only man to make love to her.

Well, well, she mused. Who'd have thought he'd be so old-fashioned?

"You're not nervous about tonight?" he asked, dragging her from her thoughts.

"Yes, I am."

"You don't show it."

"Neither do you."

One brow rose. "Who said I was nervous?"

"You usually don't have trouble doing up your tie."

"Thanks for noticing," he said wryly.

She finished her task and patted the tie. "There. That's better."

He turned away to look in the mirror. "Perfect."

Yes.

He was.

She cleared her throat. "So this dinner is important, is it?"

He reached for his jacket. "Yes and no. Alex has already made the deals to launch 'Valente's Woman' in France and Germany. I just need to keep relations agreeable between us until the launch."

Sasha realized that this must be all quite new to Nick. Previously Cesare and Isabel would have hosted any clients, and then Alex and Olivia, but this time it fell to him. No doubt he would be an accomplished host as a playboy bachelor, but this was the first time he'd be hosting a dinner in his own home as a married man.

She felt bad now for refusing before. "You'll do fine," she said, prompting an arrogant smile from him.

"I know."

And he did.

Extra fine, Sasha thought sourly an hour later as she watched Claudine, the beautiful wife of the French businessman, flirt with Nick from the moment she set foot in the house.

In the meantime the German couple just sat back and smiled, along with Jacque, who didn't appear concerned by his wife's behavior.

It concerned Sasha, especially when Nick looked thoroughly smitten by the gorgeous brunette leaning close to him and talking French in a low, husky voice.

"Ooh, Nicolah, you are teasing me," she said in her accented English, laughing sexily as she squirmed in her seat.

"No, really," he teased. "If you're going to the fashion show tomorrow make sure they don't mistake you for one of their models."

Claudine preened. "Perhaps I will need you to

come with me and protect me." She looked at Sasha. "Would you mind if I borrowed your husband tomorrow, Sasha?"

Her blatant approach took Sasha's breath away. And Nick, the rat, was sitting there smiling and thoroughly enjoying himself and probably expected she would say yes.

She'd be damned if she'd be humiliated like this.

"I'm sorry, Claudine, but I need him tomorrow," she said sweetly, smiling at Nick like her very existence depended on him.

"Ooh," Claudine pouted at Nick. "Another time perhaps, Nicolah?"

"It's a date."

Sasha could feel the humiliation rise up in her throat but she refused to look at the others at the table. A date with a married woman? Wasn't he forgetting something? Like he was now a married man himself? This was going beyond being more than a good host.

Or perhaps he just didn't care. Perhaps he was too focused on making a conquest to worry about what this meeting was all about. Worse, perhaps this was how he did business as a playboy.

A reputation well earned?

Thankfully the German woman, Freda, asked Sasha about her plans to redecorate and the conversation turned to interior design. She was busy answering questions when she heard Claudine ask Nick if he could show her where she could freshen up.

"That's okay, Claudine," she said instantly. "I can show you."

"Oh but…you are talking to Freda."

"No, that's fine. I want to freshen up, too."

The woman pouted again, but Sasha ignored it, just as she ignored Nick as she passed him on her way out the door. If he dared to chastise her later, then he was in for a rude shock.

"Your name is French?" Claudine asked as they walked down the hallway. It was the first personal thing she'd said to her all night.

"No. It's spelled S-A-S-H-A, not S-A-C-H-A."

"You are not French then?"

"No."

Claudine gave a grunt, evidently not impressed by a non-French person using a French-sounding name.

Then the woman sent her a sideways glance. "Nicolah is so handsome."

Aah, now they were getting to the main thing.

Sasha just smiled. "Very."

And he's mine, she wanted to say.

"Jacques does not like the fashion shows." She sighed deeply. "It's a pity Nicolah cannot come with me. I'm sure he would like that."

Sasha opened the bathroom door. "Family always comes first with Nick."

And as she shut the door behind the woman, Sasha realized that was the truth. His family did always come first.

Just not his wife.

Nick was glad to see the back of their guests. Now all he wanted to do was go to bed—with Sasha.

"That went well," he said, coming into the bedroom after he'd turned off most of the downstairs lights. Sasha was sitting in front of the dressing table, taking off her jewelry. She looked so right, so very feminine, and for the first time he felt thoroughly married.

It wasn't a bad feeling.

"For some," she said coolly.

Her unfriendly tone dragged him from his pleasant thoughts. "What do you mean?"

She spun around on the stool, and suddenly sparks were flying from her green eyes. "I'm sorry if I spoiled your plans for tomorrow, Nick, but I didn't think it right you go out on a *date* with another woman when you're already married to me."

He stared in amazement, then snorted. "You didn't think that was for real, did you? Claudine was just flirting."

And mild flirting at best. He'd known women who came on a lot stronger than that.

"Is that why she was practically begging me to let you go to the fashion show with her?"

"When?"

"When I escorted her to the bathroom."

He shrugged. "She's French. She does things over the top."

"Not with *my* husband she doesn't."

A crazy thought blew him away. "You're jealous!"

Her slim shoulders tensed. "Don't be ridiculous. You promised to be faithful, and I expect you to keep that promise, that's all."

Okay, so she wasn't jealous.

And now he was getting annoyed. His word was good enough for the rest of the world. It should be good enough for his wife.

"Look, I told you I take my marriage vows seriously, and I do. There's no way I'll be unfaithful to you."

"I'm trying to believe that."

He considered her tight mouth. "You've really got a thing about this, haven't you?"

She hesitated, then, "Yes, I do. I've spent a lifetime watching my father having affair after affair and my poor mother putting up with it. Not me. I won't put up with it. I won't allow myself to be humiliated in such a way."

The words were heartfelt, and something kicked inside him. "So you know about your father's affairs?"

"Doesn't everyone?" she said with a catch in her voice.

"Does your mother know?"

"We've never mentioned it, but I'm sure she does." She straightened her shoulders. "And I won't ever let myself be put in that position."

"I'm not asking you to."

Her expression clouded. "It's all about respect, isn't it?" she said, as if talking to herself. "Respect for another person."

"You've got my respect."

She focused back on him. "But I didn't always have it, did I?"

The muscles at the back of his neck tightened. She'd mentioned respect the other day, too, and he'd let the comment pass. Not this time.

"Why do you say that? I've always treated you with respect."

"If you'd respected me years ago you wouldn't have gone off with that girl after our kiss."

The comment staggered him. "What are you saying? That our kiss *mattered* to you back then?"

She held his gaze for a moment, and her delicate chin rose higher. "You gave me my first kiss, Nick. And yes, it mattered."

He expelled a breath.

"But you didn't care, Nick."

She was wrong about that.

"You've got no idea how hard it was for me to walk away from you, Sasha. But dammit, you were only eighteen. You had your whole life ahead of you."

"So did you."

"I don't deny that. I was only twenty-five. I didn't want a serious relationship. It wouldn't have been fair to you—to either of us—if I'd taken what you'd offered."

"I felt humiliated," she said quietly. "More so when you left with another girl."

He swore low in his throat. "I'm sorry. That hadn't been my intention."

He'd gotten the hell out of there with the other girl—he couldn't even remember her name now—not to humiliate but because Sasha was a siren...a little witch...who'd suddenly developed a body and a face to die for.

Knowing himself, he would have taken what was offered and moved on.

Knowing Sasha, he couldn't have done that to her.

She gave a shaky sigh. "That was the worst part. You had no idea how devastated I was."

His heart jolted inside his chest. Had this been more than Sasha testing out her newfound womanly ways?

"Sasha, did you have a crush on me?"

For a moment their eyes locked.

"Yes, Nick. I did. I was a young girl in love with the man of her dreams."

Oh hell.

Dare he ask….

"Are you still in love with me, Sasha?"

Her eyelids flickered. "I'm fond of you, Nick, but that's all." As if the thought didn't deserve any further comment, she spun on her stool to face the mirror again and began brushing her hair.

It was odd but his stomach felt like it had just been hollowed out. She hadn't missed a beat in her answer. Love definitely wasn't in her agenda.

Not that he would have known what to do if she *had* said she loved him. He hadn't figured on *that* in their plans. He'd be happy with fondness between them.

And desire.

That was enough.

He walked up behind her and put his hands on her shoulders, looking at her through her reflection. "Amazing as it may seem to you, you're the only woman I want in my life right now."

And that was the truth.

The brush stilled in her hand. "I…I am?"

Her stutter was charming and made his heart pound against his ribs. She may not be in love with him, but she was so very beautiful.

"Yes," he murmured, sliding the neckline of her dress aside and kissing her bare shoulder. "Let me show you."

* * *

At breakfast, Sasha was still recovering from Nick's questions last night.

Are you still in love with me, Sasha?

No, she wasn't, but the question had made her uncomfortable. Love wasn't an easy subject to discuss at any time, but talking about it made it seem more real, even possible.

It was a possibility she didn't want.

Just then, Iris opened the door to the breakfast room and Cesare and Isabel came walking in.

Nick put down his napkin in surprise. "Dad, what are you doing here?"

Cesare's step seemed to hesitate. "Son, I have something to tell you."

Sasha saw Nick stiffen.

"What's happened, Dad?"

Cesare sat down on one of the chairs, his face paler than usual. At the same time, Isabel hugged Nick, then straightened but kept her hand on his shoulder in a comforting gesture. Sasha swallowed hard. This was definitely bad news.

"It's your mother, *figlio mio.*" The older man paused. "She fell asleep at the wheel of her car last night and crashed into a parked truck."

Sasha gasped.

Nick sat like stone. "And?"

"She's dead, Nick. She died instantly."

Pain for Nick squeezed Sasha's heart as Isabel squeezed his shoulder.

Nick didn't move. "Had she been drinking?"

"We don't know. Perhaps."

Nick's lips twisted. "More than likely she was coming home from a party."

Cesare inclined his head. "She lived life on her terms, Nick."

"You don't have to tell me that, Dad," Nick said, jumping to his feet and going over to the patio door. He stood looking out over the sunny courtyard.

"At least she didn't suffer, honey," Isabel murmured. "None of us would want that."

Nick let out a deep sigh but didn't turn around. "No, I wouldn't have wanted that."

Seconds passed without anyone speaking as if in deference to the dead.

"They're arranging the funeral for Tuesday in Melbourne," Cesare finally said.

"I won't be going."

Cesare's mouth clamped in a thin line. "She was your mother, son."

"Really?" Nick turned around to face them, the lines of his face rigid.

"I know how you feel, but the world is made up of different people. We have to accept that."

"*You* accept it." Nick tilted his head. "Actually, you accepted that years ago, didn't you?"

Cesare stiffened. "Your mother wasn't the woman I thought she was when I married her, I know. But I did learn to accept that's how she was."

"I'm sorry, but I can't be so generous."

Cesare's gaze held his son's. "The best thing that came out of our marriage was *you*, Nick."

Sasha's throat thickened.

A muscle ticked in Nick's cheek. "Emotional blackmail won't work this time, Dad. I won't go to the funeral. I don't owe her anything."

Cesare was having none of that. He straightened his shoulders. "Julieann was a Valente, if even for a short while. She should have someone from the Valente family go to the funeral."

"You go then."

Cesare glanced at Isabel then back. "I can't. I would if I could, but—"

"His doctor won't let him go," Isabel said. "He's worried it will be too much for your father."

Cesare made a dismissive gesture. "The doctor's just being too cautious. He thinks you'll sue him if I die."

Isabel tutted. "Now, you know that's not true, Cesare." She looked at Nick. "For what it's worth I don't think you should be forced to go either."

"Thanks for your support, Izzie," Cesare muttered.

She looked at her husband. "I don't care what you

say. I don't think anyone should have to go if they don't want to, Cesare."

For some reason, Sasha thought of her own father and how she'd feel if he'd walked out on them years ago. Would she have been forgiving of him?

Probably not.

Of course, it may have turned out better if her father *had* left them. Her mother may have had a chance at a decent life.

"I'm not going, Dad."

Cesare got to his feet, his mouth firming with purpose. "Then it's up to me." He shot Isabel a look. "And no more about it from you, my darling wife. I—" Suddenly he turned pale.

"Dad?" Nick raced over while Isabel gasped, then took some tablets out of Cesare's jacket pocket.

"Here, darling. Put this under your tongue."

A short while later Cesare started to get his color back and everyone breathed a sigh of relief. If the older man had been hoping for effect, he couldn't have chosen a better moment.

Nick stood looking down at his father, his eyes unreadable. "Okay, Dad. You get your wish. I'll go to the funeral."

Cesare looked relieved. "Thank you, *figlio mio*. This means a lot to me."

"I'll go with him," Sasha said, wanting them to know she'd be there for Nick.

Nick spun toward her. "No."

"But—"

"No." Without another word, he turned and walked out of the room.

Sasha's heart sank, but she wasn't about to give up.

"Go with him, honey," Isabel said. "He needs you."

Sasha nodded. He needed someone, but she wasn't sure it was her. "I intend to, Isabel. Don't worry."

After that, the older couple left and Sasha saw them off. For all that she understood why Cesare wanted a Valente at the funeral, like Isabel, she did think it unfair to ask Nick to go. Did they really need someone to represent the family? Wasn't Cesare showing the woman more compassion than she'd shown him and their son?

But it wasn't her place to say anything.

She knocked on the study door and went in. "Nick—"

"No, Sasha."

"But—"

"I'm going alone."

She stopped in the middle of the room and glared at him across the desk. "Would you let me finish a sentence or are you taking a page from my father's book now?"

He flinched.

"Nick, look. I know we were forced to get married, and I know we didn't marry for love, but I…care about you. I'm your wife, and I should go with you at a time like this."

A nerve pulsed near Nick's temple. "It's a funeral for a woman you didn't even know, Sasha. There's no reason for you to attend."

"I may not have known the woman, but I know her son very well. *He's* reason enough for me to go."

His eyes darkened as silence hung in the air. She meant every word. She wouldn't back down over this.

Something shifted in his expression as he looked at her. Finally he said, "As you wish."

Her heart thudded with relief. "Thank you."

He picked up the phone. "Now, if you don't mind, I have some arrangements to make." Clearly he wanted to push her out, both of the room and emotionally.

Still, she hung on. "Would you like me to do all that?"

"Thanks, but my PA knows my requirements."

She inclined her head and went to leave the room. It was obvious he'd given all he had to give right now.

"Sasha?"

She stopped and turned. "Yes?"

"Thank you," he said brusquely.

She nodded and shut the door behind her, not

sure what he was thanking her for—wanting to go to the funeral with him, or offering to help. Her heart swelled inside her chest. Nick really did appreciate her efforts.

He had finally noticed.

Seven

With Alex using the family jet in England, making it unavailable to take to Melbourne, Nick was glad he'd hired another plane. At least this way he wouldn't leave the tainted memories of the funeral in the family jet and could put it all behind him once it was over.

He only wished Sasha had stayed at home, he thought, watching her in the leather chair opposite as she stared out the aircraft window. She was dressed appropriately in black and looked elegantly sedate, but he still didn't think this funeral was the place for her. He appreciated her concern, but it wasn't warranted. He could handle this by himself.

Dammit, his mother didn't deserve to have Valente representation at her funeral. Okay, so his father had wanted to do the right thing, but then, his father had always wanted to do the right thing. The older man just hadn't known there had been a price to pay.

And that *he'd* been the one to pay it.

An hour later they pulled up outside the church and a knot tightened in Nick's gut. Just as he squared his shoulders he heard Sasha gasp.

"It's beautiful," she murmured, looking up at the church through the limousine window.

He took a glance but he wasn't really interested in a building right now.

She sat back on the seat and winced. "Oh, Nick, I'm sorry. This isn't the right time to say that."

"It's fine."

She shook her head. "No, I was being insensitive. It's just that this is the type of church I always dreamed I'd be married in."

That caught his attention. "You did?"

She flushed, then gave a shrug. "Sorry. It took me by surprise when I saw it."

Just like she was taking him by surprise.

"No need to apologize," he said, as the driver opened the car door.

Nick had the strangest feeling when he saw his mother's casket near the altar. He stopped inside the door, his legs unable to move. This was his *mother,* something inside him screamed.

And then he felt Sasha touch his arm and at that moment he was truly grateful to have her with him.

The service was brief with only about twenty people who'd bothered to come. Two of the men he remembered as her husbands from years ago. Not much for a life spent with five husbands and various lovers.

A life spent on the edge.

Outside the church a man in his early sixties came up to him and shook his hand. "Nick, she would have been so happy you came."

Nick's brows flattened. "And you are?"

"I was Julieann's husband."

"Husband?" Nick bit back from asking which one.

"Her last one," the man said, reading his mind. "My name's Ted, by the way."

Ted's eyes darted to Sasha. "And this must be your new wife," he said, startling Nick, then explained, "Julieann read about your marriage in the papers."

Nick grimaced inwardly. He wondered how long before his mother would have found a way to make use of that knowledge.

"How long were you married, Ted?"

"Five years." The older man's eyes didn't waver. "She'd changed, Nick."

"Really? So she wasn't drunk behind the wheel of her car when she died?"

"No, she wasn't," Ted said firmly. "She'd been working the nightshift at an old people's home. She fell asleep because she was tired."

"My mother would never have been working. Period. And certainly not working to help anyone else."

Ted began to look upset. "I told you, she'd changed. Believe me, she had."

Nick held himself in check. Nothing would convince him of that statement. "It doesn't matter if I believe you or not. It's over."

The older man blinked rapidly, then reached into his pocket and pulled out an envelope. "I think you should have this."

Nick didn't take it. "What is it?"

"It's a letter. To you. She was planning on sending it, but kept putting it off until she felt you were ready."

Nick still didn't take it. "I don't want it. It's too late."

Ted continued to hold out the envelope but his hand shook a little now. "Then it won't do any harm for you to read it."

Nick stared hard at him. "Were you good to my mother, Ted?"

Moisture refilled Ted's eyes as he straightened. "Yes, I was."

"Then I'll take it for your sake." Nick took the envelope, aware of the other man's relief. He couldn't promise to ever read it. "I'm sorry for your loss, Ted."

"I'm sorry for yours, too, son."

Swallowing a lump in his throat, Nick cupped Sasha's elbow and walked her to the limousine. Ted had no need to offer condolences for losing his mother.

You couldn't lose something you had never had.

After dinner that evening, Sasha wasn't surprised when Nick said he was going to do some work in the upstairs study. He'd already spoken to his father about the funeral, and then Alex had called from London with concern in his voice.

She knew Nick was upset and he needed to be alone to think about the day's events. She understood he was having trouble assimilating what Ted had told him about his mother, how to fit that image into the person Nick knew her to be. She could only imagine the thoughts going through his head right now.

Of course, he hadn't needed to hear her exclaim over the church like they were attending a joyous wedding instead of a solemn funeral. Yet she hadn't been able to stop herself. The moment she'd seen it, she'd fallen in love with its picture-book setting. The perfect picture for the perfect wedding she had dreamed about.

She sighed and pushed aside her wistful thoughts as she settled down to do some work of her own. For once, time dragged. She wanted to go and see how Nick was doing.

For a few hours she held back, but at nine o'clock she couldn't wait any longer. She went upstairs and knocked on the study door, only to find him nowhere to be seen.

And then she saw the letter from his mother lying open on the desk. Her heart started to thud.

Hurrying to the window she saw his car was still parked outside in the driveway. Then she checked their bedroom but he wasn't there either. She was about to go downstairs and check the kitchen when she noticed a door open at the far end of the landing.

Nick's old bedroom.

She found him sitting on the side of the bed in the dark, the light from the hallway spilling across the center of the room, showing him with his elbows on his knees, staring down at the floor.

"Nick?" she murmured with concern, wanting to rush to him but not wanting to intrude in a private moment.

He lifted his head. "Sasha."

"Are you okay?"

A moment's silence, then he straightened. "Yeah, I am."

She took a few steps into the room. "I went to look

for you in the study." She hesitated. "Um…I saw your mother's letter was open and I was concerned for you."

"Did you read it?"

"No! I would never do that."

He grimaced. "I wasn't accusing. I thought you might have read it to see if it had upset me, that's all."

"And has it? Upset you, that is."

"Yes and no." He took a ragged breath. "No, because my mother truly was genuinely sorry for all she'd done. Yes, because it's too late to tell her I forgive her."

Stunned surprise rippled through her and she sat down on one of the brocade chairs. "You forgive her?"

He nodded. "My mother was never the type of person to ask for forgiveness. You see, she never actually realized she needed forgiving in the first place." He gave a half smile at that. "And I would've said a leopard never changed its spots, but some things happened to Julieann that had a profound effect on her."

"What was that?"

"She fell in love for the first time ever. With Ted." He gave a tiny pause. "And she got cancer."

Sasha's heart saddened for the woman. "Cancer?"

"Yes, and she recovered but it made her look back on her life and see all the hurt she'd caused. Believe me, I know the woman my mother was in her younger years, and she would never have written that letter. Never."

Sasha knew he would never let himself be fooled by anything insincere. "I'm glad she changed for the better."

"Me, too." Then his brows pulled together. "I guess for once my father was right and I was wrong. If Dad hadn't convinced me to go, I'd probably have received the letter in the mail and not read it at all. I know for sure I wouldn't have been so quick to forgive, but meeting Ted today convinced me he was genuine. And that the letter was, too."

"I liked Ted."

"Me, too. He's much better than her previous husbands. There were five," he said before she could ask. "And apart from Ted, they were all after my mother for the money she could get out of my father."

Sasha's forehead creased. "Did your father just hand over money whenever she asked for it?"

He shook his head. "No, it wasn't quite like that. From the time I was seven she'd turn up here every couple of years until I was twelve, and insist on my staying with her and her current husband for a few days while they were in town." His lips twisted. "Naturally she'd insist on being paid 'expenses' and then blow it all at the races."

Sasha listened with rising dismay. She was beginning to see why Nick had disliked his mother so much.

"My dad didn't want to stop me from seeing her, but he would always ask me if I wanted to go. I thought he wanted me to, so I did." He shrugged. "I've never told him the truth."

Her eyebrows rose. "Your father didn't realize this? He just handed you over to a woman who had no respect for anyone or took no responsibility for anything?"

"He thought he was doing the right thing. Besides, he told me years later he had someone keep an eye on me while I was away, and he thought I was having an okay time. She'd dump me on her parents, you see, while they went off to the races, so he thought I was getting to know my grandparents. They couldn't have been less interested in me if they'd tried."

Oh, poor Nick. "What did you do when you were with them?"

"Sit and watch television. I was miserable and couldn't wait to get back home." He took a shuddering breath. "It was only a few days, but it felt like a lifetime."

"And there would've always been the fear that you would never come back home again," she said half to herself.

A muscle began to throb in his cheek.

She stared aghast. "Oh my God. That's why you won't let me redecorate this bedroom. This was your sanctuary whenever you returned home, wasn't it?"

He nodded with a taut jerk of his head. "Yes. I felt safe here. I still do. I used to imagine they would never get to me here."

Her heart constricted. "Oh, Nick. I'm sorry you had to go through all that."

"Hey, it wasn't so bad," he said, making light of it now.

"Yes, it was."

A look of discomfort crossed his face. "Okay, so those times were bad, but I always made it back home and that's the important thing."

She looked at Nick and something tumbled around in her chest. She could imagine him a little boy or a young teenager putting on a brave face, terrified of going with his mother and her latest new husband, not knowing if he would ever come back to those who loved him.

The urge to hold him was strong and she stood up and went to stand between his legs, pulling his head against her breast in a comforting fashion. He didn't resist, and they remained like that for a while.

Only, suddenly, she wanted more tonight. She wanted to show him that this was their home and she was his wife and he had no need to fear being abandoned ever again.

She turned his head up to her. "Let me make love to you, Nick."

His eyes flared with desire. "Yes, Sasha," he said in a low, raspy voice. "I need you to love me tonight."

His words cut the air from her lungs.

Love him?

Oh God, she thought as she bent her head and began placing soft kisses down his cheek until she came to his mouth.

She already did.

Eight

The next morning Sasha felt Nick's lips on hers in a brief goodbye kiss, but she kept her eyes shut until she heard him leave the room. Then and only then did she carefully open them to a new morning and a new beginning, one where she knew she would have to be strong.

She loved him.

If it hadn't been for all the smoke and mirrors caused by their forced marriage she'd probably have seen it coming. As it was, it had taken a private man like Nick to share his painful past with her to make her see what was truly in her heart.

She'd never stopped loving him.

She'd merely been convincing herself otherwise because it hurt too much to admit she loved a man who would never love her back. He couldn't. He wasn't the type of man to give up part of himself for love of a woman. Even now, she knew he didn't love her. He liked her, and she was sure he liked her even more with each passing day, but there was no way she could tell him she loved him.

He wouldn't want to know.

And his rejection of her would be far worse this time. They were adults now and their feelings ran deeper and more lasting, and to bring it out in the open would ruin any chance of a happy marriage between them.

A marriage now based on friendship.

Not love.

No, she'd have to be happy with what she had. The alternative of a divorce, or of Nick feeling uncomfortable around her was too much to bear.

Better to keep it a secret.

Of course, for all her self-talk, when he returned home that night and kissed her hello, then took the stairs two at a time to go shower and change, Sasha's heart skipped a beat as she realized something. This morning's kiss before leaving for work had been the first time he'd kissed her goodbye.

And now this?

Things had definitely changed for the better between them. Perhaps one day…

No, she dared not think it.

"By the way," he said over dinner later. "I'm happy for you to redecorate my old bedroom now."

She blinked. "You are?"

"Yes. Give it a whole new look and turn it into a spare bedroom. Do whatever you want. You're the expert. I don't need it anymore."

Her insides turned soft. "No, you don't, do you?"

He seemed much more relaxed. "Sasha, I think it's time we had some fun. Would you like to go to a party on Saturday night? Friends of mine are celebrating their fifth wedding anniversary."

She liked that he was asking her and not merely expecting her to go. More importantly it was as if he actually *wanted* to be with her.

"I'd love to go to the party with you."

He flashed her a smile. "Good."

That smile made her senses spin and took her right through the week, especially when he continued to kiss her goodbye and hello every day. It was as if he truly considered her his real wife now.

There were about fifty people at the party held at a gorgeous mansion overlooking the Parramatta River. Nick's friends, Fiona and Boyd, were warm and friendly.

"We're so sorry we missed your wedding," Fiona said. "We were overseas at the time but it was a nice surprise when we came back."

"Surprise?" Boyd laughingly choked. "I was totally shocked when Nick told me he was married. Who'd have thought the playboy would ever get married, let alone so quickly?" He got an elbow in the ribs by his wife. "I mean…well, you know what I mean."

"Yeah, Boyd, we know what you mean," Nick teased and left it at that.

Sasha was grateful Nick didn't tell them the truth. She hadn't cared at the wedding if everyone had known, but now it was a matter of pride.

And a matter of love.

Over the next hour Nick kept her by his side, not leaving her for a minute while they mixed with a small group of friends. They were laughing at something one of the wives said when suddenly a blonde beauty pushed through the group.

"Darling!" she squealed, throwing her arms around Nick's neck and hugging him. She leaned back and kissed him full on the mouth before saying, "Darling, I'm back. Aren't you glad to see me?"

There was dead silence in the group.

Sasha swallowed hard as she looked at the beautiful blonde, then Nick, seeing the shock before a mask came down over his face.

Effortlessly he extricated himself from the

woman's arms and slid his arm around Sasha's waist and said, "Brenda, I'd like you to meet my wife."

The other woman gasped, her eyes darting in disbelief to Sasha and back. "Your *wife?*"

"That's what I said."

The blonde's face began to crumble. "Oh, Nick, how could you!" she choked, spinning on her heels and racing out to the patio.

The silence continued.

Nick's mouth tightened as he turned to Sasha. "I'd better go sort this out."

Sasha nodded. It was the right thing to do, the only decent thing to do, so why was she feeling uneasy about it all? He strode away, leaving an uncomfortable quiet.

Then Fiona took matters into hand. "These things happen," she said sympathetically, giving Sasha's arm a pat.

Sasha cleared her throat. "Yes, they do."

Then one of the men started talking about something else and the conversation started up again somewhat awkwardly, everyone no doubt wondering what was going on out there on the patio and none more than herself.

She held her head high and determined to keep on doing so, but inside she was feeling less than certain. Who was Brenda, and how much had she and Nick meant to each other?

It seemed forever before he returned. His jaw was clenched as he came up and slipped his arm around her waist again, pulling her close. "Right, I'm back where I belong now."

She knew he meant to comfort her but their relationship was such that she didn't know which way the wind would blow. All this could be for show.

She winced. What was the matter with her? It *was* all for show.

All at once Brenda appeared at the open doorway, tears streaming down her beautiful face as she gave a loud sob and ran through the room to the front door. Every pair of eyes watched her, then all those eyes seemed to turn and look at her and Nick.

Sasha wanted to sink through the floor.

"Let's dance," he rasped, taking her drink and handing it to Boyd. Then he led her toward an area set aside for dancing.

He pulled her into his arms. "Don't ask."

"Nick, I—"

"Later. Right now I want to dance with my wife."

She kept quiet but as she looked into his angry blue eyes she had to wonder if there was a reason he had called her his wife.

Was it to remind her that he was married to her?

Or was it a reminder to himself?

Thankfully by the time they'd finished their

dance, the commotion Brenda had caused had receded into the background. Everyone had gone back to enjoying themselves and she was touched that some of the ladies seemed to be going out of their way to be nice to her.

She just hoped it wasn't from pity. She couldn't bear that. Not when she'd seen so many others pity her mother over the years.

They stayed at the party for an hour after that, more out of pride than not, Sasha knew. Once in the car, she couldn't hold back any longer. She had to know.

"Do you love her?"

Nick's hand stilled on the ignition key. "Of course not."

"She loves you."

His mouth tightened as he lowered his hand. "She thinks she does. She'll get over it."

Just like *she* had got over him years ago?

Just like *she* would have to get over her love for him now?

"That's so hard-hearted, Nick."

"What do you want me to say, Sasha? I'm married now. I can't help her."

Pain wrapped around her heart. "Would you help her if you *weren't* married?"

He shot her a hard glance. "No."

Is that all he had to say?

"Look, she went overseas and married someone else, and now she's walked out on that marriage after six months and is pretending she still wants me? No way."

She swallowed hard. Couldn't he see what was right in front of him?

"Maybe she really does love you."

He made a harsh sound. "Sure. Brenda came back through that room knowing everyone would feel sorry for her. Don't you think a truly broken-hearted person would leave by the back door and away from prying eyes? Does all that sound like love to you?"

Her heart began to fill with relief. "No, I guess it doesn't."

"I was the one who broke it off. Brenda was a fling, that's all. I would never have married her."

"Never?"

"Never." He reached out and put his hand over hers. "I'm glad I'm married to you."

She ignored the warmth of his skin against her own. "Why?"

He blinked. "Why?"

"That's what I said."

Withdrawal came over his face before he turned back to put the key in the ignition. "There's a whole heap of reasons."

Yes, and none of them were love.

He glanced back at her. "Sasha, don't let her get to you. She's someone from my past and I can't change that. But don't let her into our future, okay?"

He was right.

"Okay."

He waited a moment more, his eyes reading hers as if to be convinced, then he started up the engine and headed for home.

"Are you sure you don't want to come with me to my parents' place?"

Sasha placed her hairbrush down on the dresser and looked at Nick. "No, I'd only be in the way."

The Valente men were getting together at Cesare's apartment now that Alex was back from London. And Isabel was having Sunday brunch with a friend, so it was no use going with Nick just to sit and listen to the men talk business.

"You wouldn't be in the way," he said, a touch of gruffness to his voice.

Tenderness filled her but she tried not to show it. She'd accepted what he'd said about Brenda and it was forgotten. Now she just wanted to get on with her life.

With Nick.

"No, I've got lots of things to do here."

He went to kiss her then stopped to hover just above her lips. "So you're okay about Brenda?"

"Yes, I am."

And she was.

He kissed her then, a long lingering kiss that was meant to reassure her.

And it did.

Until she answered the phone an hour later and a woman asked to speak to Nick.

"He's not here at the moment," Sasha said, her fingers tensing around the handset. "Do you want to leave a message?"

"Tell him it's Brenda." The woman's pause was definitely for effect. "I'm returning his call."

Sasha held on to her composure. "His call?"

"Nick called me a little while ago and said to call him back. I thought it was from this number. This is his parents' old number, right?"

Her words implied that she knew his parents' number very well.

Sasha drew herself up straighter. "Yes, this was Cesare and Isabel's house. It's mine and Nick's now. I'll pass on the message that you called."

Her hands were shaking as she hung up the phone and for a moment she felt a silly sense of triumph. Then it hit her.

Nick had called Brenda.

To meet with her?

Or to tell her to leave him alone?

All at once Sasha's doubts rose again like weeds

in a garden. She tried to mentally cut them off at the roots but they went too deep.

Was Nick lying?

She'd believed him about not being in love with Brenda, but was she being a fool to be so accepting? Had she *wanted* to believe him because of her love for him? Had it blinded her to his faults? Made her weak to his lies?

No, she didn't want to believe any of that, but the scenario was all too familiar. Memories of her parents' marriage were always at the back of her mind, her father always so glib at assuring her mother he was working when he was out with his latest girlfriend. Her mother always accepting his assurances. Sasha was certain her mother hadn't always believed him, but she'd forgiven him anyway.

Was this the same situation between her and Nick?

Was she like her mother?

And was Nick more like her father than she wanted to admit?

All at once she had the urge to go see her parents. Perhaps by merely being around them she'd find she was just being silly.

An hour later her mother's eyes lit up with surprise when she opened the door. "Darling, what are you doing here?" she said, giving her daughter a kiss. "And where's Nick?"

"He had to go see Cesare about work," Sasha said, stepping inside.

"Men! Your father's not here either. He went into the office to fix something or other. On a Sunday, too!"

Sasha turned to hide her face so that her mother couldn't read the suspicion in her eyes. Was that just an excuse? Was her father out with his latest mistress?

"Anyway," Sally said. "It's just us girls today. We can catch up over coffee."

"That would be nice, Mum," Sasha said, regretting having come now. Instead of doubting her suspicions about Nick, this visit was only reinforcing that she could never be like her mother and so accepting of her husband's lies.

And if she couldn't trust Nick, then how could she stay married to him?

They chatted over coffee on the patio until Sasha's cell phone rang. It was one of the contractors handling the renovations. "Let me just get a pen and paper," she said, looking around for her handbag, remembering she'd left it on the kitchen table.

Sally waved her toward the study.

Sasha nodded and entered by the French doors, hurrying over to her father's desk. By the time she ended the call, she had the feeling this particular contractor was going to be more trouble than he was worth.

She sighed as she turned to leave and knocked

into the bookcase, causing a large vase to fall on the carpet and break.

"Oh no," she muttered, crouching down to pick up the pieces. She hoped it wasn't irreplaceable.

Suddenly she realized there was some rolled up paper in the vase that had now spilled out. She picked it up. Her father wouldn't be pleased to have his things all over the place, though why he would tuck them in a vase like this—

A shiver of apprehension slid down her spine as the paper unraveled and the name "Valente" caught her eye. She didn't mean to pry but the words "correct figures" had been written in pencil at the top of the paper.

Then she noticed another sheet of paper underneath it, looking like a duplicate of the top sheet except that the numbers were different.

She blinked, then reread them. Was she seeing what she thought she was seeing?

She swallowed hard. Oh God. It hadn't been enough for her father that she had married Nick. Porter had falsified the numbers to win the contract by undercutting the other tenders by one hundred thousand dollars. No wonder these papers were hidden away.

God, did Nick know? Was that why they'd delayed signing the contract a few weeks ago? She shook her head. No, if Nick knew he'd have done something about it.

Definitely.

"What are you doing with those?" her mother suddenly said in an accusing tone.

Sasha's head shot up, trepidation filling her. "You know, don't you?"

Sally rushed toward her and snatched the papers to her breast. "Know what?"

"That Dad falsified the numbers to win that latest contract."

"Don't be silly."

"Mum, I saw the paperwork. It's there in black and white."

Her mother flushed, then paled. "Darling, you can't say anything. Promise me you won't."

Sasha gasped. "I can't make a promise like that. What Dad did isn't only morally wrong, it's illegal."

Sally's face screwed up. "Yes, and he could go to jail. Oh dear God."

"Maybe he should have thought of that."

She grabbed Sasha's arm in desperation. "Darling, you can't do this to your father. He can't go to jail." She began to sob. "Besides, the deal's already—" another sob "—signed and delivered and—" sniff "—no one's ever going to know. Not unless you tell them."

"I can't *not* say anything, Mum."

"He's your father."

"Yes, and I'm married to a Valente."

"The Valentes have plenty of money. They won't miss this."

Sasha couldn't believe she was hearing this. "Mum, I can't—"

"Darling, look, don't do anything yet. Think about it all first. I'm sure you'll see that remaining quiet is the best thing."

"Mum—"

"Promise me, darling," her mother said, her voice getting shrill. "At least promise me you won't do anything just yet. Give me a chance to speak to him. I'll get him to pay back the money somehow."

Sasha was torn and confused and she just wanted to be alone for a while to think things through. "I don't know."

"Getting the contract freed up other monies and your father has the money to pay the Valentes back now. He'll have to find a way to do that without raising suspicion, but I promise he'll rectify the situation."

Could she believe that?

Did she even have a choice?

She sighed. "Okay, I won't do anything yet."

Her mother hugged her. "Thank you, darling, thank you. We'll sort things out, you'll see."

Sasha made a hasty exit after that. It was hard to believe her father had done such a thing.

It was even harder to believe her mother was sticking up for him.

Nine

"Something wrong?" Nick asked, watching as Sasha jumped slightly, her green eyes looking nervous all of a sudden.

"Wrong? Why do you say that?"

He'd been watching her over the top of his newspaper. "You were quiet during dinner and didn't eat much, and now you've been staring at the television like it has you under its spell."

A hint of pink stained her cheeks. "I find this show fascinating."

He looked at the television screen and saw they had gone to a commercial. "You were watching the news, Sasha, and I wouldn't exactly call the news fascinating. Interesting, but not fascinating."

"That's your opinion."

"Let's not quibble about words. Something's the matter." He hesitated to bring this up but "If it's about the party and Brenda—"

"It isn't," she dismissed without hesitation. "And I'm not giving that a second thought, okay?"

"Okay."

There was something definitely bothering her. She was too pale and not herself.

"I guess it's the renovations," she suddenly said. "There was a lot of work to be done in the initial stages."

Why did he have the feeling she was just saying that to stop him prying further?

"Is it too much for you?"

She looked horrified. "No! That wasn't what I meant. I love it. I really do. But with coming back from England, then the wedding, then working on the redesigning, I suppose I'm just a little tired tonight."

It made sense yet….

The news returned and she pasted on a smile that surpassed the false one on the newsreader's face. "The news is back on."

"Then don't let me stop you from being *fascinated*," he drawled.

Her smile couldn't hide her wariness as she

returned to look at the screen. He still wasn't convinced there wasn't something troubling her.

He was even more convinced ten minutes later when he heard the telephone ringing out in the hallway and Sasha didn't move. She didn't even appear to hear it. Normally she would get up to answer it straightaway.

He was just about to do it himself when he heard Iris pick up the phone. Then the housekeeper popped her head around the door. "There's a telephone call for Mrs. Valente. It's her mother."

Apprehension crossed Sasha's face, then vanished. "Iris, please tell my mother I'll call her back later."

"Yes, Mrs. Valente."

Nick scowled as the other woman left. "You don't want to speak to your mother?"

She darted a look at him, then away. "I only saw her today. It can wait." She turned back to the television but there was a flush to her cheeks that gave her away.

Something was definitely wrong.

And it had something to do with Sally Blake.

Half an hour later he walked into the kitchen and found Sasha talking on the telephone.

"I said I wouldn't say anything," she was whispering, "and I won't. But—" Suddenly she saw him standing in the doorway and went pale. "Mum, er… I've got to go. Nick's just walked in." She hung up.

Nick leaned against the doorjamb and crossed his

arms. Her words had been a warning to her mother, not a comment.

"Is the hot chocolate almost ready?" he asked, reminding her why she'd come here in the first place.

"Wh-what? Oh yes. I was just about to make it." She hurried over to the refrigerator and took out the milk.

"Your mother has a problem?"

She darted him a look. "You heard?" Without waiting for an answer she turned and took some mugs out of the cupboard. "It's um…women's problems," she said, not looking at him now. "Nothing you want to know about."

So, she was using that age-old excuse, was she? How could he refute it?

"Nick, why don't you go back in the living room. I'll bring in the drinks shortly."

He nodded, then turned and let her be, but if she thought she'd convinced him that nothing was wrong then she was in for a shock. He fully intended to keep an eye on things. Sally Blake had a secret and Sasha knew what it was. And that was fine as long as it didn't impact Sasha too much.

But by her reactions, it did.

Sasha had a restless night until Nick growled and pulled her into his arms, where she promptly fell asleep.

But her thoughts returned as soon as she opened her eyes the next morning. Dear Lord, how could her father cheat Cesare that way? Not to mention the whole Valente family? How could he cheat his *own* family like that? It put her in a terrible position.

"How about meeting me for lunch today?" Nick suddenly said, doing up his tie. "You're coming into the city anyway to talk to your suppliers."

His words brought her back to the moment and Sasha rolled on her side and watched Nick finish dressing for work. He was so handsome. So virile. She loved him so much.

And she might have to give him up.

Oh God, this might be her last chance to spend time with her husband. Her world would fall apart soon enough.

She leaned up on one elbow. "I'd love to have lunch with you, Nick."

He looked pleased. "Good. Leo will come back and pick you up in a couple of hours. He can drive you around while you do your business."

"I can drive my own car."

"Leo's not doing anything until he takes me home again. You may as well make use of him."

Her lips curved upward. "Make use of his services? Yes, I think I can do that."

"Hussy," he murmured, kissing her before he left.

She lay there in bed, just letting her love for Nick

be a part of her. *He* was a part of her, and she would never doubt that again.

She had her mother to thank for realizing that. Going to her parents' place yesterday had shown her Nick was *not* like her father.

Nor was her parents' marriage the same as her own marriage. At first she'd been scared and had projected her fears onto Nick. Nick Valente would not do what her father had done. Nick was good and honest. He'd been open and aboveboard about everything. And despite Brenda's phone call, Sasha was convinced the other woman had just been trying to make trouble. If Nick had called Brenda then it had been for an honest reason. She'd bet her life on it now. Nick was to be trusted.

Her father was not.

She kept those good thoughts of Nick close to her heart for the rest of the morning. Hopefully having only good thoughts would keep the bad thoughts at bay.

"You seem to be enjoying the view," he said over lunch at the harborside restaurant.

Sasha turned to look at him with a smile. "Their menu boasts they have the most glorious view in the world. I was merely checking it out."

"And?"

She surveyed the Harbour Bridge and Opera House through the large glass windows. "I'd say their claim is well-supported."

He smiled, then, "So, what's on the agenda for the rest of the day?"

"I've got a couple more places to visit before I finish up."

He took a sip of wine. "By the way, how's your mother today?"

She dropped her gaze to her plate so he wouldn't see the panic in her eyes. She was sure he hadn't believed her last night about her mother's medical problems. If the positions had been reversed she wouldn't have believed him.

Taking a breath, she looked up. "I only spoke to her last night, so I don't think anything's changed since then."

His eyes had a speculative look. "Aren't you concerned for her health?"

"Of course, but it's nothing urgent. My mother will be fine." Time to change the subject. "By the way, you didn't tell me about the U.K. launch. Did it go well?" She'd been understandably preoccupied last night and had forgotten to ask him about it.

His gaze held hers for a second too long, as if he was considering why she had changed the subject. "It went very well by all accounts. We're launching it on the Continent next."

She was grateful he didn't mention Claudine and any upcoming launch in France.

"It's a gorgeous perfume, Nick."

"I notice you wear it a lot."

"It's my favorite."

"It's every woman's favorite."

She smiled at the usual show of Valente arrogance, and all at once he smiled back with the full power of a Valente smile. The breath hitched in her throat.

The waiter returned to refill their glasses, allowing her to mentally break free of Nick.

When they were alone again Nick said, "How would you like to go on a harbor cruise on Wednesday? We have some prospective customers visiting from the States and I need to take them out to lunch and show them the sights. They're only here for a couple of days."

For a second, sharp anxiety twisted inside her. Would her father have paid back the money by then? Or would she have to gather her strength for Friday's deadline? How *did* a person knowingly send their father to jail?

"The women aren't anything like Claudine," Nick reassured her, thankfully reading her hesitation wrong.

"It sounds like fun."

They ate in silence for a while, until Sasha's cell phone rang. She left it in her handbag, ignoring it and wishing she'd thought to put it on silent.

"Aren't you going to answer it?"

"No."

"It could be important."

Nothing was as important as lunching with Nick. Every second with him counted.

She gave an unconcerned shrug. "It's only about the renovations. I'll get to it later."

Her phone stopped ringing.

"Would you like dessert, madam?" the waiter asked, suddenly appearing at her side.

"Um…" Her cell started to ring again. She opened her handbag and went to turn it off, but not before she caught the number displayed. It was her mother.

"No, just coffee," she said, trying to appear unconcerned as she switched the phone off.

Nick asked for coffee, too, then glanced to Sasha, "Was it a contractor?"

Flustered, she said the first thing that came to mind. "What? Oh, no, it was just my mother. I'll call her back later."

Nick's eyes were full of questions. "I'd have thought you'd want to talk to her."

Oh hell. Was she giving too much away?

"It's not exactly a subject to be discussed over lunch," she pointed out.

Nick grimaced. "True."

Just then Nick's cell phone began to ring.

He glanced at it. "I don't know that number."

"Let me see." Her heart sank. "It's my mother."

He frowned. "Then it must be important if she's calling me," he said, handing it straight to her.

There was nothing for it except to answer the phone, but Sasha got a shock as she listened to her mother's tearful voice. Oh God, she shouldn't have ignored her previous calls.

"My father's had a heart attack," she whispered to Nick in an aside, then spoke to her mother again. "I'll be there as soon as I can, Mum." She finished the call.

"*We'll* be there soon," Nick said, gesturing to the waiter, and a few minutes later hurried her out to the waiting car. "What's his condition?"

"I don't know."

Could *she* have been the cause of this? Her mother would have had to tell him she knew. And having his daughter threaten him with exposure and probable jail would certainly cause him stress enough to have a heart attack.

Yet how could she *not* do something about what she knew, she wondered, feeling like she was shriveling up with stress herself as they headed to the hospital.

Nick squeezed her hand. "You know, my dad's heart attack looked bad at first but it ended up only being a mild one."

She'd forgotten about Cesare's heart attack. Suddenly she felt guilty. "Nick, you shouldn't have come with me. I appreciate it, but I don't want you to go through it all again with my father."

"Don't be silly, Sash," he said gruffly. "I'm your husband."

Warmth rose up inside her and she had to blink back tears. He'd called her "Sash"—the name he'd called her years ago. It was something she'd forgotten until this moment.

"He'll be fine." He pulled her close and she leaned into him, grateful for his presence, comforted by his arms around her, and the now familiar scent of him.

It was only as they were walking toward her mother in the waiting room that Sasha had a tense moment of apprehension. Would her mother inadvertently say something in front of Nick about how Porter had taken the news? Would she blame Sasha's ultimatum for all this? Nick would have to ask why.

"Mum?"

"Oh, Sasha," Sally cried and hugged her.

Sasha returned the hug, relief easing through her. It didn't look like her mother was about to barrage her with blame. "How is he?"

Sally moved back. "I don't know. They told me to wait here." She sniffed. "But it's been ages now and no one will tell me what's happening."

"I'll find out," Nick said ominously, spinning on his heels. "Stay here." He strode out the door toward the nurses' station.

Sasha led her mother back over to her seat. "Mum, what happened?"

Sally gave a shuddering sigh. "When your father got up this morning he said he had indigestion so he took some antacid and went off to work. The next thing I know…" her voice shook "…they called me to stay he'd been brought here in an ambulance."

"So you haven't seen him yet?"

"No."

"Mum, did you—"

Nick strode back through the sliding glass doors. "The doctor's coming out shortly to talk to us."

"Oh God," Sally said and started to sob.

They didn't have to wait long for the doctor, and Sasha put her arm around her mother's shoulders as he told them the news that it didn't look like it been a heart attack at all.

"We're running more tests, but it appears it wasn't."

"Thank God," Sally said.

"What could it have been, Doctor?" Sasha asked.

"I'm not sure. We'll be keeping him here overnight. He's in a private room and Mrs. Blake can stay with him, if you like?"

"Oh, yes," her mother said. "Can I see him, Doctor?"

"He's resting, but I don't see why not." He paused. "But only Mrs. Blake for now."

Sasha watched her mother and the doctor leave

the room. It was wonderful that her father was going to be okay, but he still had to face tomorrow.

And so did she.

"Nick, why don't you go back to work? I'll stay here with Mum until we know more."

His jaw set stubbornly. "No. You need me. I'll stay."

"Seriously, I'll be okay. Besides, it'll probably be hours." She leaned forward and kissed his cheek. "Thank you, but it's no use just sitting around here doing nothing. I'm fine."

His gaze rested on her. "If you're sure?"

"Yes. Now go." It would give her the chance to talk to her mother in private. Sasha couldn't imagine she *wouldn't* have told her husband about yesterday, but she needed to know for sure.

Hours later her father had been given a cautious all clear and Sasha was allowed in to see him, but in the end she didn't get to ask her mother anything. Sally wouldn't leave her husband's side.

And as Sasha looked at her father sleeping peacefully on the bed, she wished so much that it could have been different. If only her father was a different man…a different person.

If only he was a better husband and father.

If only she could love him more.

Sasha finally arrived home around nine and found Nick asleep on the sofa in front of the television.

She'd expected to be home much sooner, so that when he'd phoned her she had even insisted he go straight home and not come to the hospital.

Now, standing in the doorway her heart softened as she looked at Nick. He was such a part of her. He'd always been a part of her. It would be like losing a limb to do without him.

For a moment her vision blurred. She blinked back the tears and turned away to hurry to the kitchen. She wasn't hungry but Iris had put a portion of lasagna in the oven for her, so she'd have to make the effort to eat it.

But first she showered and changed into her silk nightgown and robe, then put the lasagna on a tray and took it into the living room.

Hungrier now than she'd realized, she turned the television down low while she ate her food and watched Nick sleep. She thought the smell of the food might wake him, but it didn't, and she was sipping at her decaffeinated coffee and deciding to cover him with a blanket when his eyelids lifted.

For a moment he looked disorientated. Then he sat up and ran his fingers through his hair. "Damn, I fell asleep, didn't I?"

She gave an understanding smile. "You were tired."

"What time is it?"

"Almost ten."

His eyes grew alert. "You must be exhausted yourself."

"I'm better now that I'm home." And she was.

He scrutinized her more. "How's Porter?"

"They'll keep an eye on him overnight, but they're confident it wasn't a heart attack."

His face relaxed. "See, I told you there was nothing to worry about."

"I know."

All at once his gaze noted her night attire, and the air stilled. His eyes burned into her, making her heart skip a beat. She waited for him to get to his feet and pull her into his arms.

Only, he seemed to withdraw. "I think I'll use a spare room tonight. You need your sleep."

Disappointment filled her. "I won't be able to sleep without you," she said, putting herself on the line...putting her heart on the line and hoping he didn't notice.

The light of passion flared in his eyes again but was banked as he stood up and held out his hand. "Fine. We *sleep,* and that's all."

Her heart expanded at his thoughtfulness. He wanted her yet was prepared to put her needs first. Or what he *thought* she needed.

Happy to just be able to share his bed, she put her hand in his and together they went up the stairs. He made no attempt to make love to her, but he held her

in his arms until she fell asleep. And she found that
was just as welcome as making love.

She was home.

And she was where she wanted to be.

Ten

Cesare phoned the next morning to see how Porter was doing and Nick put the phone on loudspeaker so both he and Sasha could talk while they were getting dressed.

"Dad, it wasn't a heart attack." Nick went on to explain.

"Grazie a Dio!" Cesare said with relief.

"We've just called the hospital and he's already been released," Nick continued. "Sally will look after him. I'm sure she'll make him take things easy."

"Yes, she's a good woman." Cesare paused. "Sasha, your father's a good man. He gives so much of himself to everyone. It would be a great loss if anything had happened to him. He's the consummate businessman."

Sasha wanted to choke. If only Cesare knew….

"Thank you, Cesare," she managed. "That's kind of you to say."

Cesare ended the call after that and Nick kissed her good-bye, but as he drew back he hesitated. "Are you sure you don't want me to get out of the harbor cruise tomorrow? Alex or Matt can step in."

Tomorrow was Wednesday.

Only two more days until Friday.

The thought of having to force her father's hand pressed down on her. She felt sick at heart over him cheating the Valentes out of money.

She schooled her features. "No. I'll be fine."

Nick held her gaze a moment more. "Okay. See you tonight."

"Yes," she said, putting on a brave face.

As soon as he left, she finished dressing. She would go see her parents. Now that she knew her father hadn't had a heart attack, he had to rectify the situation soon. She couldn't go on like this.

No one answered the front door when she rang the bell, despite her father's favorite music coming from inside the house. Then she realized it was coming from the back patio, so she went around the side and opened the gate.

To her shock, she found her father sitting on the lounger in the back garden, smoking a cigar and drinking whiskey. He looked like a man who was celebrating life.

Or something else?

Suddenly it hit her.

"Oh my God," she accused, seeing him jump with fright as she strode toward him. "You didn't have a suspected heart attack at all. You made it up."

The blood siphoned from his face, then he turned red. "Don't be stupid, child. Of course I didn't make it up."

"I don't believe you."

He stabbed out his cigar. "You think I'd put myself through all those medical procedures, not to mention worrying you and your mother, for the fun of it?"

"Yes! You were desperate. And you didn't give a damn about me or Mum." Sasha swung around when she heard her mother come out on the patio behind her. "Mum, I can't believe you were a part of this."

Sally's eyes widened in alarm. "Wh-what?"

"Leave your mother out of this. She didn't know."

Sasha gasped. "So it's true."

"Know what?" Sally said, looking from one to the other.

"That Dad faked his heart attack so I wouldn't tell the Valentes about his falsifying records."

"No!"

"He thought I'd feel guilty enough to overlook the fact that it wasn't actually a heart attack. No doubt he planned on milking it for all it was worth."

"Porter?" Sally whispered.

"Sally, don't look at me like that. I was only thinking of you. What will happen to you if I go to jail?"

"How magnanimous of you, Dad," Sasha snapped.

"Mind your own business, Sasha," he growled.

She stared hard at him. "You don't regret what you did at all."

"Of course I do."

She knew he didn't. He only regretted getting caught.

"Dad, unless you tell me here and now that you're going to make things right and pay back the money, I'm going to tell Nick what you've done."

He turned white. "You don't mean that."

"I do."

"But I'm your father."

"Emotional blackmail doesn't work on me anymore." She pulled back her shoulders. "Now tell me that you'll make things right, or I go tell Nick right this minute what you've done."

He blanched. "Okay, okay. I'll pay it back, but it might take me a couple of days."

"You've got until Friday." She turned and walked away, her heart so heavy she was surprised she could walk at all. She'd never had much love or respect for her father but she had even less now.

Of course, she wasn't fool enough to trust him. And how the heck was she going to believe him on Friday anyway?

Yet there was a bigger picture here.

How was she going to look Nick in the eyes for the rest of her life and pretend this wasn't between them?

Sasha could feel Nick looking at her throughout dinner but she couldn't seem to lift her spirits. A black cloud hung over her head. It was only a matter of time before it all poured down on her.

After they'd eaten and moved into the living room, she still couldn't relax. She couldn't get interested in the unfolding legal drama on television. She had enough legal drama of her own right now.

And she was terrified her mother would call and put pressure on her to give her father more time, or to beg her to change her mind. She didn't want the stress of even talking to her mother right now and certainly not in front of Nick.

An idea occurred to her.

"I think I've got cabin fever, Nick. Let's go out for a drink somewhere."

He blinked in mild surprise and put aside some paperwork. "Will one of the local pubs do?"

"Yes, there's some lovely pubs around here. And

can we turn our cell phones off, please? Let's not have any interruptions."

He shot her an odd look. "If that's what you want."

Half an hour later they were sitting in the corner at a local pub, sipping their drinks. The hotel was on the heritage listing as were many buildings in the Hawkesbury district.

"Any special reason for the cabin fever?" he asked, leaning back in his chair, his eyes watchful.

It sounded a ridiculous thing for her to say now. They'd been out of the house a lot lately and cabin fever was the last thing she'd have.

She wrinkled her nose. "I guess it's more that we haven't had much time to ourselves."

He nodded. "And all that with your father didn't help either, does it?"

She gave a silent gasp. "Wh-what?"

"With Porter being in hospital."

"Oh." She swallowed. "Yes."

His look sharpened. "You've been tense all night. Are you sure you're telling me everything? He's not taken a turn for the worse, has he?"

"No, he's fine." Panic bounced inside her. She had to get thoughts of her father out of Nick's mind and onto something else. Otherwise she might give herself way. "Brenda called me, you know."

He straightened in his chair. "What? When?"

"Sunday morning after you went to your father's place. She said she was returning your call."

The look in his eyes turned hard and dangerous. He would be a formidable enemy. "She did, did she?"

"So you didn't call her?"

"No." His gaze focused back on her. "Did you think I had? Is that why you didn't tell me before now? You've been worrying yourself sick about it."

"No, that's not it at all. I figured you just wanted to tell her to stay away from you."

"I'd already told her. And she knows the score. She was just trying to cause trouble." He stared at her. "And succeeded."

"No, she didn't." Brenda had tried to make her doubt Nick, but in the end she hadn't succeeded.

Nick's eyes were razor-sharp. "You've been upset all evening. In fact, you haven't been yourself since Sunday at the party."

Somehow she held it together. Sunday was when she'd learned what her father had done.

"I told you it's because of everything else." She swallowed past her dry throat. "I believe you, Nick. I swear I believe you."

He studied her face, taking his time to measure her words. Finally a gentle look came into his eyes. "Thank you," he murmured.

Her heart tilted inside her chest.

In the end they stayed for over two hours, talking

about nothing much in particular and listening to a folk singer. Sasha could feel the tension easing out of her as the wine took hold.

"I think that did us both good," Nick said on the drive home.

She leaned her head back against the leather seat and smiled sideways at him. "We should do it more often."

He chuckled. "I believe you're slightly drunk, Mrs. Valente."

"Enough to take the edge off my pain," she said without thinking.

His scowl was instant. "You're in pain?"

She bit her lip and thanked heaven he had to concentrate on the road. "I had a headache before," she lied. "I thought it was going to turn into a migraine."

He darted a look at her. "Do you often get migraines?"

"No." But she had the feeling she may well start after all this.

Without warning, he gave a crooked grin. "Don't worry. I'll kiss you better if it returns."

"Then it'll be worth it."

"Don't say things like that when I'm driving," he pretended to growl.

She just smiled.

They arrived home and he parked the car in the sweeping driveway, but something happened inside her as she watched him come round to open the passenger door. A sense of impending doom centered in her chest. Suddenly she had the feeling this was all coming to an end.

"Come on, milady," he drawled, holding his hand out.

She vaguely heard him. This moment was far more important than joking or teasing or anything else in this world. God, she loved this man. How could she ever tell him the truth?

She stood up and cupped his face with her hands. "Make love to me, Nick. Make me forget all my headaches."

He looked down at her, his brows drawing together. "What's all this about?"

"Nick, don't talk. I need you tonight. Make me yours."

He opened his mouth to speak, then must have thought better of it. He released his breath and lowered his head.

After that it seemed like they kissed all the way to the bedroom. And in the bedroom…dear God, in the bedroom…their lovemaking took on a poignancy she was sure Nick felt, too. There was a deeper focus in his eyes as he looked at her. A longer than usual pause as he entered her.

And when he made her *his*—perhaps for the last time—her heart hurt.

Eleven

Sasha's pace quickened as she stepped from the elevator and walked toward Nick's office in the House of Valente building just before noon. Her sense of impending doom from last night had alleviated by the time she woke this morning, making her realize it had mostly been the wine.

But not all.

There was still a heavy feeling inside her that she'd been trying to push aside all morning, and it hadn't helped that the hours had dragged until it was time to come into the city for the harbor cruise. She'd needed to keep busy.

And she'd needed to see Nick again. Hopefully being with the man she loved would help push away those demons and doubts riding on her shoulder.

"He's in the conference room," Nick's personal assistant said. "I'll just let him know you're here." She went to press the intercom.

"That's okay, Joyce. I can wait in his office."

"No, he said to tell him when you arrived. It's only the family in there anyway."

Knowing he was waiting for her filled Sasha with pleasure, more so when Joyce said to go straight into the conference room.

"Thank you." Sasha's steps were lighter as she continued along to the end of the corridor. The view of the harbor through the panel of windows called out to her and she was really beginning to look forward to the cruise today. The harbor breeze could be just what she needed right now, especially if she was sharing it with Nick.

"Come in," Cesare called out in response to her knock.

Sasha opened the door with a smile. She had to admit she really liked being a part of the Valente family. Growing up, she'd often been a little wary of Cesare but he was a good man and so were the others.

"Well, well," the older man in question said as she came toward three of the Valente men sitting at the conference table. Nick was standing at the window looking out, his back to her. "You're just in time."

Sasha's steps faltered at his tone. "I…am?"

Why hadn't Nick turned to face her?

"In time for what, Cesare?"

"For me to have your father arrested for fraud."

Sasha's heart dropped to her toes.

"We've found out what he's been up to. Did you think we wouldn't?"

Sasha couldn't find her voice.

"I can't believe Porter thought he could get away with it," Cesare continued. "Does he think the Valentes are stupid? And you were in on it, too, weren't you, girl?"

She gasped at the accusation, aware of three sets of eyes upon her, but the eyes that mattered—Nick's eyes—were still turned away from her.

"And I, fool that I am, wanted Nick to marry you. I thought you were perfect for my son." He gave a harsh laugh. "No wonder Porter wanted you to marry Nick, and no wonder you agreed to the marriage. If it was all in the family he'd get that contract, no questions asked. Of course you had to say no first, didn't you? That way you could dangle yourself as bait in front of Nick and—"

"Enough!" Nick spun around, his face taut as he glared at his father. "You're accusing Sasha without any evidence. You don't know she was involved in any of this."

"Then ask her, *figlio mio*," Cesare said. "Ask her, and then we will know."

She watched Nick hesitate, and felt like she'd been slapped in the face.

He doubted her.

Then he straightened his shoulders and walked toward her. "Sasha," he said, his voice quiet but firm, his eyes with a hint of pleading in them. "Please tell me you didn't know about any of this."

A moment crept by. The others receded into the background. There was her and Nick.

Only her and Nick.

And soon....

She trembled. "I...I...can't."

He sucked in a sharp breath.

"Nick, I—"

His glare silenced her. "No excuses."

"But—"

"This was your sick way of getting revenge, wasn't it?" Disgust filled his eyes now. "Very clever, Sasha."

"Revenge? I don't know what you mean."

"Remember that kiss in the gazebo? Remember how you thought I'd rejected you? You wanted to pay me back for that, didn't you? You wanted your revenge."

"No!" she whispered, her voice threadbare.

"Yes."

At that moment, she knew it was over. He wasn't prepared to let her explain any of this. He wasn't even prepared to ask if there were extenuating circumstances, nor give her the benefit of the doubt.

And could she really blame him?

Giving a small cry, she spun away and ran from the room. It was over.

"I'm sorry, *figlio mio*," Cesare said, coming up behind Nick and putting his hand on his shoulder.

"Not as sorry as I am, Dad." Nick's gut was one big knot of pain. He'd trusted Sasha. Trusted her like he'd trusted no other woman.

He should have known she'd let him down.

Cesare's mouth tightened. "*Santo cielo,* I'm going to see Porter myself!"

Alex jumped to his feet. "No, Dad. We can handle this."

Cesare clenched and unclenched his hands. "I want to see his face. He was my friend, and now he's a traitor."

"You're getting upset, and that's not good for you. Matt and I will go see Porter. Let Nick take you home."

"No," Nick growled. "I'm going to see Porter." He had more than a vested interest in all this.

Alex nodded. "Then Matt can take Dad home."

Cesare complained but he was shaken and obviously realized it was best he not be there to confront his now ex-friend. He left with Matt, and Nick and Alex took off for the Blakes' house.

Sally turned white when she opened the door to them. It was evident she knew why they were here.

Porter was eating dinner, and he went white, too, as Nick and Alex strode into the dining room.

Alex spoke first. "Porter, I've come to tell you that we're filing charges for fraud against you."

Sally gave a wailing cry behind them, but they ignored her.

The older man's face screwed up. "So Sasha told, did she? I should have known not to trust that daughter of mine. She finds out a couple of days ago and threatens to blow the whistle unless I—"

Nick stiffened. "*What* did you say?"

Porter made a harsh sound. "I said my daughter was going to blow the whistle on her old man. Can you believe it?"

Nick looked at Porter. "Yes, I can." Then he looked at Alex, who nodded in understanding.

"Take my car," his brother said, tossing the keys at him. "I've got a lot more to say to Mr. Blake."

Somehow Sasha managed to find some semblance of control by the time Leo dropped her off at home. She'd never been more grateful for the dark glass panel between them as she huddled in the corner of the back seat, unable to stop the tears from flowing.

Iris took one look at her face and was full of concern. "Mrs. Valente, is there something wrong?"

Sasha almost laughed out loud. Everything was wrong. And nothing could make it right.

Not ever.

"Are you ill? Would you like me to call a doctor?"

Sasha headed for the stairs. "I'd just like to be alone, Iris."

The housekeeper was clearly reluctant to accept that, but inclined her head. "If you wish, Mrs. Valente."

"I do."

Sasha made her way to the bedroom, sick with anguish. She threw some water on her face, hoping the coldness would take away her inner pain, but knowing it was a losing battle. She was burning up inside, her despair like a flame inside her, growing higher and more intense. An iceberg could not put it out.

She knew what she had to do. Nick would no longer want her in his house or in his life and she wouldn't wait around for him to kick her out. He would be glad to see her gone. No doubt he would even get someone else in to oversee the redecorating.

Her throat tightening, she began to throw some of her things in a suitcase. She would get the rest later.

Or better still, leave them for charity. She wouldn't want any reminders of her marriage.

Just then there was a tap at the door and she swallowed a moan. "Come in."

The housekeeper's eyes widened when she saw the suitcase on the bed. "Um…your mother's on the phone, Mrs. Valente."

Sasha's nerves tensed. "I don't want to talk to anyone right now, Iris."

"She says it's urgent."

Sasha winced, then realized it was best to take the call. She felt too raw to give her mother the support she needed right now, but once she pulled herself together, she'd manage it in the future.

Somehow.

She picked up the phone. "Mum, I—"

"Sasha, how could you! You said you would give your father until Friday and now you've gone and told the Valentes. You've betrayed your own family."

She then went into a tirade about Porter going to jail and that her daughter had sent him there, and at that moment Sasha finally understood something. No matter what her father did, her mother would always make excuses for him.

And her daughter would come a poor second.

Sasha quietly hung up. Her mother was welcome to do what she wanted with her life, but *she* wasn't about to help her do that any longer.

It was over.

Just like her marriage to Nick.

There was only one place where she'd found a measure of peace before. She would go back to London. There was nothing for her here.

Nick drove home as fast as he dared. Last night when Sasha had begged him to make love to her, she must have known something was about to happen. She should have told him the truth. She should have said something.

Anything.

Then he remembered how she'd tried to tell him the truth back in the conference room, only he hadn't wanted to listen. He'd accused her of revenge.

Dammit all to hell.

He took the stairs two at a time, not believing Iris's words that Sasha had packed her things and gone. Then he saw some of her clothes missing from the wardrobe and the dresser now empty of her possessions.

And he felt empty deep inside.

So empty he wasn't sure if he could live without her. *Not when she'd taken his heart with her.*

He sucked in a lungful of air. He hadn't seen it coming, but he loved her. It hit him fair and square between the eyes. He could not deny it.

And now he couldn't even tell her. He had no idea where she'd gone, except that he knew she wouldn't go home. After what he'd seen, her parents wouldn't want her.

Well, he *did*.

He strode to the telephone beside the bed and called Joyce. He'd turn this city over until he found the woman he loved.

Twelve

Sasha tightened the belt of her bathrobe, then began toweling her hair dry as she walked into the bedroom. She probably should order something to eat except that she didn't have an appetite. It was going to be a long time before—

"Sasha."

Her head shot up, her heart slamming against her ribs at the sight of her husband standing in her hotel room. "Nick!"

Their eyes locked, but she could tell nothing from his expression.

"Yes, Sasha. It's me."

Her mind tried to take it in. He was here. Oh God, Nick was really here. But how? Why? She dare not hope. No, not even the tiniest bit.

Placing the towel on the table, she pushed back her wet hair and faced him. "How did you find me?"

"You used your credit card to book the hotel, and then again for your flight to London tomorrow."

She hadn't thought he'd be looking so she hadn't given it a second thought. Then she realized why he'd come looking for her. The disappointment was immense.

She thrust back her shoulders. "Look, if you want more details about my father, you've had a wasted journey."

"I already know the details."

Her forehead creased. Was he playing some sort of game with her? "Then there's nothing to say."

"There's plenty to say." He paused and suddenly regret seemed to cut through him. "I'm sorry, Sasha."

"S-sorry?"

"For not trusting you."

She swallowed hard. "I don't understand."

"I shouldn't have been so quick to believe you'd have anything to do with what your father did."

She searched his eyes. "You believe me?"

"*Now* I do. But it wasn't until Porter inadvertently told us your involvement that I realized I'd misjudged you." He took in a lungful of air. "I'm sorry, Sasha. I'll say I'm sorry every day for the rest of our lives if that's what it takes."

Her heart began to wobble. "You want me to come back to you?"

His expression opened up fully for the first time ever. "How can I live in that great big house without the woman I love to share it with me?"

"Nick, are you—" She moistened her mouth. Dare she say the words? "Are you saying you *love* me?"

"Yes."

Her heart jumped with joy but still she held back. She was too scared to believe it. There had to be another reason.

"Is this your revenge, Nick? Are you going to get me to admit I love you and then walk away?"

There was a flash of pain in his eyes. "No. The only direction I'm walking in is *to* you." His steps did exactly that. And then he stood in front of her, his gaze achingly intense. "Do you love me, Sasha?"

She looked up at him and could fight it no longer. "Yes, Nick, I do. I've always loved you. I always will."

He pulled her close. "Oh God, I love you, Sash," he said thickly, his deep voice caressing her ears.

"Nick," she murmured, love swelling within her.

He drew her close and kissed her. She inhaled him in like he was the very air, his heartbeat merging with hers, his touch purring along her skin, his scent mingling with her own. She'd never felt more alive.

Or complete.

He moved back but held her within the circle of his arms. "Last night I knew there was something going on with you, but I didn't know what. And today, I didn't know if you could forgive me." His lips brushed hers. "I just have to say it again. I love you."

"I'll never get sick of hearing you say it," she whispered, the love in his eyes stealing her breath. "I love you so very much, Nick."

He hugged her tight for a short while, then eased back. "I had some bad moments on the way over here, let me tell you."

"Perhaps I gave in too easily then?" she teased.

His lips twitched. "If you hadn't, I'd be a nervous wreck by now."

"You a nervous wreck? Never!"

"You're right," he said, making her smile at his Valente arrogance. "I'd never be a wreck because I wouldn't have let you go in the first place."

"I can't fault that reasoning."

His hands tightened on her waist. "Speaking of giving, you give so much of yourself, trying to balance it all so that no one will get hurt. Your parents don't deserve you. *I* almost didn't."

"Nick, I should have told you as soon as I could,

but I was torn. How could I be responsible for sending my father to jail?"

"You weren't responsible for anything."

"I was responsible to you as your wife. I should have made him tell you in the first place."

His mouth tightened. "Your father is the one who should have been responsible."

She winced, then, "You know, I'm glad it's over now. It would have always been between us because *I* would have known."

"I can guarantee it won't be between us now."

Her heart rolled over as she looked up at him. "Oh, Nick."

"Call me darling."

"Darling," she murmured. Then she remembered something else. "What about your family?"

"They'll know the truth by now. They won't hold anything against you."

"But Cesare—"

"Loves you like a daughter. It's the reason he was so hurt. He will apologize and no more will be said about it."

His words gave her joy. "I love your family, Nick."

"As long as you love me more."

"Oh, yes! Far, far more."

He glanced at the bed. "Seeing that you've already paid for the room…"

She arched one of her eyebrows. "Are you suggesting I go to bed with you, Nick Valente?"

"Do you have a better suggestion, my darling?"

"Not a one."

With their hearts finally open to each other, he drew her down on the bed beside him and at that moment she finally acknowledged something to herself. Loving Nick was no longer the worst thing that could happen in her life.

Loving Nick was the *strongest* part of her life.

Epilogue

Nick watched his very beautiful wife come toward him in the church and his heart swelled with love. He'd ruined Sasha's dreams seven years ago, and then almost ruined them again more recently. This time he was going to make sure her dream came true.

A lump formed in his throat when he saw her blinking back tears during the service. He never knew life could bring such happiness as he'd had the last few weeks with Sasha.

"Darling, thank you," she murmured after they walked back down the aisle past the Valente family, who were their only guests. "The church is so beautiful."

He'd searched high and low to find the perfect church for her and finally found it up in the mountains. The historic church had stained glass windows that looked out over the valley to the ocean where the heart of Sydney could be seen many, many miles away.

Outside the church his family…no, make that *their* family…gathered round to congratulate them and have their picture taken for posterity.

"There's one more thing I want to do," he whispered in her ear.

"What's that?"

"I'll show you later, my love."

And he did.

That night the moonlight shone over the silhouette of a couple kissing in the gazebo. And this time when Nick left to go back to the house, he wasn't alone.

He had Sasha by his side.

As it always would be.

* * * * *

millsandboon.co.uk Community

Join Us!

The Community is the perfect place to meet and chat to kindred spirits who love books and reading as much as you do, but it's also the place to:

- **Get the inside scoop from authors about their latest books**
- **Learn how to write a romance book with advice from our editors**
- **Help us to continue publishing the best in women's fiction**
- **Share your thoughts on the books we publish**
- **Befriend other users**

Forums: Interact with each other as well as authors, editors and a whole host of other users worldwide.

Blogs: Every registered community member has their own blog to tell the world what they're up to and what's on their mind.

Book Challenge: We're aiming to read 5,000 books and have joined forces with The Reading Agency in our inaugural Book Challenge.

Profile Page: Showcase yourself and keep a record of your recent community activity.

Social Networking: We've added buttons at the end of every post to share via digg, Facebook, Google, Yahoo, technorati and de.licio.us.

www.millsandboon.co.uk

2 FREE BOOKS
AND A SURPRISE GIFT

We would like to take this opportunity to thank you for reading this Mills & Boon® book by offering you the chance to take TWO more specially selected books from the Desire™ 2-in-1 series absolutely FREE! We're also making this offer to introduce you to the benefits of the Mills & Boon® Book Club™—

- **FREE home delivery**
- **FREE gifts and competitions**
- **FREE monthly Newsletter**
- **Exclusive Mills & Boon Book Club offers**
- **Books available before they're in the shops**

Accepting these FREE books and gift places you under no obligation to buy, you may cancel at any time, even after receiving your free books. Simply complete your details below and return the entire page to the address below. You don't even need a stamp!

YES Please send me 2 free Desire stories in a 2-in-1 volume and a surprise gift. I understand that unless you hear from me, I will receive 2 superb new 2-in-1 books every month for just £5.25 each, postage and packing free. I am under no obligation to purchase any books and may cancel my subscription at any time. The free books and gift will be mine to keep in any case.

Ms/Mrs/Miss/Mr_____ Initials _____

_____

Surname _____
Address _____

_____
_____ Postcode _____

Send this whole page to: Mills & Boon Book Club, Free Book Offer, FREEPOST NAT 10298, Richmond, TW9 1BR